C000153834

# THE
# DEVIL'S
# DUE

## L.D. BEYER

**OLD STONE MILL**
Publishing

This is a work of fiction. The events that unfold within these pages as well as the characters depicted are products of the author's imagination. Any connection to specific people, living or dead, is purely coincidental.

Copyright © 2016 by L.D. Beyer
All rights reserved. No part of this publication may be reproduced or transmitted in any form or by any means, electronic or mechanical, without written permission.

*Cover and interior design by Lindsey Andrews*
*Maps design by L.D. Beyer*

ISBN: 978-0-9963857-5-6

**OLD STONE MILL**
Publishing
Battle Creek, MI
*www.ldbeyer.com*

# THE
# DEVIL'S
# DUE

*For my mother Ann, who understood the Irish soul.*

"THIS SON OF MINE WAS DEAD AND IS ALIVE AGAIN,
HE WAS LOST AND NOW IS FOUND."

*—Luke 15:20*

# Preface

In 1919, after seven hundred years of British oppression, a slumbering rage awakened as the Irish people rose up to claim their freedom and their land. Poorly trained, vastly outnumbered and severely short on guns and ammunition, a relatively small force nonetheless brought the battle to British forces in Dublin, Limerick and Cork, and on the lonely roads and fields in between. As the fighting raged, Frank Kelleher and Kathleen Coffey—a young couple from County Limerick with plans for the future—were torn apart. This is Frank's tale: his fall from grace, his dreams, and his quest for redemption.

If you are interested in learning more about the historical context for the story, please see the Author's Note in the back of the book. I've also provided several maps to help the reader get a better sense of time and place as well as a "Historical Cheat Sheet" to fill in some of the blanks.

I hope you enjoy the pages that follow.

L.D. Beyer
June, 2016

# Chapter One

It was such an odd thought for a man about to die, but, still, it filled my head. *Will I hear the gun? Will I feel the bullet?* I stared at the floor of the barn, the dirt soaked with my own blood. The earth was cold against my cheek, and I could hear the pitter-patter of rain on the roof. *God pissin' on us again. Only in Ireland.* The light of the oil lamps danced a waltz across the wall and, in the flickering light, I saw a pair of boots, then trousers. Nothing more, but I knew it was Billy. One of my eyes was already swollen shut, and I couldn't lift my head from the dirt to see the rest of him. I didn't have to; those were Billy's boots.

"Fuckin' traitor!"

I tried to raise my hand, as if that would stop him, but still the boot slammed into my ribs. I heard a cry, no longer sure if it was me lying on the ground or if I was a spectator watching some poor soul being beaten. Choking, I spit out more blood and tried to catch my breath, but the boot came again. Through one eye, I saw the feet, the legs, dancing with the light, then the flash of Billy's boot striking me in the chest, the stomach, the arms. I heard the thuds, felt my body jump, each kick like a bolt of lightning, agonizing bolts of pain coursing through my body. Unseen hands began to pull me down into the darkness. Yet still I wondered. *Will I hear the gun? Will I feel it? Probably not,* I thought. *A bright flash then, what? Nothing? Blackness?* I sighed and waited for the bullet, wondering how I would know when it finally came.

There would be no Jesus waiting for me on the other side, that was for sure. No Mary, no saints, no choir of angels. Good Irish Catholic lad that I was, I had done enough in my short life to know that heaven wasn't in the cards. Not for me, anyway. My head exploded in a flash of colors, and the darkness beckoned me. *Probably just the darkness,* I decided. Maybe that wasn't so bad.

It was strange, but I wasn't afraid anymore. Not of death, certainly. Billy had beaten that out of me. I wasn't afraid of hell either. Despite all that I had done—and what happened two days ago was sure to seal my fate—I wasn't sure I believed in the Church's view of hell. Seven hundred years of oppression under the British was hell enough. Eternal damnation, I suspected, was in the here and now, in the pains and tragedies of everyday life. And, surely, I was in pain. Billy had seen to that. Pain and regret were all I felt now.

I suppose any man about to die has regrets, and I had my share. A sudden sadness overwhelmed me. I would never see Kathleen again.

I don't know how long I lay there with Billy kicking me, cursing me, calling me a spy, a traitor. It didn't matter what I said; he would never believe me. At some point I stopped feeling the kicks, stopped feeling the pain, and surrendered to the darkness. Maybe I was already dead and didn't know it.

Then from the shadows, I felt a hand on my face, surprisingly gentle, brushing the hair out of my eyes. *Kathleen?* Then a hiss.

"Oh Jesus, Frank! What has he done to you?"

*Liam?*

Hands grabbed me below the arms and lifted me up. I heard a grunt, then a curse—Liam's voice. My head spinning, I tried to stand but couldn't. It took a moment to realize that my hands and feet were still strapped to the chair. I felt something pulling then pushing, hands on my sides again—Liam? A jolt of pain shot through me. Shaking with spasms, I hissed and coughed up more blood. Surely, I thought, I had a few broken ribs thanks to Billy's boot. I squinted through the tears and blood; there was Liam, his own eyes wet. What was he doing here? Had they sent him—my closest friend—to put the bullet in me?

My head hung limp, then I felt Liam's gentle hands on my chin. Through one eye, I watched as he dipped the cloth in the pail and began to wipe my face. I gasped when he got to my nose. Liam pulled the cloth away, stared at it for a second, his own face a grimace. In the flickering light, the cloth was dark red, stained by my own blood. Liam shook his head and dropped it in the pail.

"Do you want some water, Frank?"

Not waiting for an answer, he held the cup to my cracked and swollen lips. I coughed again and most of the water ran down my neck to join the blood on my shirt. The little I drank tasted of copper.

"Jesus, Liam," I hissed. "Is it a bath you're giving me or a drink?"

Liam just shook his head.

"I thought you were one of us, Frank."

I coughed again and squinted through the pain. "I am, Liam." I coughed once more, my voice hoarse. "I am."

He shook his head again, and I could see the pain in his eyes.

"That's not what they're saying, Frank. Three of our boys dead..." His voice trailed off, his eyes telling me what he couldn't say. *How could you do it, Frank?*

"And now the British have our names," he continued, choking on the words. He sighed and wiped his eyes. "They'll hunt us down. Is that what you want?" His eyes pleaded with me, and I knew what he wanted to say but couldn't. *Do you want to see me with a bullet in my head too, Frank?*

"Liam..." I coughed again—a spasm—bright, hot pain slicing through me.

He shook his head sadly. "You were one of us, Frank." There was a hurt in his eyes that matched my own. *How could you betray me?* his eyes seemed to ask. He sighed, dipped the cloth in the pail, then wiped my nose again. "I thought you were one of us…"

"Liam…"

He leaned close and whispered in my ear. "For the love of God, Frank! He's going to kill you anyway. You know that. Why don't you tell him what he wants?" He sniffed then turned away and wiped his eyes. "I can't watch this anymore."

"I didn't do it, Liam."

He stared at me for a moment then leaned close again. "Ah, Jesus, Frank. Don't you see? It doesn't matter. You know that. If they suspect you're an informant, you're an informant."

He was right, but still I protested.

"I swear on my father's grave, I didn't do it, Liam."

"But you're the only one still alive."

A small doubt, but his eyes, like his words, told me it was hopeless. If Liam didn't believe me, Billy and the others surely wouldn't. And why should they? It was supposed to be a simple operation. But something had gone wrong—terribly wrong—and now here I was, waiting for the bullet. Better that it would be coming from one of my own than from the fuckin' British. For some reason, that made me feel better.

"I know, Liam," I wheezed. "I know. But I didn't do it."

Liam shook his head, unsure what to do.

"Did you write your letter?" he finally asked, choking on the words.

My letter. My last chance to speak to Kathleen, to tell her in my own words what had happened. Billy hadn't given me the chance, though.

"Just tell Kathleen I love her." I looked up into my friend's eyes. "You'll do that for me won't you, Liam?"

He nodded slowly. "Aye." He paused, his eyes telling me there was more. "And your mam?"

*My mam.* What could I say to a woman I hadn't spoken to in three years? Would she even care?

Suddenly, there were shouts from outside, and I flinched at the sharp crack of a rifle. This was followed by two more, then shouting again. *What was happening?* I tried to piece it together. I knew what it was, I told myself, but the answer seemed to be lost in the clouds in my head. I stared up at Liam. Before I could ask, the clatter of a machine gun filled the air.

"Oh, Jesus!" Liam screamed. "It's the Tans!"

The clouds suddenly vanished. *The Black and Tans!* The fear came flooding back, and I forgot about the pain of Billy's boot. For the last year, the scourge of the British army, wearing their mismatched uniforms, had sacked and looted our towns and terrorized our people. Ex-servicemen, soldiers who had seen time on the Western front—and many who had seen the inside of a British jail—they had been sent to supplement the ranks of the Peelers, the Royal Irish Constabulary. These were war-hardened men, more than one of whom had been languishing in prison for one crime or another. And now, Britain had cleaned out their jails and sent their criminals to be our police. In April, they had gone on a rampage in Limerick; in December, they'd burnt the city of Cork.

"Liam!" I pleaded.

Before he could answer, bullets tore through the windows of the barn, chipping stone, ripping into the wood. The cows and sheep screeched, slamming into the cart and threatening to finish what Billy had started. I saw the flash above, heard the tinkle, shards of glass raining down on me. Seconds later the hay was on fire. One of the oil lamps had been hit, I realized. Liam slammed into me, and I howled in pain when I landed back on the blood-soaked dirt. He was screaming as he clawed at the ropes that bound my hands. The fire raged as chips and splinters flew. Soon the sparks hit the ceiling and the thatch began to smolder, the sheep and cows shrieking all the while.

"Come on, Frank!" Liam screamed as he struggled with the ropes that held me.

I felt his arms pulling, dragging me through the dirt to the cow door in the back. He kicked it open, peeked outside, then pulled me through.

"For fuck's sake, Frank! I'll not be dragging you the whole way! Get up! Run!"

I struggled to my feet, the emotion and adrenaline masking the pain. I limped after Liam across the field, scrambled over the stone wall, falling once and crying out in pain. But somehow, I got up and kept going. Behind me, the guns went silent, but the screech of the animals, the shouts and the sounds of motorcars carried across the fields. I lost sight of Liam, knowing he'd done his part in setting me free. I was on my own.

I stumbled but kept running, unsure where to go, just wanting to get away. But I couldn't run all night, not with broken ribs and the life nearly beat out of me.

As the sounds died behind me, I stopped for a moment to catch my breath. Hands on my knees, I looked back across the field, expecting to see British soldiers, or worse, Billy. But in the darkness I saw nothing. I turned again then hesitated. As I debated what to do, where I could hide, I realized there was one thing I had to do first.

———

I crept along the alley, careful to stay in the shadows. Then a *putt putt*, and I froze as the sound of a motorcar echoed off the walls. In a panic, I ducked behind the rubbish bins as the noise grew louder. For a moment, I was sure the lorry would turn into the alley, but then the motor began to fade as the lorry passed by. The city was worse than the countryside. Every sound startled me—every scrape of a foot, every bang of a door, every clop of a horse's hoof on stone. The curfew meant that the only people who should be out were the

British. That thought sent a shiver up my spine. Just the British and me.

I snuck around to the back of the house and, as I passed the darkened window of the scullery, I caught a glimpse of myself in the glass. In the faint glow from the gas lamp in the alley behind me, I could see the damage Billy had done: one eye dark behind a puffy slit, the other anxious, scared. My cheeks and lips were swollen, and blood still oozed from my broken nose. Other than that, my face was mostly clean; thanks to the cold water from the stream I had stopped at an hour before. My trousers were still damp and my boots sloshed from the crossing, but so far I had managed to avoid capture.

The chute was open, thank God, and I swallowed a groan as I crawled through the trap door into the coal store. *Big Frankie*, the boys called me, with a laugh. But I could fit in places most men couldn't. On my hands and knees, I waited several moments, listening for noises in the house, but all I heard was the occasional creak and groan. The banshee and the ghosts I could deal with; it was the living that frightened me. Thankfully, the house was quiet. I brushed the coal dust off as best I could then crept upstairs. The stairway protested under my weight, but no one seemed to notice. It was plain luck—I was too cynical to believe that Jesus and Mary were watching over me. Kathleen's room was on the third floor, in the servant's wing. The lock took but a moment, and then I was inside.

I know I gave her a fright, placing my hand over her mouth, whispering into her ear, but it couldn't be avoided. It took her several moments to calm down. Then a sly smile.

"If it's the bed you're after, Frank, you shouldn't have come. I have work tomorrow."

Good Catholic girl that she was, she hadn't seen me for two weeks. I shook my head.

"Nay, Kathleen. I'm not here for that."

She smiled wickedly until she saw past the coal dust. She gasped.

"Jesus, Frank! What have you been in to?"

I winced when she touched my cheek. I took her hand.

"I need to go away for a while, Kathleen."

First confusion, then fear, then a scowl, her eyes dark, her face cross.

"What did you do?" she demanded.

"It doesn't matter, Kathleen. But I have to go. Now. Before they find me." I paused as I searched her eyes. "I'll be back, I promise."

"How long?" she asked with a worried frown.

Not sure what to tell her, I shook my head.

After a moment, I could see the resignation in her eyes. She nodded slowly. "Where will you go?"

I shook my head again. "I don't know."

She was quiet for a moment, waiting for more, expecting me to tell her that I had a plan, to tell her that everything would be all right. When all I could give her was silence, she frowned and shook her head.

"What about Liam? He'll help you," she protested. "And the lads? They'll see you're taken care of?"

The lads. The IRA. They had hidden many a man on the run from the British.

I sighed. Before I could answer, there was a shout outside and we both turned to the window. After a moment, I heard the quiet singing, the sounds of drunken men on their way home from the pub, one that should have closed hours ago. I shook my head; it was a dangerous game they were playing, breaking the curfew. But who was I to talk? I turned back to Kathleen and shook my head again.

"Nay," I answered. I took a breath and forced myself to say it. "They're the ones after me." It was a lot for her to digest—it was a lot for me to digest—and the early hour didn't help. "I'm on my own."

Kathleen gasped, her breath catching in her throat, then she looked away. Her shoulders slumped, and she leaned forward, her face in her hands. I waited for tears that never came. When she looked up, there was something else in her eyes; the fear I expected, but there was a sadness too.

"Frank," she began slowly. She held my gaze for a moment, then turned her head and stared at some unseen spot on the floor. She pulled a chain from the collar of her gown and absentmindedly rubbed the medal between her fingers.

It was a foolish thing to do and I knew it before the words came out of my mouth.

I reached for her hands. "You have to come with me."

Kathleen looked up and dropped the medal. She frowned. "What?" she demanded, her voice rising. "Have you lost your mind?"

I nearly had to clamp my hand over her mouth again but, thankfully, she stopped. I waited, knowing she wasn't done.

"How can I leave?" she whispered, then nodded toward the door. "What about them?"

A domestic servant she was called, one of six girls who kept house for a rich Protestant family. Her days were spent scrubbing yesterday's dirt from the tile floors and polishing the dark wood moldings that filled the house. She washed and mended the linens, cleaned out the fires, and restocked the coal. At four, after she brought Mrs. Cavanagh her afternoon tea, in a china cup served on a silver platter kept polished as the missus demanded, she put the baby in the pram and took the three children for a walk.

"Kathleen." My whisper was urgent. "You know what will happen if you stay."

It was only a matter of time before Liam told the boys about Kathleen. He was my friend after all, and Billy would come for him next. I didn't think Billy would do anything to Kathleen—what could he do, her sister being Mary and all?—but I didn't tell her that. I couldn't stay in Limerick, but I didn't want to leave Kathleen behind.

There was a thump in the house. She gasped, and I had to clamp her mouth again. A door squeaked, then loud footsteps right outside the room. A second later, the creak of the stairs.

Kathleen pulled my hand away and leaned close, her lips touching my ear.

"It's Eileen," she whispered, "going to the privy."

I stared at the door and listened to the footsteps fade. A moment later, there was the far-off clunk of the privy door shutting outside. I turned back to Kathleen and, in the dim light, I could see her face was clouded with doubt.

"Come with me," I said softly.

"No," she said, shaking her head. "I can't."

"Why not?" I asked as I searched her eyes. I nodded toward the door. "They mean nothing to you."

"I can't," she said again. She hesitated, looking away for a moment, before her eyes found mine once more. "I can't."

Before I could say anything more, her eyes narrowed. "And where would we go?" she demanded. "With the IRA after you." She continued to scowl. "And likely the British too."

"I don't know. Tipperary? Tralee? Dublin? What does it matter?"

"What does it matter?" she repeated as if I were daft.

She was about to say more but stopped as the sound of a motor drifted across the darkness. I glanced at the window. The sound grew, the motor whining. Soon it became a roar. My heart quickened as I reached for the drapes. I froze at the squeal of the brakes. Doors banged open and the night was filled with voices. British voices.

"Go!" Kathleen hissed in my ear.

I turned back. Her eyes were filled with panic. She gripped my hands.

"Now! Before they find you."

I held her gaze for a moment—her eyes pleading with me—before I nodded. I leaned forward and kissed her gently on the forehead. I turned and rose, then felt her hand on mine once more.

"Go," she said softly, nodding toward the door, all the while still holding my hand.

There were shouts from below the window, then the sounds of running feet. She dropped my hand and nodded toward the door once more.

"Go."

Silently, I made my way to the door.

It was a foolish thing to do; it was better to get the parting over with. But I couldn't help myself, and I glanced back once more before I slipped outside.

Kathleen had pulled her knees up to her chest, the linens draped over. She was biting her lip and staring at something—nothing—on the floor between us. She pulled the medal from her gown again, and I watched as she turned it over and over in her hands.

She looked up once, shook her head as a tear slid down her cheek. *Go*, she mouthed.

I felt a lump in my throat as I quietly stepped outside.

———

I managed to sneak out of the Cavanaghs' without disturbing the family or the other servants, or worse, drawing the attention of the British patrol. The fog was thick, and I was thankful for that as I made my way down the alley. Still, I hid in the shadows, afraid not only of the Peelers and the IRA but wary of the gypsies and gangs that would surely try to beat and rob me given the chance. As I approached the street, the murmurs of voices and the bang of a hammer caught my attention. Heart thumping in my chest, I slipped back into the alley. After a moment, I peered around the corner and, in the glow of the gas lamp, spied the green uniforms of the Peelers. A constable was standing in front of the telegraph pole, a hammer in his hand. One more stood behind him, his rifle held ready. Three more plus a driver sat in a lorry. They were hanging another notice;

more orders, no doubt, more new laws from London designed to put us back into our place. The aristocracy in London was looking to squash the latest insurrection as they had all the ones for centuries before, all the while trying to appease us ignorant peasants with promises of Home Rule someday. I hid in the alley waiting for them to finish, my heart thumping in my chest all the while.

It was but a moment later that they were done. With a growl from its engine and a grinding of its gears, the lorry disappeared into the mist. I slipped out of the alley and made my way to the pole.

*One thousand pound reward*, the notice said. I shivered as I stared at the picture, at the grainy black and white image.

"Jesus!" I hissed.

I jumped at the loud bang somewhere off in the darkness but, after a moment, realized it was nothing more than a backfire from the British lorry driving away. I turned back and stared up at the poster, stared up at my own face.

*Francis Kelleher. Wanted for murder in Ireland.*

# Chapter Two

We were to burn down Argyll Manor—a stately home that belonged to a rich Protestant landowner—before, it was rumored, the RIC moved in and converted it into a new barracks. Lieutenant Dan Buckley was in charge and Tom Sheehy, Sean Murphy, and I were ordered to assist. Under cover of darkness, Dan and Tom broke the lock on the door while Sean and I kept watch for the Peelers. This far out in the country, we didn't expect them, but the dead before us had taught us to be careful. I heard the whistle—two long, low notes was the signal that Dan and Tom had been successful—and I took one more look down the lane before I stood nervously. Lugging the mine—fifteen pounds of gelignite and gun cotton packed in a wooden box—and the haversack with the other things we would need, I followed Sean. He wobbled side to side, an awkward step due to the two tins of paraffin he carried. I was no better, watching my own feet, not wanting to trip, careful with the package in my arms. I didn't tell the boys, but the mine scared me, and the sooner I could lay it and get away, the happier I would be.

We slipped inside and while Dan issued hushed orders and kept watch, Sean carried a tin of paraffin to the second floor. Tom was responsible for the first and began spreading the paraffin—kerosene— over the furniture, the walls, the drapes, and the doorways. Leaving the others to their tasks, I set the mine in the center of the parlor, checking the distance to the door. We planned to detonate the bomb from outside, protected, we hoped, by the heavy wooden door and the thick cut-stone walls. I only had forty yards of detonator wire in my haversack. I had wanted more, but supplies being what they were, that was all the quartermaster could spare. As I unwound the wire, working my way back to the door, I hoped I remembered everything I had been taught. Stepping outside, I knelt on the stoop and pulled the detonator from my haversack. Two nights earlier, we had pilfered the coil from a Model T Ford. This I had fashioned into a detonator, a box with a plunger, and a flashdamp battery, a device that the man from GHQ—General Headquarters in Dublin—assured me would work. I attached the wires, carefully twisting the nuts, mindful of the plunger the whole while.

Without warning, there were shouts from inside and I flinched. Then came the gunshots, first one then two, then the roar of a volley. My heart thumping in my chest, I peered around the door and saw two British soldiers, their weapons blazing up the staircase where Sean had gone. Tom and Dan were lying on the floor, two more British soldiers standing over them. Dan was still; Tom was screaming in pain, clutching his stomach. Then I heard a shout from upstairs. With a sinking feeling, I realized Sean too had been shot. I reached for the haversack and began frantically searching for my revolver. Why didn't I carry it in my coat pocket like the other lads? I'm not sure how he saw me, but suddenly one of the soldiers turned and leveled his gun. Forgetting my own, I lunged to the side, slamming my hand on the plunger as I leapt out of the doorway.

For several days after, I replayed the scene over and over in my head asking myself each time if there was anything different I could have done. Surely, Dan was dead and Tom soon would be, if not from the bullet he already had taken then from the one he soon would— the British, as they had done many times before, would later claim that he was shot while trying to escape. And surely Sean had no chance, wounded as he was, and me without a gun in my hand and ready at the time, I was no help. And surely the British had reinforcements in the area, waiting to rush in and shoot any IRA men still alive. Surely, I told myself again and again, there was nothing else I could have done.

There was a terrible bang and a bright flash followed by a roar, and suddenly the world was raining down on my head. Deaf and blind, I struggled for several moments, praying for the first time in years to Jesus, to Mary, to the saints, to anyone who would listen. When I finally pushed the door off me, I could hear the muffled screams as I pulled myself to my feet. I slapped at my own burning clothes then, dazed, I stared back at the doorway, feeling the heat from the growing inferno inside. I stumbled backwards when the flames, unhappy that I had somehow escaped their wrath, began to lick out the door, searching for me. A moment later, they shot out the broken windows on either side and then from the windows on the floor above.

From behind me, I heard the shouts and the sound of the lorries, muffled in my ringing ears but loud enough to startle me. With one last look at the burning doorway, I turned and ran. I scrambled over the wall, then darted across the field, waiting the whole while for the bullets to find me. Somehow they never came. Still I kept glancing over my shoulder to see if I had been spotted. By the time I reached the crossroads, the screams from inside the manor house had gone silent.

———

It's a strange thing to know that someone wants you dead. Sure I knew that one day I might find myself on the wrong end of a British rifle and, like many before me, I might become another nameless face, another worthless Irish peasant, an *enemy of the Crown* killed in a gun battle. But it was a risk I was willing to take, for ours was a cause worth dying for. That the British wanted me dead, just as they wanted every Irishman like me, was not a surprise. Like all new Volunteers, I was told this repeatedly during training. *If the*

*British catch ye, yer dead! But just as sure, lads, if they learn who ye are, they'll hunt ye down and ye'll be just as dead!* Hiding who we were behind the facade of farmers, ironmongers, coal porters—good citizens all—was the means of our survival.

But as I had learned earlier, the British now knew who I was. In many ways, perhaps, it was inevitable. Events that had taken place years ago had set the wheels in motion.

It was on a warm summer night two and a half years earlier that I had found myself in the stable facing a dozen men.

*"I do solemnly swear that to the best of my ability, I will support and defend the government of the Irish Republic against all enemies, foreign and domestic, and that I will bear true faith and allegiance to the same. I take this obligation freely without any mental reservation or purpose of evasion. So help me God."*

I remember pausing, taking a deep breath before glancing up at the faces around me, at Billy, at Liam, at Patrick, at Mick, Tom, Sean, Roddy, and Dan, people I had known all of my life. They stared back at me, their voices silent, their faces stern. Then Billy stuck his hand out.

"Good to have you with us, Frank."

Suddenly there were claps on my back and laughing; a light time, a camaraderie despite the seriousness of the moment. Thinking back on it now, there was never any doubt that I would join. Ours had been a rage seven hundred years in the making. Centuries of massacres and attempts by the British to crush us had surely left us weakened but had never darkened our dream. Even while our land was being taken and our food was being shipped to England—all while our own children starved to death—we continued to fight for what was ours. Even when our language was denied to us and when they tried to squash our heritage and our faith with their so-called Penal Laws, we held firm. Certainly the Irish Catholic Church was as bad as the British government but it was *our* church. Then, finally, on one fine morning, the day after Easter, one hundred and thirteen years after Robert Emmet hung from a British noose, Patrick Pearse and James Connolly led a band of men—Fenians and Irish Brothers all—into the center of Dublin and awakened our slumbering rage. Suddenly, it seemed, the dream of our fathers and of our father's fathers was within our reach.

My own contribution began three years after Pearse and Connolly and fourteen others faced a British firing squad for proclaiming Irish independence. There I was, with just nineteen years of age, joining my friends, my fellow countrymen, taking up arms in the fight for freedom. Doing my part for Ireland.

———

With my picture posted on the telegraph poles and the lampposts around the city, I couldn't wait any longer. In the cold darkness before dawn, I began my journey, hitching a ride on a milk cart. Wet and dirty from the long night and with the pain of Billy's beating becoming a dull, throbbing ache, I fought the pull of sleep. The air was cold, and I shivered as the city faded behind us. The driver was content to listen to the sounds of the horses, their steps rhythmic and somehow peaceful. It was just as well—I didn't want to talk, lost as I was in my own thoughts. And what was there to say anyway? With my own friends against me, there were few places I could go. Sure I could hide—for a while—but it would only be a matter of time before someone discovered who I was.

Yesterday's papers had denounced *the atrocities perpetuated by the dangerous criminal element that calls themselves the Irish Republican Army*. Dan, Tom, and Sean had been identified, as had the dead Black and Tans, and authorities were looking for the accomplices who were seen escaping after setting the explosives. While the papers hadn't mentioned me by name, the poster I had seen earlier confirmed the British were hunting for me. The mood in the country left me with few choices. There was still an element within the Irish that was more afraid of what the Tans might do in retaliation, and sacrificial lambs—real or imagined—were offered as appease-ment. My only option was to run.

I listened to the horses, their steps softened by the fog, as the plan began to form in my head. As I put the pieces together, the heavy weight I had been carrying since Billy first accused me of be-ing a traitor, began to lighten. But that was replaced by the burden of what I was leaving behind. My plan was dangerous, I told myself, but less dangerous than staying. Besides, what choice did I have anyway?

My mind made up, I settled back into the seat and stared off into the fog. I had a long way to go before I reached the coast, longer still because I couldn't risk being seen. Not by the Peelers, not by the Tans, not by the men who were once my friends.

———

I shook my head trying to chase the dark thoughts from my mind. Despite all that had happened, the morning was quiet and peace-ful. The gray mist that surrounded us, the rhythmic clip-clop of the horse and the rattles and squeaks of the cart provided a strange comfort. My head bobbed and I shook it again to clear the cobwebs, telling myself I had to stay awake. I sat up and stared out at the countryside, at the gray light of dawn, too tired to talk and not sure what to say anyway.

Three nights with no sleep and Billy's beating had taken their toll. The soft darkness continued to pull at me, but as soon as I be-gan to slip away, sharp jolts of pain would startle me awake. I went on like that for some time, see-sawing between sleep and pain, each rut and bump reminding me of Billy's boot. I finally gave up fight-ing, letting the waves of darkness wash over me. Sometime later I let out a cry, waking to the pain that shot through my ribs.

"We're here," the driver said. He poked me with the buggy whip again.

I looked up. The cart was stopped at the crossroads; the lane to the right led to the farm. I thanked the driver as I climbed down. He nodded once then flicked the reins. I watched as he turned and disappeared into the fog, his early morning delivery to the creamery done. I sighed, glanced once behind me at the road we had traveled on, then back in the dim light of early dawn over the hills toward where the city lay, lost now in the fog. With a sigh, I turned. As I began walking in the other direction, a cold rain began to fall. I turned my collar up and tugged my cap low. So much had happened in the last sixteen months, I thought as I made my way down the road, and now here I was leaving my home, leaving the fight for freedom to my brothers.

––––

I had thought that I would have my savings, enough money to pay for the boat fare. But with my picture posted all over Limerick, it wasn't safe to wait for the post office to open. I had no way of knowing if Billy was still alive or if he had been captured by the British. Liam had escaped, I hoped, and as for the others? I didn't know. But one thing I knew for certain: no British jail could hold Billy. He was one of the most ruthless men I had ever met and if he hadn't escaped, he was surely dead. But I also knew that dead or not, he was sure to come after me. That was a fear that kept me going.

It was a tough journey; I spent four days and three long nights making my way to Cobh—what the British called Queenstown— some eighty miles away in County Cork. Whenever I heard a motorcar or a lorry, I hid. Many times I laid quietly behind stone walls as a British patrol drove by. When I was certain it was safe, I hitched rides. But mostly I walked.

In the ever-present winter rain, I slogged through the wet grass while the cows and sheep grazed. I climbed over countless stiles and stone walls and trudged through the endless bogs and planting fields, barren and muddy now in the winter. I sloshed down the rain-soaked boreens, hidden, I hoped, by the mist. I slept in churches and barns when I could, and, when I couldn't, I huddled in the fields, finding what warmth I could in the hayricks. I begged for food along the way, and when my requests were met with cold stares, I stole what I needed. No, heaven wasn't in God's plans for me.

By the time I reached Cobh, the pains of Billy's beating began to fade. But the worry hadn't, and Kathleen was never far from my mind.

———

Standing in the shadows, I pulled the watch from my pocket. Feeling the weight in my hand, the smooth metal, I let out a breath as my father's voice filled my head. *When a thing is wrong, you have to make it right.* I stared down at the watch and ran my thumb across the cracked lens. Despite the crack and despite the worn metal— tarnish I couldn't see now but knew was there—the old timepiece still worked. Steady and rhythmic, the *tick-tock* of the gears and the sweeping hand both informed me of the present and reminded me of the past. It had been my father's watch.

It was a quarter till three in the morning and I was standing on the dock, looking for a man I didn't know. The quay was crowded, even in the middle of the night, full of frantic activity to prepare the ship for sailing in the morning. I watched the men as, one after another, they wheeled the crates and steamers up the gangplanks. There was a metallic clank and then a groaning as the provisions for the journey were hoisted by crane to the deck. The deck itself was busy as crewmembers scurried about, checking this and that all while under the watchful eyes of several officers. I studied the dockers coming and going, not sure which was the one.

"Frank!"

I jumped at the sound. Heart pounding and ready to run, I turned.

A man I didn't know, dressed in the clothes of a docker, was waving. He didn't seem to be looking at me. I turned in the other direction and saw another docker on the deck waving back. I let out a breath and turned my attention back to the loading. After a while, another docker appeared and stepped over into the light of the gas lamp. He lit a cigarette and, as I studied his face, I tried to remember the description I had overheard.

By the warehouse was a lone guard, sitting on the back of a cart. Every now and then I caught him taking a sip from a flask. The loading continued and, when the guard's head finally dropped to his chest, I approached the docker—the big man smoking the cigarette below the light of the lamp.

"Would you tell where I might find Paddy O'Hurley?"

Up close, he was bigger than I thought. He was a head taller than me and had the large arms and the broad back that came from years of heavy work. He turned and eyed me, his eyes narrowing. Muddy, wet and dirty from the journey as I was, he had every right to be wary.

"And who would be asking?"

"Michael O'Sullivan," I said without a pause. It was the name of a boyhood friend who had died when I was nine. "From Limerick." I had prepared myself for the question.

He regarded me for a moment. "I'm Paddy," he said. I caught the challenge in his voice, a warning that told me he was busy, to state my business or be gone.

Before I could say anything, there was a shout and a curse and Paddy turned. Two men were struggling to attach the rigging to a large crate. The rigging dangled below the crane, the men on deck watching impatiently while the two on the wharf scrambled to secure it. Paddy shook his head and turned back to me.

Taking a breath, I explained my situation, telling him I was on the run and, with the British after me, had to leave the country as soon as I could. I prayed the whole while that he truly was the Paddy I had been looking for and that I hadn't made a mistake. If there was a code word, I didn't know it. He asked me several questions and those I answered truthfully. Something told me it wouldn't do to lie.

Paddy's eyes narrowed. "You know Billy Ryan, do you?"

I felt the hairs on the back of my head stand up at the name. "Aye. Billy's the O.C." I answered. The Officer in Charge. "But I'm not even sure if he's still alive."

"Argyle Manor?" he asked, his eyes boring into mine.

I shouldn't have been surprised. Even as far away as Cobh, the newspapers surely had carried the stories of the bombing. I sensed there was no use in lying. "Aye." I nodded. "Argyle Manor."

Paddy glanced over his shoulder once, then looked at me and nodded.

I told him what I needed.

"Meet me back here in an hour," he ordered then disappeared.

An hour later I made my way back, wondering the whole while if I was walking into a trap. I had seen two British patrols earlier but thankfully neither had seen me. When I reached the quay, there were no soldiers, no constables waiting for me. That didn't mean that the IRA wasn't lying in wait. I buried myself in the shadows and kept an eye out for Paddy. My eyes darted around, and I tried not to appear nervous, tried not to jump at the shouts and the commotion around me.

It was another thirty minutes before I saw him. We spoke quietly and he pointed over to the cart. The guard I had seen earlier was gone but sitting in his place was a small trunk. More importantly, Paddy gave me two names.

———

Thanks to Paddy, the clothes had been easy but the travel papers and ticket had taken some effort. Cleaned up as best I could and with new clothes, I waited outside the hotel, studying the people coming and going, looking for a man who was close to me in size, and catching snippets of conversations until I found what I needed.

"Oh, wasn't Paris grand, Desmond?"

A nod and a smile. "Aye, Maureen. But it will be good to lie in our own bed again."

"And what time is the train?"

"At nine. Tomorrow morning."

It didn't take much to find out what room they were in, or to break in for that matter. The IRA had trained me well. And it didn't take much searching to find the travel papers. These were below the trousers and shirts in the bottom of one of the trunks. There was also a purse and, although I was tempted, I left it. The missing passports might not be noticed for a day or two, or so I hoped. But the purse was different. Had both the purse and the passports disappeared, surely a robbery would have been reported and the Peelers would have been alerted. But what thief would take the passports only and leave the money? Surely the travel papers were only misplaced.

Now that I had their passports, neither Desmond nor Maureen could travel. But I could. Having served its purpose, when no one was watching, I dropped Maureen's passport into the harbor, taking pains to weight it with a stone so that it would sink quickly. I kept Desmond's safe in my pocket.

I wasn't sure what I would do for money, but my good luck continued as, later that morning, I found myself with a purse full of pounds. Cobh was a busy town with ships coming and going. The hotels and restaurants were full and the streets were crowded with horses and carriages, motorcars and lorries, carts, and people all fighting for space. On my way back to the hotel, still several blocks away, I came upon an opportunity.

The carriage was askew, the rear wheel broken; steam was rising from the front of the motorcar. A well-dressed woman was sitting on the ground, sobbing and holding her head. The blood ran down her fingers, and the sleeve and front of her dress were stained red. Another man, the carriage driver it appeared, was lying face down on the ground. He too was bleeding from a wound to the head, the cobbles stained red below him. Two men, well dressed in their derbies and suits, were shouting and pushing at each other. When one hit the other, I rushed forward, joining the small crowd that had gathered.

Ignoring the donnybrook, I looked inside the motorcar and then the carriage before I found what I needed. Leaving the two injured people in the street and the two angry men cursing and swinging at each other, I made away with the purse.

I was already going to hell, what did one more sin matter?

———

"It's a rich man you are," I told myself as I smoothed my hair then placed the derby on my head. "Rich and smart," I continued. In the mirror, a stranger stared back. I touched my hair, once brown now black, dyed to match Desmond's, then I adjusted the wire-rimmed glasses I now wore, just as he did. Paddy O'Hurley had done a fine job with the trunk. The tweed vest and brown pinstripe sack coat I wore hadn't required much from the tailor, but as I was shorter than the man they belonged to, the trousers did. Still, he had done a fine job with the pins and the stitching. For a pig farmer from Limerick, I had never known such finery.

Minutes later, I was heading down the street searching for one of the names Paddy O'Hurley had given me.

Trying my best to look like a gentleman out for a noonday stroll, I studied the signs above the store fronts as I remembered what Paddy had told me. It wasn't but a short while before I found the photographer, next to the chemist, just as Paddy had said. I had to wait for several carriages and motor cars to pass before I could cross the street. I had just stepped off the curb when the sound of a horn caught my attention. I paused as a Model T raced past me. The driver nodded and I saw him shift gears. The sharp bang startled me and, for a moment, I thought it was a gun, but then I saw the motorcar lurch. There was a puff of black smoke from the back. I let out a breath, smiled to hide my nervousness and tried again to cross the street. As I dodged the carts and carriages and motorcars, I tried to calm nerves that were on edge. *It was only a backfire*, I told myself. But that didn't stop the tingle in my spine. I glanced behind me to see if I was being followed. No one, thankfully, seemed to be paying me any mind.

I had just reached the other side when I heard the whine of another motor followed by the grinding shift of gears. I felt the hairs on the back of my neck as I remembered the British lorry below Kathleen's window. Suddenly there were shouts and I glanced behind me. A lorry skidded to a stop in the middle of the street and several Peelers, all wearing the mismatched uniforms of the Tans, jumped out. They surrounded a carriage and began to shout at the driver and passenger. I turned quickly and hurried along the curb, away from the men who would surely kill me if they discovered who I was.

"Hold it! You! Stop!"

I froze and turned slowly. My heart began to hammer in my chest. The Tan was pointing directly at me.

He marched over, stopping a foot away. I could smell the tobacco and sweat from his clothes as his dark eyes bore into me. He studied me for a moment then glanced at the papers in his hand. I felt the panic rising. The RIC in Limerick, I realized, figuring I would try to escape, had sent my picture and description to the obvious place: the port. Standing calmly—or so I hoped it appeared—with my hands by my side, I waited. He was older than me but not much taller. Behind him, the rest of his patrol was questioning random people in the street. One, I saw, frisked the couple they had pulled from the carriage while another searched inside. There were six of them, and they all had guns. Fighting my way free wasn't an option. While I might be able to get the better of the one who had taken an interest in me, I had to worry about the others.

"Your name," he demanded when he looked up.

"Michael O'Sullivan," I answered, hoping he didn't notice how nervous I was.

He regarded me with a skeptical eye. "Where are you from?"

"Birr," I answered. "County Offaly." This was an answer I had practiced too. Birr was more than a hundred miles from Cobh and at least sixty miles from Limerick.

"Where are you traveling to?"

I shook my head. "I'm not," I answered. "I'm here to meet my brother." My brother, I told him, was a medical doctor living in London.

The Tan stared at me but said nothing.

"Has something happened?" I asked.

Ignoring my question, he turned then shouted at someone else and hurried away.

I slowly let out the breath I had been holding then turned and hurried down the street.

———

Paddy had given me two names. The first was for a photographer, one the IRA had used from time to time. I decided it was best to wait several hours for the commotion in the street to subside before I approached him. When I finally did, using Paddy's name, I explained why I was there.

"And you're the one the Tans are looking for, are you?" he asked, nodding to the window, where, hours earlier, the Tans had been causing a ruckus right in front of his shop. His eyes told me that he knew and I was unsure how to answer.

"Aye," I finally said, sensing it would do me no good to lie.

"And a fine looking man such as yourself?" he asked with a smile, a joke to ease my tension.

I smiled back.

"Well then, we'd better take care of that."

He led me to the back, behind the black curtain, where he took several photographs of me. He told me to return the next day.

When I did, I offered to pay him.

"Just doing my part," he insisted as he handed me an envelope.

I shook his hand.

"Mind yourself now," he cautioned, nodding again toward the window.

I thanked him again and left in search of the second name.

———

"Two days," the engraver said when I explained what I needed. I handed him Desmond's passport and the new picture. While I waited, I passed the time in the hotel, telling the chambermaid that I wasn't feeling well. I only ventured out when necessary—for food and newspapers—but for two days I lived in luxury with the money I had stolen.

On the second day I got the news I had been waiting for. The paper announced that the *Celtic* was leaving Liverpool that afternoon. It would stop in Cobh, take on passengers and, on the following day, depart for New York. I purchased a standby ticket. If there was room, I planned to be on the *Celtic*.

I'm not certain how the engraver did it, somehow removing Desmond's photograph and inserting mine. Even the embossing and rubber stampings looked like they had been done by a government official. I shook my head and, when I asked the engraver for the bill, like the photographer, he refused to accept any money. I knew I wasn't the first that he had helped to escape.

I boarded the next morning, catching the first skiff out to the steamship—the *Celtic* forced to drop anchor out in the bay. I found my room, stowed my trunk and made my way back to the deck. Standing there, while the crowd around me prattled on excitedly, I kept a watchful eye on the skiffs ferrying passengers from the wharf, expecting anytime to see the Peelers searching for whoever had stolen Desmond's and Maureen's passports. I held my breath for a long six hours but, thankfully, they never came.

The low moan of the boat's whistle startled me and I felt the deck shudder. There was a low, painful groan from somewhere deep inside the ship, and the deck lurched again. Ten days after I listened to the dying screams of my friends in the manor house and eight days after I felt the blows of Billy's fists and feet, I stood silently on the deck as we slowly sailed out of Cork Harbor. The towns and farms slipped past us as the ship made its way out the mouth into the sea. As the ship turned east, a stiff wind hit us.

We followed the coast for a while and I stood there for a long time watching the only land I had ever known slip away. When the green hills finally disappeared into the mist, my eyes teared up. I wondered if I would ever see Kathleen and Ireland again.

# Chapter Three

I woke to the cry of the neighbors' baby and the chill of the December air. *Jesus!* The cold here was worse than the one I had known in Ireland. With the linens and blankets cinched up around my chin, I stared into the darkness and listened to the creaks and groans of a building that was surely as weary of us—the mass of people who filled its rooms and called it home—as we were of it.

The baby, no doubt now cuddled in his mother's arms, soon quieted. But now that I was awake, thoughts filled my head, and I knew I wouldn't be falling back to sleep. Too early to get up for work, I laid in bed, searching the shadows for answers that I knew weren't there. Instead the dark gloom held a sadness, one that always seemed to find me in the early hours, as thoughts of Kathleen filled my head. I missed her sorely and wondered if she too lay awake in the darkness, when sleep eluded her. Did she think of me then? As I had done many a night, I thought back to the events that had separated us—events that had brought me here, thousands of miles from home, shivering in the darkness in a dirty tenement in lower New York.

———

Compared to what I found when I landed, the crossing had been a holiday. I had traveled in relative luxury with my forged papers, dressed as a wealthy and successful man, one who told people who asked that he had made his money in linens. Despite that, my accommodations were in second class, the only berth I could secure with a standby ticket. Still, with a private bath and comfortable berth, it was a far cry better than the unsanitary and overcrowded coffin ships my ancestors had endured only twenty years earlier. For eight days I pretended I was Desmond, but I was careful not to say more than I needed to, fearful that someone would expose my charade.

As the *Celtic* made its way into New York's harbor, Ellis Island lay in the distance. The worry that I had managed to chase away while we were in the open ocean suddenly refused to be ignored. I had smiled at a few of the passengers—ones I had dined with a handful of times during the journey—sharing none of my fears and instead spoke of the excitement to come. My travel papers had received only a cursory review in Cobh before I boarded and, while they certainly looked real to me, I wasn't sure if they would withstand a more thorough review by American authorities.

I needn't have worried. The men on Ellis Island had been more concerned with the diseases we Irish might be carrying than with our papers. And since I had money left after the voyage, they weren't concerned that I would become a ward of the state. But while the passing was grand, once I left Ellis Island, I joined the ranks of thousands of other immigrants who had come ashore with me: each in search of a job and a place to stay.

———

Lost in the bustling streets of Manhattan, I couldn't help but think of my father's farm. Only nineteen acres, it was a peaceful place in the country where several days might pass before we saw a neighbor. Limerick City, just ten miles away, was filled with tall buildings, its streets crowded with people and carts and motorcars all fighting for space. Even after I joined the cause and spent more and more time in Limerick on IRA business, I always felt out of place, a stranger in a foreign land. And although I had seen other cities—Cork, Cobh, Dublin—nothing had prepared me for what I found in New York.

*America: the land of milk and honey, where everyone was a millionaire!* I soon found out that most of what I had heard about America—what we Irish called *The Golden Door*—wasn't true. Sure, we were escaping the disease, the poverty and British oppression, but the dirty tenements, the gangs, and the corruption in New York were things we had never heard about when we dreamed of better lives. We had left the British behind, but even America had its share of disease and poverty. Still, with all that, America offered the Irish something that had been denied us for centuries: opportunity.

It's difficult to describe New York, a place so big yet so small at the same time. When I first arrived, shortly after the New Year in 1921, some five and a half million people—almost twice as many as in all of Ireland—had arrived before me. And with each passing day, thousands more came. The English, the Poles, the Jews, and the Germans had all come before the Irish, and it had taken us several generations to earn our place. But earn it we did. Not bothered by pride, we took whatever jobs we could, for the certainty of weekly pay was something we had never known, toiling each day on our farms, unsure if this was the year when the crop would fail again. We worked with our hands and our backs, unloading cargo from ships, laying track for railroads, and riveting steel, miles from the safety of the ground. Irish women made trousers and dresses and shirts by the thousands, their feet nonstop on the treadles while their hands fed yard after yard of cloth through the sewing machines of the garment factories. Still others could be found as servants in countless hotels and houses, cleaning and minding the children of the rich. Laborers we were, and we swelled the ranks of the trade unions, bringing an activism all our own. By the time I arrived, names like Murphy, O'Connell, and Daugherty were already common in government buildings and in the police stations and firehouses throughout the city.

———

I made my home in a single room in a crowded tenement with nothing but clotheslines and laundry to see out the only window. The building was just south of the Gas House district, a dangerous area of slums and gangs on the Lower East Side, where the air was filled with the foul smells from the tanks and from too many people in too small a space. Cautiously, I made contacts in the Irish community to learn what I needed to know to survive in this new land.

Being a pig farmer, I was able to find a job as a butcher's apprentice in one of the slaughter houses in the Meatpacking District. It wasn't close to where I lived, but I didn't mind the walk. The pay was poor, barely enough to cover the rent, but with what I was able to steal—mostly food from the slaughterhouse and the farmer's market nearby—I survived.

At nights I would lie awake, listening to the sounds of life in the tenement—the laughter, the shouts, the arguments, the fights. And with so many people came a stench, the foul smells of the street drifting through my open window. Even that didn't stop my thoughts from drifting to Kathleen. It had been almost a year since I had last seen her, huddled below her linens, her fingers fidgeting with the medal she wore as she stared at the floor.

———

There was good reason few knew that I was courting Kathleen: she and I were cousins. A marriage between close family bloodlines, although common in other countries, was a sin in the eyes of the Catholic Church. A rich man might receive dispensation in exchange for a generous contribution, but such options were not available to someone like me. Sin wasn't something I spent much time worrying over; my fate was known. But it worried Kathleen.

I had known Kathleen since we were children. One year older than me, she was the daughter of my mother's brother. For years, we only saw each other on special events: at weddings or funerals and occasionally on fair days. But like many our age we stuck to our own kind, Kathleen preferring the company of the women and the girls while I got into one form of mischief or another with the boys. That changed in my fourteenth year, when I met Kathleen on a fair day at the end of September.

On a bright, clear day, my father and I left at dawn with two cows, headed to Rathkeale, some eight miles away. We arrived at noon and, while he bartered their sale, I wandered the streets looking for fun. I passed the pens by the railway station, half full of cattle waiting to be shipped. The crowds from the pubs spilled out into the street. The laughter of men, taking a break from their toils with a pint, filled the air. The horse races were about to start, and as I made my way over, I passed the blacksmith shop. The blacksmith, a man Kathleen called Uncle John, was standing outside, glancing at his watch. Fair days were big events for a blacksmith and rare it was for him to leave his shop. But then again, John was not one to miss the races.

"Ah, Frank," he said when he saw me. "Kathleen will be along in a moment. You won't mind waiting?" Before I could say anything, he patted my shoulder. "Now there's a good lad." He smiled. "I'll see you at the races." And then he was gone.

Frustrated at having to wait, I stood in front of his shop, watching the stream of people making their way to the fields at the edge of town. I heard the bang of a hammer on anvil, John's apprentice busy inside. I shook my head. I had never missed a race before and had no intentions to miss this one, cousin or no cousin.

"Hi, Frank."

The words startled me, sounding strangely seductive, more like music than a voice. To hear my own name like that was something I had never experienced before. Excited and nervous at the same time, I turned, feeling the flame in my cheeks as I did.

"Kathleen?" I said, "Is it yourself?" The Kathleen I remembered was a wee lass, one who had never paid me any mind before. But now, in front of me stood a grown woman and a beautiful one at that. And she was talking to me and smiling, something the Kathleen I knew had never done before, or if she had, it was something she hadn't done for me.

Kathleen laughed at my obvious surprise. Years later, I would realize that she was pleased with herself and pleased too with my obvious discomfort. The prospect of talking to a girl was something that frightened me, but after an awkward start I found talking to Kathleen was easy. The streets slowly emptied, but neither of us seemed to notice.

We talked for a long time—I had no way of knowing how long—and Kathleen told me of the things that had happened since the last time we had seen each other. She was still in school—rare enough for any girl or boy our age—and she was still living with her sister, Mary.

There was a noise from the crowd, and then excited shouts and I looked over my shoulder knowing the races were about to begin.

"Please don't go, Frank," she said. I felt her hand on my arm, a strange feeling coursing up to my shoulder, filling my chest.

I turned back. Kathleen wasn't smiling anymore and I saw something different in her eyes: an uncertainty, a vulnerability I hadn't noticed earlier.

"Not yet," she continued, her voice suddenly soft and quiet and strangely uncertain.

I felt a lump in my throat. Then her hand slid down my arm and grasped my own. She stepped closer, and I could feel the heat of her body.

"And not until you kiss me first."

---

We Irish honor our traditions, and slow we are to change. Like the rituals surrounding death, courtship and marriage had their own rituals and rare it was that they weren't followed. Matchmakers, chaperones, the *walkings* and dowries were things long ingrained in our culture. Alas, such customs were not possible for Kathleen and me. There was no father to ask for Kathleen's hand as her own—my uncle—had died years ago. There were no brothers or uncles—Uncle John, the blacksmith, was really her brother-in-law and he had died several years ago too. The only family Kathleen knew—the only one that mattered—was her sister Mary. And while I had a mother, I wasn't certain if she even knew if I was still alive. And if she did, I wasn't certain if she cared.

There were practical reasons why we couldn't marry, or so I told myself at the time. I wondered now if I had made the right decision. Kathleen was a domestic servant, and it was rare for a married woman to work outside the home—a custom that favored men in more ways than one. While Kathleen wasn't opposed to this, I was. The Irish Republican Army had called us Volunteers for volunteers we were. When I first joined, I had been able to work during the day and train and fight with the Volunteers at night. But for the few months before I had been forced to flee, the British had kept us on the run. We were called a *Flying Column*, going wherever the IRA sent us to wage our war, finding shelter in someone's barn at night or sleeping in the fields if we had to. As the war wore on, we spent more time away from our homes and away from our occupations. Without some way to put bread on the table in the evenings, I had been reluctant to have Kathleen leave her job. I could make do with the kindness of those who supported our cause, but would it be enough to support a wife too? The war had turned uglier with each passing day and with me on the run, getting married hadn't made any sense.

It was one of the many regrets I carried with me through the streets of New York.

———

I had posted a letter a week after I had arrived, a long note filled with stories about the wonder and excitement of New York—the type of letter an Irishman far from home was expected to write. I signed it Michael O'Sullivan, a name I hoped Kathleen would recognize. The IRA had men in the post office who read the mail, always on the lookout for spies and informants. And always on the lookout for traitors like me.

I didn't know how long it would take my letter to reach Kathleen—four to five weeks I suspected. Maybe more. Still, I continued to send letters each week, anxiously hoping that each new day would bring her response.

It was eight long weeks before her first letter arrived. It was a Saturday evening, and I had just returned from the day's work anxious to clean the blood and grime from the slaughterhouse off my hands and face. I got the fire going in the stove and set the water on top, waiting for it to heat up for my bath. I sat in front of the stove and shivered, the fire not yet hot enough to drive the cold and damp from the room. There was a slam in the hall and, a moment later, a sharp knocking on my door. I flinched.

"Mr. O'Sullivan?"

I recognized the voice and let out a breath. My fear of both the IRA and the British had followed me all the way to New York. I opened the door to a short, thin woman, an apron poking out below the heavy black sweater she kept wrapped around herself to ward off the chill.

"Good evening, Mrs. Hirsch." I did my best to smile. I had never seen her smile back, and tonight was no different.

I had met Mrs. Hirsch shortly after I moved into the apartment. I shivered involuntarily, but it wasn't from the cold. Mrs. Hirsch's cheeks were sunken and her eyes seemed almost too large for her face. Like many, she carried pains from the past, and her eyes betrayed the sorrow that had followed her. She reminded me of my mother.

"I found this in my box," Mrs. Hirsch said, pulling an envelope from inside her sweater. I felt my heart skip a beat.

"A letter from home, it would seem," she said as she handed it to me.

I resisted the urge to grab it and tear it open.

"Thank you, Mrs. Hirsch." I smiled again then stared down at the letter in my hand. I ran my hand across the return address, touching Kathleen's name, feeling her writing. I coughed and turned my head, not wanting Mrs. Hirsch to see the tear in my eye.

"The soup will be ready in thirty minutes," she said, apparently oblivious to my reaction or more likely choosing to ignore it. She continued standing in my doorway and it took me a second or two to remember why.

"A moment, Mrs. Hirsch," I said as I retrieved the package from the table.

Wrapped in brown paper and tied with twine, the package would last her for several days.

She nodded once—silently—as she took the beef shank. She pulled the sweater around her once more and turned away.

We had an arrangement, Mrs. Hirsch and I. I brought her meat—stolen from the slaughter house—several times a week. In exchange she made me supper and washed my clothes and linens.

I closed the door and, forgetting about the chill and the bath water warming on the stove, carefully opened Kathleen's letter. I unfolded the single page and held it to my nose, hoping to find something— the sweet scent of Kathleen, the earthy, damp smell of Ireland. Maybe it was the day's soil still on my hands and in my clothes, but I found nothing, at least nothing that I had been hoping for. I stared at the pages. The curls and loops of Kathleen's writing flowed across the paper, and I ran my fingers across the words. On the bottom, I saw where

Kathleen had signed her name and sighed when I touched it. I pulled a chair over, sat by the fire and began reading.

From the very first line I could see that Kathleen had been cautious, careful with her words so as not to put either of us in jeopardy.

*Dear Cousin,*

*I received your letter of 24 February and it gave me great pleasure to hear from you and learn that you are well. I thank God that you arrived safely and am pleased to hear that you have been getting on. America sounds like a dream, but sadly it's one that I will have to content myself to experience only through your letters.*

*There has been much rain here but Mary and I have managed to survive. I left the Cavanagh's and Mary and I are getting on, mending and doing laundry and with the little we manage to get from our farm, it's enough.*

*I now understand why you had to leave. The troubles that you left behind continue and life in America is surely better for you than it would be here. There is no peace here and no hope in sight. But I am safe so please don't worry about me. Most of the troubles are in Limerick and Cork and Dublin and in the North. In Kilcully Cross, Mary's home, there is nothing worth fighting for anyway.*

*I've not heard from your friends since you left but I am sure they are fine. I wouldn't trouble yourself writing to them directly as you know how they are. One day here, the next somewhere else. I will inquire for you and let you know in my next letter.*

*I long to see you but I know it is not meant to be. I'll have to content myself with your letters. Please write again.*

> *Mind yourself,*
> *Your cousin, Kathleen*

I turned the page over, looking for more. *That's all?* I stared at the words, each one carefully written below the light of the oil lamp in her sister's cottage. They brought neither hope nor comfort. I told myself that she was only being careful, saying no more than she needed to let me know that she had received my letter and that she was well. I told myself that it was an intelligent thing to do. Still, it wasn't what I wanted to hear. I read the last few lines again and sighed as the finality struck me. Her words were filled with a resignation, the same one that always found me in the darkness of my room when sleep wouldn't come. Events beyond our control had cast us apart and there was nothing we could do to change that.

———

Despite my loneliness, New York was an adventure, as confusing as it was exciting and as frightening as it was grand. Each day brought something new. I soon learned which grocer to trust and which would sell you the vegetables too rotten for their own table. I learned how to avoid the gangs of young boys who would gladly stab you with their rusty knives for the few pennies you had in your pocket. And I learned that the past had a way of finding me, even thousands of miles and an ocean away, in the dirty streets of New York.

It was only one week earlier, on a Friday evening, and I had stopped in the public house, to have a pint with the lads after a long day's work. Butchers all, we frequented a place owned by a man named Burns, popular with the Irish who worked in the slaughterhouses and produce markets nearby. It was always a quick pint at the end of the week before we each went our own ways.

I had given up the wire-rimmed glasses and dark hair that had been my disguise on the voyage over, but I was careful not to use my real name. As I had done in Cobh, I told people my name was Michael O'Sullivan.

I planned on only staying for a short while, knowing full well the dangers of staying too long. One pint too many and tongues loosened; stories would be told and the signing would start. Another pint would be poured, and the process would start all over. It was a mistake I had made once, several months after I'd arrived. The next day, not certain what I'd said or to who, I vowed not to make the same mistake again.

That night, after two pints, I made my farewells. Although it was a cold night, I welcomed the walk home. I made my way across town, from one river to another, from the Hudson to the East Side, but at First Avenue, I turned south. Several blocks before the Williamsburg Bridge was a bakery that I frequented. Although there were other bakeries closer, this one was owned by an old couple from Clare. The woman reminded me of Kathleen's sister Mary, and I often found myself there, talking of home.

I had just stepped out of her store, a loaf of stale bread below my arm—I would crumble it later and boil it in milk—when I heard the voice.

"Frank Kelleher."

I froze. It was so unexpected, hearing my name like that and after so long. The man stood two feet away and, although his hands were in his pockets, his eyes told me he would use them if he had to. I took a step back.

He nodded, apparently satisfied that his suspicions had been confirmed. He took a step toward me and, although he was much bigger, this time I held my ground. He had a scar on his chin, a straight purple line that curved up on one side. The color told me it was recent, maybe a year old, and although many things could have caused a scar like that, I suspected that it had come from a knife. His lilting voice told me he was from home, but by the sound of him, I knew he wasn't from Limerick. I stared at him, at his eyes, at the scar, unable to shake the feeling that we had met somewhere in the past.

"Fancy meeting you here," he said with a sneer, "in America."

"It seems you're mistaken." I responded calmly as I considered my options. The street was crowded, as it always was. Several people glanced our way, curious at the tension between us.

"Is that it then?" he asked as his eyes narrowed. "Have you've forgotten about Sean too?"

I flinched again at Sean's name and the image flashed in my mind: Sean Murphy's father laid out on the table, the women keening nearby. I stared for a moment as it came to me. His name was Jack, a cousin of Sean's from Galway who had come for the waking. With Sean himself now dead, and by my own hand, I knew why he was here.

Several men paused, their entertainment often found in the day-to-day of the street. A fisticuff would be talked about for days to come. I glanced at them then back at Jack as I considered my options.

"It's someone else you're looking for," I said, tensing, knowing now that there was no way to avoid the fight I didn't want.

"You don't remember me?" he asked, his glare and tone telling me he saw through my lie.

I shook my head anyway.

"Oh, but I remember you." he said with a snarl. He must have seen the truth in my eyes. "You're the fuckin' traitor who killed Sean!"

And with that he lunged. The iron pipe came at me and I stepped forward, thrusting an arm up in defense, the bread forgotten now, soon to be crushed beneath our heels. I drove my other hand into his chin, hearing a crack as his head snapped back. A sharp pain shot through my other shoulder as the pipe connected. Ignoring it, I hit him again in the stomach and he let out a grunt. There was a clang behind me, and I knew he had dropped the pipe. I hit him once more, this time in the nose, and he fell backward. Grabbing the pipe off the cobblestones I stepped forward.

"The last thing I would ever do," I hissed at him, shaking the pipe in his face, "is betray my friends."

It was then I noticed the crowd, swelling now with men from a nearby pub, full of drink, excited to see a fight.

"The last thing I would ever do," I said, "is betray the cause."

The shouts and jeers from the crowd rose, and I knew Jack was sure to have friends nearby. It was time to leave. I shook the pipe again and he flinched.

"Stay away from me," I warned. Then I pushed my way through the crowd and ran up the street, hoping and praying no one would follow.

———

I shivered in the darkness and knew I should get up and light the stove. There was a creak in the floor above me, then a door closing. As I listened to the footsteps—a neighbor going to the water closet—I rubbed my shoulder, still feeling the pain from last week's scuffle with Jack. It was a strange thing, I thought as I took in the sounds and smells of the tenement slowly coming to life: the heavy foot, the hushed voices, a slammed door, eggs frying. A year ago, I was being chased, by the British and by my own men. *Surely if I could reach America*, I had thought at the time, *I would be safe*. But even so, someone from the IRA had found me and I wondered. With the Treaty that the papers said would soon be signed, was Ireland now safer than America? But that was dishonest I knew—even with the Treaty, would Ireland ever really be safe for someone like me?

I knew it wouldn't be long before Jack found me again and, when he did, I was certain he wouldn't give me a warning before his pipe found my head. I was considering leaving New York and finding work in Philadelphia or Kansas City, somewhere where my past wouldn't follow me. As much as I wanted to go back to Ireland, staying in America made more sense. It was something I had been telling myself since I had arrived.

I climbed out of bed and lit the oil lamp—the single gas lamp on the wall hadn't worked since the day I had let the room. Shivering,

I opened the stove and stirred the ashes from yesterday's fire. After I threw in a few small pieces of wood and a handful of coal, the fire began to smolder and I put the kettle on for tea. I picked up the newspaper, the one I had purchased the day before, and read the headline again. *King Calls Party To Ratify Irish Peace; Amnesty to Sínn Féiners.* The Treaty, if approved, would end centuries of British rule and oppression in Ireland, or at least in most of it. But it was a steep price that Britain demanded. They had laid claim to the six counties in the north, to most of Ulster. Like many Irish in New York, I was angry with that provision. I had hoped that the negotiators Eamon DeValera had sent to London would be able to secure more. But, if the Treaty was signed, the twenty-six counties of the south—including Limerick, Dublin, and Cork, and the cities I had known—would soon be free.

Since the truce in July, just five months earlier, I had learned what was happening back home from the newspapers and on the radio that Mrs. Hirsch played in the evenings while we ate. Daily, it was discussed and debated on the streets and in the saloons of the Lower East side. But to see it in black and white brought a finality to what I and so many of my Irish brothers had fought so hard and so long for.

As the room began to warm, I dressed for the day's work. The kettle hissed and I poured myself a cup of tea. I took a sip. Distracted by the news and what it meant for Ireland, and more importantly what it might mean for me, I hadn't let the tea cool long enough. Cursing, I put the tea down. As I ran my tongue over the burn on the roof of my mouth, I wondered if now was the time.

Ever since I had arrived, although I had made a new life in a new land, my old life was calling me home. The political tensions were easing and, although many were upset about the six counties in the north, most of Ireland, the papers seemed to say, was prepared to lay down their arms and begin anew.

Kathleen wasn't the only reason I wanted to go back. There

was unsettled business—the events of a year ago and those that had taken place well before wouldn't rest. The thought of going back continued to nag me. And if the Treaty was signed, I wanted to be part of what was taking place. I wanted to do my part to help build a new nation.

I didn't know what to do. I sipped the tea, careful this time to avoid another burn. It was a difficult decision and one that I would have trouble making. But as I would learn later that evening, it was one that had already been made for me.

———

It was six o'clock when I returned home that evening. I climbed the five flights of stairs to find Mrs. Hirsch waiting for me in the hall.

"Good evening, Mr. O'Sullivan," she greeted.

"Good evening, Mrs. Hirsch." I smiled but received only a nod in return. A few months ago, I had learned why Mrs. Hirsch never smiled, not anymore at least. I had asked about the photograph on the wall in her apartment. In it, Mrs. Hirsch was smiling as she stood next to her husband. Both were smartly dressed as were the children in front of them. The boy and the girl—I couldn't tell who was older, but they couldn't have been more than nine or ten years old at the time—were smiling as well. The only one who wasn't was Mr. Hirsch. The photograph was from 1912 and I wondered later if perhaps Mr. Hirsch knew then what was to come. Both children would have been my age now, but it wasn't meant to be—they both had died of the Spanish Flu two years ago. In some ways, I suppose, I reminded Mrs. Hirsch of the children she had lost.

Less than a year later, Mr. Hirsch would fall below a horse and carriage as he was crossing Broadway. A heart attack, the doctors had said. He was no longer able to get out of bed. Mrs. Hirsch worked in one of the garment factories sorting buttons for a few hours each day, just enough, I suspected, to pay the rent. The rest of her day was spent caring for Mr. Hirsch.

"Another letter," She said as she pulled the envelope from her sweater.

I hid my excitement. Kathleen's letters had come once a month, and all, like the first letter, had been cautiously written, with only passing mention of the troubles at home and no mention at all of our relationship. After the truce had been announced, I had asked several times what it meant, but her neat, plain handwriting only provided vague answers. I handed Mrs. Hirsch the package—beef tongue was all I could steal today—and she handed me the letter.

"A woman dropped this off this morning."

I looked up at Mrs. Hirsch. She frowned, and I couldn't help but think that something was wrong. I looked at the envelope and felt a sudden emptiness in my stomach. It was addressed to Frank Kelleher.

"Is that you?" Mrs. Hirsch asked. "Frank Kelleher?" She was still frowning, her gaze was steady on me.

"Yes," I heard myself say. Someone knew my real name and where I lived. Sharing my secret with Mrs. Hirsch hardly seemed to matter.

I looked at the envelope again. There was no stamp from the post office. I stared at my name but didn't recognize the handwriting. I flipped the envelope over. There was no return address.

Frowning myself, I looked up at Mrs. Hirsch.

"She wouldn't give me her name," Mrs. Hirsch continued. "She only said it was important that I deliver that to you."

I turned the letter over in my hand as my mind raced. I couldn't stay here—after Jack and now this letter, it was no longer safe. I wondered again about Philadelphia and Kansas City and whether I could find a job there.

"Supper will be ready in thirty minutes," Mrs. Hirsch said. I looked up, and she held my eye then nodded once before turning away. My secret, it seemed, would be safe with her. But was that enough?

I unlocked my door, the letter feeling heavy in my hand. I lit the oil lamp but didn't bother with the fire. With a sense of dread, I slid my fingernail, still dirty from the day's work, below the flap.

*Dear Mr. Kelleher,*

*We've been introduced once before but you wouldn't remember me. It doesn't matter. I'm from Ireland. I came to New York six months ago.*

*I knew Kathleen Coffey in Limerick. I visited Kathleen and her sister Mary in March, before my journey. Kathleen made me promise not to tell anyone and I wanted badly to honor that promise. I have had a long time to think and pray about this.*

*When I saw Kathleen, she was with child. She didn't want to tell me but I wouldn't let her be until she did. I know you and Kathleen were courting.*

*God willing, the baby has come safely. I've written to Kathleen but I couldn't ask directly. I'm sure you know why. I pray for Kathleen and the baby every Sunday and I light a candle in the church when I can. I pray too that Kathleen and God will forgive me for this letter. But the world is not kind to women such as Kathleen, Mr. Kelleher. I'm sure you know that.*

*I've done what I set out to do and whatever you decide is your business.*

*Sincerely,*
*A Friend*

I let out a heavy breath when I finished reading. I pictured Kathleen as I had last seen her: three in the morning and she had been sitting in bed, her knees pulled up to her chest. Her fingers had been playing nervously with the medal dangling from the chain she wore around her neck. I realized now that the fear I had seen on her face wasn't only for me, it was for her too. As I slipped out the door, she had continued to twist the medal around and around.

I should have known then. I had seen the medal clearly but with the excitement of the night, with the IRA after me and with the British right outside Kathleen's window, it hadn't made sense. I glanced at the letter again. It made sense now. Kathleen had been wearing a St. Brigid medal—*St. Brigid, the patron saint of mothers and babies.*

# Chapter Four

It was cold and gray when I first saw Limerick in the distance. Like they had been when I fled, the fields were barren, waiting for the first planting in six weeks' time. Hayricks dotted the landscape, and trails of smoke—white swirls against a dark sky—rose from the chimneys of the white-washed stone cottages that we passed. In the hills, I noticed an old man tending a flock of sheep. They were clustered together under the watchful eye of a collie who circled the flock, keeping the strays from wandering too far. I thought of my grandfather.

In addition to the pigs, my grandfather had tended a flock, some three dozen sheep. When I was eight, it became my job to help shear them, once in the spring and once in the fall. It was tough, dirty work, but so were most things on the farm. Like the man I now saw out my window, my grandfather had a collie to help him. I think that dog understood my grandfather better than my grandmother ever did. Using nothing more than hand signals, sometimes over great distances, my grandfather and the dog worked as a team and never lost a single animal. My grandfather died in my tenth year and my father—sick himself I later realized—sold the flock the day of my grandfather's funeral. Like I would do years later, the dog disappeared one day, broken-hearted I'm sure that both the man and the sheep he loved were gone. Four years later, my father, God rest his soul, died of consumption, and the responsibility for running the farm had fallen on the shoulders of a scrawny fourteen-year-old boy named Frank Kelleher.

Big Frankie indeed.

———

"Look!"

The sound of the woman's voice brought me back to the present. I glanced behind me and smiled. The young mother, holding the baby in her arms, was pointing out the window to the steel gray surface of the river as the train entered the valley.

"That's the Shannon," her husband said.

I had spoken to them briefly when we boarded. They were from Wexford and were visiting the man's relations in Limerick, something denied him for the last few years due to the war. His wife had never traveled farther than Waterford and, to her it seemed, Limerick was a world away. Relying on the name I had used for the last year, I had introduced myself as Michael O'Sullivan from New York. We had chatted about Ireland. They were tired of the war and supported the Treaty, even if it meant an Ireland divided.

They chatted excitedly, and I half listened as the husband told her about the river and what lay ahead. I stopped listening. I already knew what lay ahead on the river, but I wondered now what lay ahead for me. On the journey over, I learned that although the fighting had stopped and the British would soon be leaving, the mood in Ireland was changing. For two years we had fought side by side, united in our desire to drive the English out of our country. But now, there were growing tensions between those who supported the proposed treaty with Britain and those who didn't. The supporters, *Free Staters* they were called, celebrated our independence, a victory that had been centuries in the making. But the Anti-Treaty faction saw that the freedom Britain offered wasn't free at all. Ireland was to remain a dominion of the British Empire, and the Irish government would be required to take an oath of allegiance to the throne. *How was that different from today?* I wondered. Worse, Britain laid claim to three of Ireland's most valuable ports and proposed transferring a portion of their debt to a fledgling nation that had no means to repay it. But it was the partition above all else that caused the most debate. The six counties of the North—most of Ulster—would remain part of Britain. It was no surprise that the British wanted to keep Belfast and the North for themselves. While Limerick and the south and west were primarily farms, Belfast had foundries that made iron, textile mills that made linens, and boat yards that made ships. These businesses were controlled by Protestants whose loyalty to the King had been an economic decision as much as an ideological one. They were invaders—English and Scots—who had been given the land that British occupiers had stolen from us. Under the Treaty, Ireland would be forever divided. In exchange, Britain would withdraw its forces from the twenty-six counties of the south.

"It's the best we could hope for," a man I met on the ship had argued, something I would later hear time and again. "It's a path to freedom."

I was careful to avoid the debates, not wanting to draw attention to myself. But I didn't agree. So long as Britain required that we bow to the king, so long as they kept a strangle hold on our economy, and so long as they kept the north, we would never be free. It seemed that the country I had dreamed of during the dark, lonely nights in New York was a myth.

"Look, there's Limerick!" the woman said as she pointed to the buildings in the distance.

*Limerick*, I thought, both excited and worried. I had to be careful. Even with the war over, the year I had been gone hadn't been enough to ease the grudges. We Irish were pretty good at hating— we'd been hating the British for over seven hundred years. I suspected there was enough hate left over for me, for a traitor.

To the gentle swaying of the train, the rhythmic shush of the steam engine, and the clackity-clack of the wheels, the baby in the woman's arms behind me had fallen fast asleep and remained so for the last three hours. Like the mother and father, I'd kept my own window up lest the black smoke from the coal boiler soil the baby's dress. I was a father now too, a thought I still hadn't grown accustomed to. As I had since the moment I had received the letter, I wondered again about my own son. That the baby was a boy was certain. I don't know how I knew, I just knew. *What did he look like?* I wondered. Was he fair like Kathleen? Or did he have my own dark features?

There had been no time to ask. The day after I received Eileen's letter—she was one of the Cavanaghs' other servants and I was certain the letter had come from her—I had written to both Kathleen and her sister Mary, telling them that I was coming. I gave them no time to protest: two weeks later I stood on the deck as the boat sailed out of the harbor and New York faded in the distance behind us. I hoped my letter arrived before I did. But to be safe, I had sent a telegram from Cobh after the boat reached port.

With a loud hiss of steam, the train pulled into the station. There were dozens of people waiting on the platform, many waiting to board and others waiting for friends and relatives to get off. Out the window, I spotted the tall, fair-haired woman dressed in black standing on the platform. I was relieved to see that Mary had received my letter. She was by herself and I wondered where Kathleen was. She must be waiting with Tim by the cart, I reasoned.

Mary was searching the windows of the cars as the train slowed. I smiled and waved until she saw me. She caught my eye. Her curt nod told me that she wasn't pleased to see me, and I worried that something was wrong. Mary, twelve years older than Kathleen, was more of a mother than a sister to her. Many times I had found myself the target of her sharp tongue. Mary, I suspected, would be angry with me for the way I had left Kathleen, regardless of the circumstances. I glanced at Mary again and this time I saw something more in her eyes. Her brow was furrowed and she glanced once or twice toward the rear of the train. I frowned. It was a look I was familiar with for it was one I had seen on my own mother.

Once the train stopped, the passengers in my car began climbing out of their seats, their excited voices filling the air. I peered out the window again. Mary was looking down the platform toward the rear of the train. She bit her lip, then seemed to catch herself. I realized I had misread the tension I had spotted before. Something was happening outside. When she turned back, she held my eyes and shook her head twice.

What was happening outside I didn't know. I turned to the family behind me, looking for something to delay getting off the train until Mary signaled that it was safe.

"Here, let me," I said with the biggest smile I could manage. I helped them with the luggage and the pram, holding it steady as the mother laid the baby inside. All the while, I kept one eye on Mary. She glanced my way and shook her head again. I felt a prickle on the back of my neck as I sat back down. Outside, two men passed Mary and they too glanced over their shoulders toward the rear of the train. The worried looks on their faces were a match for that on Mary's. They quickened their pace and hurried away. A moment later I knew why. I heard the scrape and staccato clack of footsteps— sounds that could only be made by hobnailed boots. Then I heard the voices—British voices—and a moment later six soldiers appeared. I spun away from the window, tilting my head down, trying to hide my face. *Wasn't there supposed to be an amnesty?* In a moment of panic, I wondered whether the truce had failed. I watched the soldiers out of the corner of my eye. Except for the officer who carried a revolver in his holster, they weren't armed like the ones I remembered. *What type of patrol is this?* I wondered. As they passed by the car, Mary bit her lip and glanced down the platform again. As the soldiers disappeared, I realized that something else troubled Mary.

"Is everything alright here?"

I spun at the voice. The conductor frowned. He held a small silver watch in his hand, the chain connected to his waistcoat. Letting out the breath I'd been holding, I told him I would be off in a minute. He glanced at his watch, slid it back into the pocket of his vest, nodded once, and then left to check on other passengers. Most of them were gathering their luggage and making their way to the door and the steps that led outside. From the platform, I could hear the high-pitched voices of people who hadn't seen each other in years.

Unsure what to do, I waited for Mary's signal. The soldiers had disappeared, but Mary still wore a worried look. Cautiously I pressed my face to the glass, trying to see down the platform. I felt the shiver creeping up my neck again and a moment later I knew why. I jerked back at the sight: the broad shoulders; the dark, hooded eyes, filled more often with menace than they were with laughter; the thin upper lip that sat over a square jaw; the crooked nose that came from Liam's stone. It was Billy.

Better the devil you know than the devil you don't, my mother would say. But as I ducked below the window again, fussing with my boots now—or so I hoped it seemed—I knew she was wrong. It was the devil I knew that caused me worry. Eyes darting around, I searched for some means of escape.

I slid out of my seat. Leaving my luggage, I kept my head low as I made way through the car to the rear, dodging the few remaining passengers, hearing a few rebukes in my wake.

"Here now!" I heard the conductor shout behind me. I ignored him too.

How could he have known? My mind raced as I debated what to do. The train would continue on to Abbeyfeale but there were several stops along the way. I could ride the train to Patrick's Well, get off there, and find a farmer or someone heading back to Limerick and ask for a ride. I stole another glance out the window and felt my stomach sink. Billy was now talking to Mary. But if she was nervous now she hid it well.

"What's this all about?" the conductor asked again.

I turned, narrowed my eyes and coughed, my hand on my chest. "I'm…" I said and coughed again. "I've been sick," I said in a weak voice. Then I turned, doubled over and coughed once more.

Eyes wide, the conductor backed away. Like many, he feared the consumption or whatever disease I might be carrying.

I wiped the non-existent sweat off my forehead, let out a loud breath, contorting my face.

"I only need a moment….." My voice hoarse, I never finished the sentence, unable due to the bout of coughing that had overcome me.

The conductor took another step back.

"Just a moment," I continued, trying my best to wheeze, "and then I'll be gone."

He glanced back up the now empty train car. He was confused and that was all I needed. Ignoring him, I put my face up to the glass again and let out a soft moan, hoping the conductor would go away. The whole while, I could feel his eyes on my back.

Mary was by herself now, staring down toward the front of the train. After a moment she turned, searching, then her eyes found mine. She glanced down the track once more then back at me. Finally she nodded. Billy was gone.

———

It was several minutes later when I stepped onto the platform that I let out the breath I'd been holding.

"Mary!" I said. "It's grand to see you."

"You shouldn't have come," she said, her voice sharp.

Without another word, she turned on her heel and led me away. I realized that she had probably been angry with me since the day

I had fled. I held my own tongue, knowing that she had earned the right. As much as I wanted to ask about my son, I couldn't. Not yet and not until she had a chance to say her piece.

Outside the station, Mary's son, Tim, was waiting by the cart. But Kathleen and my son were nowhere to be seen. Let down, I smiled anyway.

"Tim!" I said. "How are you, lad?"

"Getting on," he said softly.

As quiet as I remembered him and with barely a glance my way, Tim took my steamer and, without another word, hefted it up on the cart. *Was he angry too?* I wondered. Or had he become more sullen the year I was away? His own mood seemed to follow his mother's.

I sighed. The reunion I had pictured in my head had only been a dream. I had hoped Kathleen would be here too, to meet me at the station. I had pictured holding my son as Kathleen told me all about him. I counted again, as I had done numerous times. My son would be eight months old now. I didn't know much about caring for a child, but I knew it was difficult and maybe Kathleen had decided it was best to send Mary and Tim to meet me.

My steamer loaded, Tim stood waiting by the cart. I turned to Mary to help her up.

"You shouldn't have come," she said again. She stood before me, hands planted on her hips, daring me to disagree. I wasn't sure what I could say to ease the tension. Mary stared at me, waiting for my answer.

I shrugged. "How could I not, Mary?"

She shook her head. "Do you have any idea what you've done?" she asked, her voice shrill.

I felt the fear rising in my chest again. *Have I been wrong about Mary?* I knew well the fate that waited for unmarried mothers. At the first signs that they were pregnant, young girls were sent away. Tainted for life, the baby and mother were left to languish in shame at the Magdalen Laundry or a home run by the Sisters of Mercy.

Reform schools the Catholic Church called them. Somewhere out in the country; out of sight, out of mind. The Church was good at sweeping its problems under the rug. But I never thought Mary would do that, not to her own sister.

"She hasn't been sent away? Has she?" I searched her eyes.

Mary said nothing for a moment, then dropped her hands. She shook her head.

*Thank God,* I said silently.

"Kathleen and the baby?" I asked. "They're well?"

"The baby," Mary said softly, she looked down for a second before finding my eyes again. Then she shook her head. "The baby died, Frank."

"Died?" I said, not quite believing my ears. I felt a tightness in my chest. *Died? How can this be?* Ever since Eileen's letter, I had pictured my son. I had thought of all the things I would teach him, the things my own father had taught to me. *My son is dead?*

"It was two days," Mary explained, "and poor Kathleen, she tried Frank, but the baby wouldn't come. When she finally did I could see something was wrong. It was all too much." Mary shook her head again. "The baby died two days later."

The news came like a blow and I stood there staring blankly at Mary. *Dead? How can this be?*

I don't recall climbing onto the cart, but at some point I found myself sitting next to Mary as Tim, his hands on the reins, steered us over the bumps and ruts in the road, away from Limerick. Mary and Tim were both silent, which was just as well for I had nothing to say. The only sound came from the snorts of the horses, the clop of their feet and the creaks and groans of the cart. I stared ahead, hardly noticing the sights and scenes that had occupied my dreams for the last year as a jumble of thoughts and emotions swirled in my head.

# Chapter Five

"Oh Frank," Kathleen said as she sobbed on my shoulder. "She hadn't been baptized. We never had a chance." I held her tight, her body shaking as she sobbed. I felt a tear run down my own cheek.

From a young age, both Kathleen and I, like most Catholics, had been told of the horrors that befell babies who died before they'd been baptized. They were forever damned to the eternity of Limbo, Father Lonagan had told us. Although we never knew exactly what Limbo was, I had a vague yet terrifying image of souls in anguish, chased forever by demons. In many ways, Limbo sounded worse than the fire and brimstone of hell that Father Lonagan had repeatedly assured me I was destined to see firsthand. Many babies died before their first year, something I had seen not only here in Ireland but in America too. That was painful enough. What made it worse was that Kathleen and I had never married. To many priests, unwed mothers were sinners, and the babies they bore were the product of that sin. An unbaptized child, and an illegitimate one at that, if I believed what Father Lonagan had preached, our baby would suffer for our sins. Despite my own views of Father Lonagan and the church, I understood Kathleen's anguish.

We were standing outside Mary's house, a small cottage on twenty acres, nine miles south of Limerick City in an area known as Kilcully Cross. There was steam rising from the washtub. Kathleen, when I first saw her, had her sleeves rolled up, her forearms red from the scrubbing. Now as she clung to me, her body wracked by sobs, I didn't know what to say. The dreams that had kept me awake for hours—what I would find when I returned to Ireland, my reunion with Kathleen, meeting my son—had been nothing more than that. Just dreams.

"Did the baby have a name?"

Kathleen lifted her head from my shoulder, wiped her eyes, and nodded. "Margaret," she said.

"Margaret?"

Kathleen nodded. It was my mother's name.

I let out a heavy breath. The child that I thought would be a son had turned out to be a girl. She must have known the world that awaited her. That's why she fought so hard against being born—and almost killed Kathleen in the process, Mary had said. Then when she first saw Ireland for what it was, she decided it wasn't a world she wanted to live in.

"And you?" I asked. "You're alright are you?"

Kathleen nodded. "The midwife said the baby wasn't ready, that she had turned the other way. That's why she wouldn't come." She wiped a tear from her cheek. "But I'm fine now." She took my hands. "I wanted to tell you, Frank, I did. That night at the Cavanaghs'?" She looked at me, searching my eyes to see if I understood. "But you wouldn't have left if you knew. And if you stayed"—she shook her head—"Billy or the British, one or the other, would have found you." She sighed. "And when I received your letter from America, I wanted to write back and tell you then. But I couldn't."

"Kathleen, I…" I started, choking on my own words. I took her hands in mine. "I'm sorry. I never meant for any of this to happen."

"I know," Kathleen said, nodding as she put her arms around me again. "I know."

——

I reached out and touched the metal, the large circle intersecting the cross. It was cold, but I kept my hand there anyway. Someone— Mary? Kathleen?—had attached a small piece of wood, carved with the inscription. I ran my hand across the words.

*Margaret Coffey*
*July 12, 1921 – July 14, 1921*

Before I knew what I was doing, I was silently mouthing the words to a prayer, as a tear ran down my own cheek. I felt Kathleen's hand on my shoulder.

"We couldn't hold a wake, and we couldn't have a funeral in the church. Father Lonagan would never have permitted it." I heard Kathleen's sigh. "But Mary arranged with Father Leahy to say a mass right here. And Mary arranged for the cross."

"Father Leahy?" I asked, looking up.

"He's from Abbeyfeale, a friend of Mary's. He's the one who has agreed to wed us."

I nodded. Trapped in the unforgiving and rigid rules of the Catholic Church, Kathleen had had no choice but to bury Margaret here, below a large oak on the highest point of Mary's farm.

"When we can, we plan to move her, to a churchyard for a proper burial. I want to speak to Father Leahy again when we see him."

I stood and took Kathleen's hand.

"I should have been here," I said softly.

"There was nothing you could have done, Frank. The baby would have died anyway."

I shook my head. "I should have been here." I looked back at the marker, at the grave where the daughter I had never met had been buried. "What was she like?" I asked quietly.

Kathleen leaned into me.

"Mary said she looked like me," Kathleen said as she wiped a tear from her eye. "But she had dark hair, like you."

We stood quietly as dark clouds built overhead and the wind rustled through the grass around us.

———

I listened to the *shoosh* of the rain on the thatched roof and the staccato splatter of drops off the stones outside. I stared out the window, at the hill, lost now in the rain, at the large oak I knew was there but couldn't see and at the grave that was sheltered below it.

"Frank," Kathleen said. I turned. Standing in front of the stove, she held the kettle up. I nodded my response and turned back to the window. I heard the clang of the kettle on the stove. A moment later, I felt Kathleen's hand on mine. She led me away from the window to the chairs in front of the stove.

"Frank. There's something else we need to talk about." She waited until I nodded. "You've been gone a long time now, and they might have forgotten about you." Her eyes narrowed. "But you can never be sure."

I nodded again as I thought about seeing Billy at the railroad station. It had just been a coincidence, but one that had left me shaken nonetheless. And the British soldiers, the ones I had seen on the platform? When Mary, Tim, and I had left the station, they had been standing out front, watching with bemusement the comings and goings of a people they had, until recently, terrorized.

"They certainly haven't forgotten about him," Mary said as she joined us, the door banging shut behind her. She shook off her wet cloak and hung it on a peg by the door. While Kathleen and I had been visiting our daughter's grave, Mary and Tim had been tending the chickens and the cow and the other livestock that had kept the three of them alive over the last year. She stood in front of us now, her eyes darting back and forth between us before settling on mine.

"We may have a truce and a treaty, but that doesn't mean we have peace." She waited a moment to see if I would argue. When I nodded, she turned and took four cups off the shelf. Kathleen got up to help, but Mary put a hand on her shoulder and Kathleen sat again.

"Things are calm now," she continued as she looked over her shoulder at me, "but it wouldn't take much." Men who had fought together for the last two years, she explained as she prepared the tea, were now taking sides. Commanders were doing all they could to hold the companies together, in case the truce didn't last.

"Still," Mary added. "Some are choosing to go with the new Free State Army that Michael Collins is forming, while others say we should keep fighting."

I didn't need to ask which side Mary had chosen.

"And as for you"—she pointed her finger and gave me a stern look—"you'll do no such thing as choosing one side or the other, not with Kathleen to mind. So don't go getting any wild notions in that head of yours."

I didn't argue, not that it would have made a difference. After nineteen years of acting the mother, acting the mother-in-law came naturally to Mary. If she had her druthers, she and some of my old comrades would carry on the fight while Kathleen and I made our home as far away from Limerick as we could. I hadn't thought about taking a side when we set sail ten days ago, but if I had to choose, I would keep fighting until all British forces, in the north as well as the south, were gone. I would keep fighting until all of Ireland was united in freedom. I nodded at Mary. For now, I would have to keep that to myself, lest I upset her any more than I already had.

"You'll be going to Abbeyfeale," Mary announced. She went on to explain that she had arranged for Kathleen and I to stay on a small farm owned by the Maloneys, relatives of her dead husband John. The Maloneys' farm was 40 miles from Limerick City and a world away. But even in New York, I remembered, thousands of miles from Limerick, the IRA had still managed to find me. If they found me there, they could find me in Abbeyfeale. It was a thought I kept to myself.

"I know a priest who will wed you," Mary continued, "but it can't be here." Kathleen and I had already discussed this, but I let

Mary have her say. That we would be getting married was never a question, but Mary wanted to be certain that I knew my obligations.

"I'll need to get my money first," I said when she was done. I had left so quickly the year before there had been no time to get my savings. I would have to visit the post office. I wondered again if the IRA still had men inside.

"It'll do you no good if you're dead," Mary snapped. She gave me another sharp look, making sure I understood. "For now, it'll be safe where it is."

I nodded. Fierce when crossed, it wouldn't do to question Mary, certainly not now. Besides, she was right; the money could wait until I understood just how much Ireland had changed since I'd left.

I wondered about my things, but I didn't ask. The IRA, I suspected, had taken everything. Coats and boots were in short supply, and the Volunteers commandeered whatever they could. Now that I was back, I realized I'd had left nothing of value when I'd fled. In my coat pocket, I wrapped my hand around my father's watch, feeling the reassuring *tick-tock* of the gears. It was the only thing from my past that I still owned. The only thing that mattered.

While Mary talked about Abbeyfeale and the wedding and her plans for us, one way or another, before we left Limerick, I had unsettled business to tend to. I had come back to Ireland for Kathleen and for the baby. But now that I was here, I knew it was more than that. Now that I was in Limerick, I couldn't leave without facing my past. And the first thing I needed to do was to track down the man who had saved my life.

Unfortunately, that would have to wait for two more weeks.

———

Although she didn't say it, I think Mary saw how happy Kathleen was to have me there. The last year had been difficult for both of them and I suspected that it had been a long time since either had laughed or even smiled.

Like many in Ireland, Mary had her share of sorrow. Her husband John Reidy, a blacksmith who had quietly supported the IRA, had been killed by the British almost two years before. He hadn't been shot or hanged, but his blood was on their hands the same as if he had been. Although he wasn't a Volunteer, he had steadfastly refused when the RIC had asked him to forge steel shutters for their barracks. Then one night, in reprisal for an IRA raid, the Black and Tans set fire to several businesses, including John's smithy. Told by the Tans that his apprentice was inside, John had rushed into the flames. While he frantically searched the smoked-filled shop, the inferno grew. John would never learn that his search was futile, that while he battled the flames, his apprentice was safe at home having supper.

Mary never had time to grieve. With a dead husband and the smithy—and her home along with it—reduced to ashes, she had been forced to leave Rathkeale, the only village she had ever known. She found a farm for rent—almost twenty acres—some twenty miles away in Kilcully Cross, a small quiet crossroads nine miles south of Limerick City. Far larger than she and Tim could manage on their own, they only raised a small crop, and Mary had been forced to take in laundry, leaving her hands permanently raw from washing and mending clothes.

Mary was the only family Kathleen knew, their other siblings long gone, one to Boston, another to Philadelphia, the rest to England and Australia. I didn't know if Kathleen's mother was still alive, but it didn't matter. She was a tired and bitter old woman who had given birth to twelve children. By the time Kathleen came along—she had been number thirteen—her mother had been too worn out to worry about another child. She left the mothering to her then twelve-year-old daughter, Mary. Kathleen's father, like many Irish men, had given up too and found the only solace he could in the drink. Too many years of poteen—what Americans called moonshine—had killed him before his time.

That was why, I suspect, Mary was so protective of her sister. Sure I was a cousin, but Mary never saw it that way. To her, Kathleen and Tim were the only family she had left.

———

Two days after I returned, I was repairing a section of wall where the stones had fallen. It was hard, heavy work, but a work I enjoyed. My hands in Irish soil once again, I smiled despite the pains in my back. I spent the days doing the odd chore around Mary's house: mending the thatch on the roof, fixing a broken lantern, whitewashing the fowl-house and then the barn.

Kathleen was busy at the stove, the rabbit I had caught in the morning now a stew in the pot. I laid a final stone on top of the wall and stepped back to admire my work when I heard the creaks and groans of the trap.

I turned to see Mary and Tim coming up the lane. Tim, his hands loosely on the reins, let the horse lead the way. Head down, the old mare plodded along, the lane to the cottage as familiar to her as her own stall in the barn. I watched Tim, the awkwardness of a boy growing into a man's body. Tall and thin, he looked nothing like his father. Except for the hair. Tim, like John, had curly black hair, the hint of a Mediterranean ancestor in his Irish blood. I saw the faint lines of the scar on his chin. Awkward, even as a child, Tim had tripped and fallen in his father's smithy, catching his chin on the anvil. Some seven years later, the white line of the scar still ran along the side of his jaw.

I left the stones, wiped my dirty hands on my trousers and hurried over. They would have news from Limerick

"They did it," Mary said as she climbed down. Mary was a member of the Irish Women's League—an auxiliary of the IRA—her Republican sympathies coming on the heels of her husband's death. She had been in Limerick City for a meeting.

It wasn't difficult to figure out what she meant. The *Dáil*—the Irish revolutionary parliament in Dublin—had been debating the Treaty with Britain, and we had been awaiting the vote.

She handed me the paper. The picture said it all: General Michael Collins, proud and triumphant in his uniform, as the British turned over Dublin Castle to the new provisional government.

"DeValera walked out," she said.

Eamon DeValera, the President of the *Dáil* had resigned in protest. The fracture within the IRA—the one everyone had feared—had occurred.

"The *Cumann* supports it," she added.

The *Cumann na mBan*—the Irish Women's League—supported the Treaty? That surprised me.

Mary sighed. "Maybe it *is* the best for now," she continued.

I frowned. *Now Mary supports the Treaty too?* What had changed? I wondered. The last two weeks had been filled with talk of nothing but the Treaty, and Mary's views had been clear. She was a Republican, not a Free-Stater.

She was biting her lip, a habit of hers when she was nervous. "We don't have the men or the guns to continue," she said more to herself than to me.

"A path to freedom?" I asked, not believing what I was hearing.

She looked up, her eyes narrowed. "Aye," she said with more than a touch of sarcasm in her voice. "A path to freedom."

I glanced at the paper again. It was what Michael Collins had said: the Treaty offered us a path to freedom, something so many, including Mary, were now repeating. I stared at his picture again then suddenly Mary's finger was in my face. She shook it.

"Don't you go getting any ideas in that foolish head of yours, Frank Kelleher. You'll be going to Abbeyfeale." She wagged her finger to make sure I understood. "Tomorrow," she said, leaving no room for protest. Then she turned and stomped into the house.

# Chapter Six

Despite what she had said, Mary's insistence that we go to Abbeyfeale right away softened. Sure, she worried about the tensions brewing in Limerick and wanted to keep me away from the IRA. But I think she enjoyed seeing her sister happy—for the first time, I suspected, since I had fled. Besides, as long as I stayed at the farm, away from Limerick City and the places where my old comrades were sure to be, there was no immediate danger. The Treaty had been signed, but the debate continued in Dublin as it did in Limerick and in cities and villages all across Ireland. For now, I thought, we were safe.

Mary must have felt the same. The days that followed were peaceful and I found pleasure in the repairs that needed doing and in tilling the few acres Mary had, preparing them for planting. Despite how controlling she could be, Mary was happy to have Kathleen living under the same roof. That would change once Kathleen and I were wed, but for now, she wanted her sister close by.

While the women were content, by the end of two weeks, I was restless. The sights, the sounds, the smells of Ireland brought with them memories of another life. With each day, the call of my past had grown, and I knew now that my return had been inevitable. News of Kathleen's condition had been the push I needed.

I kept thinking about Liam, our time together as lads and our time together fighting. The last time I had seen him, we had been trapped as the barn burned around us. With the animals screeching and British bullets flying, Liam had risked his own life to save mine. He could have saved himself, but he hadn't, not until he had untied me and dragged me to the door, giving me a chance to escape. I owed my freedom and my life to Liam. I had to see him, to make sure he was alright. I had to thank him for saving me. And I had to tell him the truth about Argyll Manor.

"Where can I find Liam?" I asked Mary one morning.

She glared at me. Her frequent warnings over the last two weeks told me that she had been afraid this moment would eventually come.

"Where is he?" I asked again.

She shook her head. "It'll do you no good to go stirring up the past. What's done is done."

"He saved my life, Mary. I have to see him."

She squared her shoulders and raised her finger, prepared to give me a piece of her tongue. I glared back, stopping her before she could.

"I'm not going to Abbeyfeale," I said quietly. "Not until after I see him."

She wanted to argue, I could see, but she hesitated, and I caught something in her eyes. When she didn't answer, I asked again.

"He's in Castleconnell," she finally said, "at his brother's house." She paused, and her eyes narrowed. "They released him two months ago."

I was relieved to hear that he was still alive but was troubled by her tone. She explained that Liam had been captured by the British the very night he had set me free. As I was making my way to Limerick City, he had been caught by the Peelers. He had been found on the side of the road, confused and bloody, having crashed the bicycle he had stolen to aid his escape. After learning who he was, the British had tortured him for information.

"What they did to him, Frank..." she said with a shake of her head. He had been held for almost a year. "I hear he's not the same anymore."

Later that evening, I lay awake in bed. I couldn't sleep. Mary's words continued to haunt me. *He's not the same anymore.*

———

I took Kathleen's hand as we followed the path below a sky that was dark from both the threat of rain and the late hour. Returning from a visit to Margaret's grave, we discussed our future.

"Maybe it's not safe here anymore," Kathleen said.

"Why do you say that?" Mary wanted us to go to Abbeyfeale, but I had things I needed to do before I left.

"Maybe we're better off in America. After the wedding, maybe we should go."

I stopped and looked at her. "I just came back and now you want me to leave again?" I grinned. It was a poor attempt at humor, a mask to hide my shock. I was surprised to hear Kathleen mention America. Although the words were hers, I could hear Mary's voice behind them. I gestured to the land around us. "Could you leave this?"

"I don't know," Kathleen said. She bit her lip and looked away.

I took both of her hands in mine, and she looked up again. "New York is not what you think it is," I said, searching her eyes to see if she understood. She continued to bite her lip but said nothing.

"Would you leave your sister here?"

Kathleen shook her head. "I don't know," she said again. She held my eyes this time and I could see the fear.

"Margaret won't be the only one. Surely you know that. Once we're married, we'll have other children."

She bit her lip again. "I don't know if I want my children to be born here, to live with the threat of another war. Maybe they'll be safer in America."

I nodded, finally understanding.

"Mary says it's not safe," she said.

"I know what Mary says, Kathleen," I snapped. "It's all I hear from her, how there'll be another war." I took a deep breath. I hadn't meant to sound cross. I was frustrated with Mary's nagging, not with Kathleen. "I'm sorry," I said, offering her a weak smile.

She nodded.

"We *will* go to Abbeyfeale, Kathleen. We will get married. And we will baptize Margaret and give her a proper burial." I searched her eyes, finding only doubt. "We will, Kathleen. I promise."

She nodded, and we turned and began walking again. I glanced over the stone wall on the side of the road and saw the furrows in the earth, the lines made by the plough that the horse had dragged through the rich soil. Although they could have planted more, Mary and Tim only farmed one acre. Mary had insisted that Tim complete his schooling, a rare thing for a child his age. The school was in Patrick's Well, some nine miles away, and with walking there and back and with the schoolwork, Tim hadn't the time for more. Over the last few days, I had begun ploughing additional acres. I planned to plant the crop for them, then, if I was still here, bring it in in the fall.

We stopped at the stone wall that surrounded Mary's cottage. In the faint light, I could see the smoke curling up from the chimney. A flicker of light peeked out from around the shutters. I leaned on the wall and took a deep breath, filling my lungs with the smell of the newly tilled soil, the manure Tim and I had begun spreading, and the peat from the fire inside. It was a rich aroma, one I had missed during my year in New York. It smelled of home.

"Are you still wanting to see Liam?" Kathleen asked, interrupting my thoughts.

"Aye, Kathleen. I have to."

Even in the dim light, there was no mistaking the worry on her face.

"Can't it wait?"

I sighed but said nothing. I could hear my father's words: *When a thing is wrong, you have to make it right.*

Kathleen bit her lip, and I reached for her hands again.

"I have to see him, Kathleen. You know that. He saved my life. And I have to tell him what happened at Argyle Manor."

"Ahh, it's a stubborn one you are, Frank Kelleher," she said softly. "You'll be sending me to an early grave with the worry you cause me."

I pulled her close; she laid her head on my shoulder.

"I only need a few days, Kathleen. But when I return, we'll go to Abbeyfeale. We'll wed. Then we'll find some land and build a cottage. Somewhere in Limerick." The picture was so clear in my mind, this dream I had carried with me to New York and back. "We'll have sheep and cows and chickens. And pigs," I said with a grin. "Aye, we'll have pigs. I'll teach the children all the things my own father taught me. We'll buy a spinning wheel and a loom." I paused as I felt Kathleen's body pressed against mine as the dream danced in my head. I hadn't held her like this in over a year. Without warning, there was a stirring in my loins and I realized then how much I longed to hold her, to be with her. I glanced back at Mary's cottage. Before I could suggest that we take a walk, that we find a quiet spot away from everything else, Kathleen stepped back and gently pushed me away.

"We can't, Frank. Not now." She shook her head. "Not here."

I reached out, but she shook her head. "We can't. Not anymore. Not until we're properly wed."

"But, Kathleen," I protested. "I came back for you. I came back for us."

"Aye, you did. But it's a proper woman you'll make me first." She scolded me softly then turned and left me standing there. A minute later, I heard the door close. I stood alone, outside, in the silence.

———

One soggy Monday morning, despite Mary's protest, I set off to find my friend. The latest paper said that the British would begin withdrawing their forces from around the country. In Limerick, the City Council vowed to establish a new police force that would take over from the RIC, but until then, the Peelers would still function to keep order. With the truce and Treaty in place, I hoped that their focus would shift to the normal police functions of protecting the city instead of terrorizing it as they had done when the Black and Tans had infiltrated their ranks. And while British patrols were still a daily occurrence, as we had seen at the station, the soldiers appeared to have laid down their arms. The patrols seemed to be more out of boredom and curiosity than anything else.

I was more worried about Billy and the IRA than the British soldiers and the Peelers when I set off to find Liam that morning. The dye in my hair on the boat over was now gone. Kathleen had washed it out with mixture of eggs, vinegar, and carbonated ammonia, a mixture that had tingled my scalp and left me smelling strange for days. Gone too were Desmond's glasses. Now that I was back, I didn't think I would need the disguise any longer.

Liam's brother lived in Castleconnell, some eleven miles from Kilcully Cross and Mary's house. I had borrowed a bicycle from Tim, and it had taken me three hours of patching holes in the tires and fixing a broken chain before it was in any condition to use.

The rain had stopped before I set off, but the roads were slick with puddles and mud. Thirty minutes later, I was making my way down a long stretch of lane, a route that would keep me away from the city, when I heard a motorcar. I pulled to the ditch to let the car pass; it wouldn't do me any good to be run off the road. Glancing over my shoulder, I felt a moment of panic as the British lorry drove up behind me, slipping and sliding in the mud. The driver blew his horn and waved as he passed. I flinched involuntarily and turned my head, tucking my chin low into my chest. *Easy now,* I told myself, *they're not here for you.* I stole a glance. The soldiers in the back, like the ones I had seen at the station the day before, were unarmed.

Several smiled and waved as they drove by. With my heart thumping in my chest, I watched as the lorry disappeared around a bend. Only then did I let out the breath I'd been holding.

Shaking my head at my own nerves, I scolded myself. *Things were different now. The war was over.* With another sigh, I set off again but still I couldn't shake the feeling. *Were things really different?* Outwardly they seemed to be, but I sensed it would take more than a few months before seven hundred years of hostility was replaced by peace.

I crested a small hill and saw the lorry again. For some reason, the patrol had turned around and was driving slowly back toward me. My heart began to pound inside my chest. *Nothing to worry about,* I told myself as I coasted slowly down the hill, all the while weighing my options. The tall stone walls that lined both sides of the lane left me few. I tugged my cap low and kept my head down. The lorry was driving slowly, too slowly for my comfort. Thirty feet from me, it suddenly stopped. I stamped down on my brake, sliding and almost falling in the mud. Regaining my balance, I straddled the bike, staring up at the six faces staring back at me. The soldiers in the back were no longer smiling; the two in front regarded me warily. I had made a mistake, I suddenly realized, and now I was trapped.

The door opened and an officer climbed out. I didn't know who he was, but I remembered his face from the train station. Then a soldier from the back climbed down, soon followed by the rest. Only the driver remained in the lorry, and he peered at me through the windscreen. I glanced from the officer to the soldiers behind him to the driver, uncertain what to do when the officer reached into his tunic. I tried not to flinch.

*So this is how I'm to die,* I thought as he walked toward me. *Killed by the British on a lonely rain-soaked boreen. And with a truce no less!*

"And a fine day it is," I said with what I hoped was a smile when he stopped two feet away. His eyes bore into mine. Without a word, he handed me a piece of paper. Still smiling, I took it, doing my best to hide my fear. My hand shook slightly as I unfolded it. I felt my stomach drop.

*Francis Kelleher. Wanted for murder in Ireland.*

"You're fucking lucky, Kelleher," he said, poking me in the chest. "If it weren't for the Treaty, I'd kill you right now."

# Chapter Seven

"They told me you had gone to London."

There was no hiding the accusation in Liam's voice. He and I sat in the kitchen of his brother's house. Cold and wet from my ride—it had started to rain again shortly after my encounter with the British—I was only too glad to be inside. But even with the fire in the stove, the smell of peat filling the room, I shivered as I stared into Liam's eyes.

When I arrived, I almost didn't recognize him sitting at the table, thinking him a stranger, a relative of Tara, Seamus's wife. Liam, someone I had known since we were both lads, was different now. He'd always been thin, but now he was gaunt. An ugly purple scar ran down from his ear to his nose, a slash from a British bayonet no doubt. But it wasn't the scar that made him different. It was his eyes—they were those of an older man and betrayed the harshness of the last year and the bitterness that had been left behind.

While Tara fixed us tea, he told me about the eleven months he had spent in a British *gaol*. Daily, he was beaten and tortured. At first, the British were convinced that he knew more than he did. Later, it seems, they beat him for fun. His hand shook when he picked up the tea, and I could see the ugly scars where his fingernails had grown back crooked and deformed. That was a favorite of theirs, the civilized British, taking the pliers to the fingers of a boy who had already told them weeks earlier what little he knew.

I shook my head. "I went to New York."

He stared at me for a moment. "Is that what you're telling people now?" He paused and when I hesitated, he continued, "Is that what you'll be telling Dan's wife? And Sean's mother? And Tom's?"

I sighed. When I opened my mouth, the things I had wanted to say, the words I had rehearsed on my ride over were lost.

He slammed his fist on the table. "Don't lie to me, Frank!" His cup spilled and crashed to the floor. "You owe me more than that!"

Not sure what to say, I waited while his brother's wife cleaned up the spill. Without a word, Tara swept up the broken cup, then wiped up the tea that had splattered all over the stone floor. She put a new cup in front of Liam, but he ignored it. Once again, I found myself staring into the eyes of a stranger.

"Liam," I began softly. "The stories you heard about me aren't true." Before he could say anything, I held my up hands. "At least listen to me first before you condemn me."

Eyes still dark, he sat back, folding his arms across his chest. I told him the story as best as I could remember and felt myself slipping back to a quiet road in Adare on a dark night just over a year ago:

*Two miles from the manor house, we stopped, hid ourselves in the heather along the side of the road and waited. Dan, the only officer amongst us, had seen the most action of our group, but we had all tasted the fear and excitement of battle. I felt a hollow pit in my stomach, a nervous feeling brought on by adrenaline and fear. I did my best not to let the others see my nervousness.*

*We hadn't been there for more than ten minutes when we heard the bicycle. A moment later, the scout appeared then passed us by. Dan ordered us to stay where we were while he cautiously made his way down to the road. We could see a distance in both directions. The road was quiet; the scout was alone. We heard a short whistle, and I turned in time to see the scout stop. He climbed off the bicycle and walked slowly back to where Dan was standing in the middle of the road. We watched the road, Sean one*

*direction, Tom and I the other. We were close enough to hear their words.*
*The scout, a boy of sixteen, told Dan that the road ahead was clear; that*
*a British patrol had been sighted an hour earlier but was miles from the*
*manor house now.*

*We waited until the scout climbed on his bicycle and continued on his*
*way. Then Sean, Tom, and I climbed out of the heather, lugging our haver-*
*sacks and supplies with us. Forty minutes later, I was crouched behind the*
*wall near the manor house while Dan and Tom broke in. Fifteen minutes*
*after that, I was standing in front of the burning house, my own clothes*
*smoldering, as I listened to the muffled screams of my friends dying inside.*

"We never had a chance, Liam. The Tans were lying in wait for
us. It was a trap. They knew we were coming." I shook my head.
"And, we made a mistake. We should have taken more men, maintained surveillance on the house for a couple of days before we went
in. We should have had lookouts." Forever short of men and supplies, so many of our operations were like this: a hastily crafted plan,
a few men with a couple of revolvers taking on the British Army.

Liam said nothing, and I found myself wondering what was going on in the head of a man I once thought I knew as well as I knew
myself.

"If it was me," I persisted, "if I was the traitor, would I have
allowed Sean and Tom to spread the paraffin while I set the mine,
knowing that the Peelers would be busting in any second and with
me standing right in the middle of it all?"

Liam continued to stare but said nothing.

"If it was me, would I have killed the three Peelers too?"

I saw something flash over his eyes. *Doubt?*

"If I was a traitor, would I have come back, especially now with
the threat of civil war? Me?" I said, my voice rising. "Of all people,
me? A traitor? If anyone knows what happens to traitors, it's me,
Liam." I paused and stared hard at my friend for a moment. "I'm
guilty alright, but I'm not guilty of that." I sighed. "I'm guilty of
killing Sean and Tom and Dan"—my voice broke—"but they were

as good as dead already. I'm only guilty of killing them before the British had a chance to finish the job." My voice was a whisper now. "Liam, I had no other choice."

My friend stared at me for several long moments. Eyes still dark, he reached up and rubbed the scar on his cheek. I sighed again as I realized that my words had no effect. It was a mistake to have come. I pushed my chair back and stood to leave. He coughed, a spasm, and I hesitated, turning back for a moment. He wiped his mouth, and I noticed the glisten in his eyes but whether it was from the coughing or from my words, I wasn't sure. Then he looked up at me, and his face softened. He pointed to my seat. As I sat again, he said something to his sister-in-law, and a moment later two glasses and a bottle of poteen appeared on the table.

We sat silently for several minutes. I took a sip, felt the burn in my throat, felt the heat rising in my chest and thought of all of the years we had between us, Liam and myself. A moment later, I put my glass down, and Liam's sister-in-law quietly refilled it. I nodded my thanks but left the glass where it was. I didn't want the whiskey to tell the story that I had to tell myself. I told him about my escape, about my journey to Cobh, about the voyage to New York, and about my life in America. I told him about Kathleen and our daughter. I told him everything.

He listened quietly, nodding now and again. When I finished, I took another drink.

"That was the last operation, you know," Liam said after a while. "The rest of the company was reassigned." Billy, he said, went on to become OC—the Officer in Charge—of another company within the brigade, the boys that remained joining him.

"And what about you?" A glass of poteen wasn't enough. I needed to hear the words from his mouth.

He sighed. "I spent the last year thinking about you, about why you did it. Every time they took their clubs to me, I cursed you." He held up his mangled hand, "every time they took their pliers to me, I cursed you." He rubbed his scar. "Every time they took their knives to me, I cursed you. But through it all," he paused a moment, his eyes on mine, "I never told them about Kathleen. I never told them about you."

Then, for the first time that night, he smiled.

We talked till the wee hours, and I didn't leave till the following day, the poteen helping to mend our friendship but demanding a penance all its own in the morning. As I made the journey back to Limerick, the storm raging in my head to match the one in the sky above, Liam's warning continued to ring in my ears.

I had just climbed on my bicycle when he suddenly reached out and grabbed hold of my arm.

"If this is the price for a free Ireland," Liam had said, holding his mangled hand up in front of my face, "it's a price I'll gladly pay. But, things are different now. Soon it is we'll be fighting each other. Another war's coming, Frank, and there's nothing can be done to stop it." He stared at me for a long moment. "There's nothing here for you anymore. There's nothing for anyone. Take Kathleen and go back to America."

———

A land of dreamers we Irish are, and many a night it was when Liam and I, just lads, would listen to the old folks tell their stories and talk of the better times to come. We would sit on the stairs while the men gathered in the kitchen, chairs arranged in front of the fireplace. They'd talk about Wolfe Tone and the uprising in ninety-eight. They'd talk about Robert Emmett and the uprising only a handful of years later. They'd talk about the Fenians and the land wars and Charles Parnell. They'd talk about how different life would be when the British finally granted us Home Rule.

But dream was all they did. The centuries of living under British rule, with its brutal policies, left them struggling day to day. We were Catholic, which meant we were tenant farmers and had no rights to the land we lived on and toiled over daily. Our land had been stolen centuries before, and we had been reduced to mere peasants, forced to work the fields that we once owned. Sitting around the fire, while Liam and I listened at the top of the steps, my grandfather would talk of the *great hunger*. Then a young boy himself, he remembered the mound of black, rotting potatoes—a mountain taller than the stables—and wondering why God was angry at them. He remembered his father telling him he couldn't eat the few good potatoes—the ones that somehow had survived—because they were all the family had to pay the rent. He remembered the constables forcing neighbors from their homes, while angry landlords burnt down their cottages. No crop meant no rent.

My grandfather's stories both mesmerized and haunted me. His voice dropped as he described the sharp angles of his own father's face, of his chest, of his arms, the bones all but poking through the skin. He remembered seeing his sister and his mother, both overcome by the famine fever, die within hours of each other, too sick to lift themselves off the floor. He remembered going to bed and praying for a few hours of sleep, a few hours of relief from the constant pain in an empty belly, only to lie awake for hours, crying silently so his father wouldn't hear. And for years to come, he remembered the fear in his father's eyes and in those of his neighbors, all wondering if this would be the year when the *great hunger* would return.

Liam's conversion from dreamer to soldier had come earlier than mine. His father, himself a farmer, had been brutally beaten by British soldiers when he was slow to move his cart off the road so their lorry could pass. While his father lay bleeding in the dirt, they set fire to his cart. Liam, then only sixteen, joined a newly formed company of Volunteers. My own conversion came later, a few years after my mother remarried.

Sixteen years then myself, I'd spent two years running the farm, and my mother's new husband didn't like having someone else around the house making decisions. An ex-British soldier, he had been wounded in Verdun. It was because of his wounds, perhaps, that he liked his poteen, a way to ease his constant pain. Many was a night when, in a drunken rage, his anger at the life he had been forced to live was taken out on me.

One night, my lip split and my nose broken again, I ran out the door, tears in my eyes at the injustice. I walked and walked and with each step my anger grew, the hate filling me with a rage. When I returned, I found him asleep on the floor in front of the stove, the empty bottle on the table. Grabbing the irons from the fire, I was prepared to beat him to death. My mother, God bless her, threw herself on top of him. Two men couldn't live below the same roof, she told me. It was time for me to leave. My mother had made her choice clear. Without a second thought, I left. I met Liam that evening at the crossroads and decided that was the last time I would let anyone—my drunk stepfather, the Peelers, the British—take from me what was mine. The farm my stepfather could have—we were only tenants anyway—but my blood was mine to give, not his to take.

It was two years I was gone. Traveling around the country, taking odd jobs where I could. I found jobs tending to the sheep and pigs or working the stables and minding the horses—work I knew. Many a night it was when I went to sleep hungry for no work was to be had. And many a night it was where I begged or stole what I needed to survive. I wandered the country, from Galway to Tipperary, from Waterford to Dingle. The whole while the mood of the country was changing, slow at first then building, and I often thought of my father's final words. *Promise me, Frank!*

The Easter Rising, as it was now being called, was initially met with both shock and contempt, labeled an act of treachery, of anarchy, perpetrated by criminals. The Brotherhood and the Sínn Féiners, men who had taken up the cause, had been met with open hostility by a citizenry who feared the retribution that was sure to come more than they desired freedom. The former was something they had seen with their own eyes while the latter was something they had never known. But when the leaders of the Rising were court martialed and executed—a rushed farce that the righteous British called justice—the very same citizenry was shocked. And as dozens more were sentenced to death and thousands of others were arrested and sent to prison—all the while London pushed to conscript Irish men to fight the Germans in France—the British charade was laid bare. Dirty and uneducated we were, a lawless people, good for nothing but cannon fodder for the British Empire.

After two years of wandering, Republican thoughts and my father's words had taken root. I made my way back to Limerick, thinking that if I was going to join the fight, I wanted to fight with men I knew. It was late spring when I returned and met up with Liam.

I had returned on a Saturday and, after spending the night at Liam's, we decided to go to the crossroads dance Sunday afternoon. Although public meetings were illegal—one of many liberties the British had taken away—it was a common enough event in the country at the time. The boys and girls, the young and the old, would gather at the intersection, the music coming from a fiddle and a hornpipe or two, while couples danced the sets.

We had just arrived, and it was a welcoming scene. The sweet sounds of the fiddles filled the air, a handful of couples dancing, others lounging on the stone wall, the smiles and laughter infectious. I was talking with Liam and two other boys—people I hadn't seen for several years—when something caught my eye. I saw the blue dress and the long, golden hair, and my heart started to race. She was standing by the wall, talking with two other women. I hadn't seen Kathleen for over two years and, when she turned and smiled, it was as if we were the only two in the world. From that moment, my life would never be the same.

# Chapter Eight

"Let sleeping dogs lie, Frank," Liam had warned me.

But I couldn't and two days later I found myself wishing I had.

"It's the devil, you are!" Mrs. Sheehy screeched. In the courtyard outside her cottage, she dropped her pail and came at me, her arms swinging, hands slapping at my head. I put my arms up in defense as I backed away, the hens and rooster scattering behind me. This only seemed to further enrage her, and she came at me with a fury.

The commotion drew Tom's sisters out of the cottage and while Angela, the older sister, held Mrs. Sheehy back, Colleen ran to the stables. Mrs. Sheehy began to wail.

"Leave now, while you still can." Angela warned with a snarl.

But I didn't, and a moment later I found myself surrounded by shovels and pitchforks, Tom's father and brothers spread out around me. I had made a mistake. With the stone wall behind me, I was trapped. I wouldn't be able to scramble over the wall before a shovel or pitchfork found me.

"So now that the war's over, you came back, did you?" Mr. Sheehy growled as he held the pitchfork steady, pointed at my chest. "And for what purpose? To torment the family of a man you sent to his death?"

"I did come back, sir, to pay my respects and to tell you the truth about the night Tom died."

Before Mr. Sheehy could respond, Pete let out a growl.

"You killed my brother!" he shouted. A year younger than Tom but a head taller than me, Pete's eyes filled with rage. Suddenly, he lunged at me with his shovel. I stepped to the side, dodging the blade, and hit him once in the head. Pete dropped to the ground and his brother Barry rushed forward. It was only Mr. Sheehy's bark that stopped him.

"No!" he shouted.

Barry stopped in his tracks. Mr. Sheehy didn't want to see any more of his boys hurt. Small as I was, he had seen me take on lads much bigger than myself.

"There'll be no killing here!" the father continued, more to mollify Barry than anything else.

Barry hesitated, his shovel held menacingly close to my face. Three years younger than Pete and four years younger than me, he was my size. I contemplated disarming him, but as close as he was, it was Mr. Sheehy's pitchfork that had me worried.

"See to your brother," Mr. Sheehy ordered.

I stared at Barry's shovel, at the dirty blade that would surely cut me or bash my head given the chance, and then at his dark eyes. After a moment, he cautiously stepped back and, watching me the whole time, nudged Pete with his foot. As Pete struggled to his feet, Mr. Sheehy called over his shoulder to his youngest daughter.

"Colleen," he ordered. "Go fetch Billy."

I let out a nervous breath as I considered what to do. Billy lived seven miles away. If Colleen found him, it would take an hour and a half at least before Billy was there.

"Mr. Sheehy, sir," I pleaded as Colleen ran to the side of the cottage. "The stories you heard about that night are not true."

"We'll see what the IRA has to say about that," he answered as he jabbed at the air between us with his pitchfork. Pete rubbed at his cheek, now swollen red, and glowered at me, contemplating, I was sure, his revenge. While his father and brother watched me warily, he picked up his shovel. Out of the corner of my eye, I saw

Colleen climb on her bicycle. Legs pumping, her feet furious on the pedals, she disappeared down the lane.

They escorted me to the stables, Pete on one side, his shovel held cautiously, Barry on the other and Mr. Sheehy behind me, prodding me along with the fork. The stable, a small stone building with a thatched roof, was beyond the cottage, past the fowl-house and next to the cow-house. In addition to two horses, a rooster, and a dozen hens, the Sheehys, I remembered, had a cow and several goats. As we stepped through the gate, following the path to the barn, Mr. Sheehy poked me again.

"You can try and make your peace with Billy," he said unnecessarily, "but the IRA doesn't have much use for traitors."

It was something I knew all too well.

———

It was just a year and a half ago, late summer, several months before I fled. We had planned to ambush the shipment to the quarry. Recognizing the risk that gelignite and blasting materials posed to them, the British provided escorts for all such shipments lest they fall into our hands. Commandeering and stealing what we needed was the only way we could arm ourselves. If it wasn't guns, it was black powder and detonation cord, paraffin and rope, clothes and food, bicycles and boots—whatever it was, if we needed it we took it. For those who were Catholic and sympathetic to our cause, we issued receipts in the hopes that someday, a free Ireland would be able to repay them. For those that weren't, they received no such commitment, even though the receipts probably weren't worth the paper they were printed on.

We had lain in wait for most of a day, expecting the convoy between twelve and one, but that hour had come and gone. Our ambush site was a stretch of road with a sharp turn where the convoy would be forced to slow down. Dan, Sean, Liam, and I were positioned behind a wall before the turn; Billy, Padraig, Roddy and

Tom were similarly positioned around the bend. The plan was for our group, led by Dan, to let the lead lorry pass. Once they made the turn, Billy's group would engage them while we engaged the rear lorry. The blasting supplies, normally on a horse-drawn cart, would be caught in the middle. Once we disposed of the British, the gelignite would be ours for the taking.

It was just after five in the evening when we received word from one of our scouts that the convoy had been spotted. This was relayed up the road to Billy's team. We hunkered down behind the wall, checked our weapons again, and fought the nervousness that always came before battle. Moments later, we heard the sound of the lead lorry. Dan peeked over the wall but even though the noise of the motor continued to grow, he couldn't see the convoy.

Suddenly, there was the crack of a rifle, and we heard a scream from around the bend. Instantly, we knew that we'd been out-flanked. As more gunshots rang out, we scrambled over the wall into the road and ran towards the bend. The lorry, which had been waiting just over the crest of a hill, out of our view, was now racing down the road toward us. Around the bend, we saw the rest of our group scrambling over the wall; all except Roddy. Shouting and waving, Billy directed us across the road, over the wall on the far side where we took up a defensive position. What had been planned as an offensive strike now had us running for our lives.

It was a fierce fight that lasted some thirty minutes. Luckily for us, Billy had grabbed the machine gun from Roddy as he lay dying, slumped over the wall. Between that, our rifles, and the Mills bomb Liam had thrown below the wheels of the lorry, we succeeded in keeping the British at bay. The soldiers from the disabled lorry had scrambled over the wall on the opposite side of the road, where we had been hiding only moments before, using the wall and the over-turned truck as a screen.

Luckily no one else was hit, except Padraig, who caught a piece of chipped stone just below his eye. Seeing we were running low on ammunition, Billy ordered a retreat. Half of us ran back across the field and found defensive positions and provided cover fire for the rest. We alternated like that until we had successfully escaped. Only later did we learn that the British had two machine guns, one on the lorry and one in the hands of the flanking party. Fortunately for us, they both had jammed. Had it not been for that, more of us would have joined Roddy, dying before we had a chance to fire our own guns.

We met after the funeral, the seven of us remaining, and it was then that Billy shared with us what we all suspected. The British had known of our plans. Besides three people in brigade headquarters, only five other people knew of our mission, the scout we had positioned on the road leading to the ambush site who was to warn us of the convoy's approach, another scout who was similarly positioned around the bend who was to warn Billy's team if anyone approached from that side, and three men who were situated behind both of our teams and who were to protect our rear. The scouts and the men who were providing cover behind us were from a different brigade. We knew them, but the animosity between the brigades had been growing and it was only a rare occasion that we worked together. Had we not been short of men, we wouldn't have been forced to borrow from their ranks.

Two of the men protecting our rear, we learned later, died in the first volleys of gunfire. The third man, the only one unaccounted for, was a twenty-year-old volunteer named William Conroy.

We found Conroy three days later, hiding in the fowl-house at the farm of a cousin. As soon as he saw us, he broke down and admitted his betrayal. He had been picked up by a British patrol, part of a random roundup designed both to intimidate and to gather information. They threatened his family—a tactic they often used—and Conroy, believing he had no choice, told them of our plans. After the court martial, we led a handcuffed Conroy to a desolate field, and while the rest of the company took up security positions, Liam and I led him sixty paces farther behind a grouping of rocks.

Liam had been assigned the task. We positioned the prisoner so that any bullet that missed or passed through him would not deflect off the rocks back toward us. Conroy slumped forward, weighed down by the weight of his crime and his pending punishment. Liam took up his position, ten paces away. I watched my friend as he raised his arm; he had gone pale and his breaths came rapidly.

"Any last words?" I asked.

Conroy shook his head and let out a sob. Liam's hand shook, and I could see the tears in his own eyes. A moment later he turned his head away and lowered his arm. Without hesitating, I took the revolver from my friend's hands and, after a single shot, Conroy slumped back against the rocks. I stepped forward and, as he looked up at me, both fear and pain in his eyes and with blood seeping from his mouth and running down his chin, I shot him once again, this time directly in the heart. I stood over him for a moment, let out a breath, then handed the gun back to Liam. With tears in my own eyes, I knelt by a man I had known for the last two years, one I never would have thought would have done such a thing. I wiped my eyes, took the note from my pocket and pinned it to Conroy's shirt.

*Shot by the IRA*, it read. *Spies and informers beware.*

Neither Liam nor I ever mentioned to the others what had happened.

———

I approached the stable, prodded along by Mr. Sheehy's pitchfork. When I stepped inside, I was temporarily blinded, my eyes struggling to adjust to the darkness. I lunged to the side, hoping the stable hadn't changed since the days Tom and Liam and I had played together as boys. I blindly grabbed the horseshoe off the peg on the wall—thankful that it was still there—and swung it as Mr. Sheehy stepped inside. With a grunt, he doubled over and dropped to the ground. Pete, as hot tempered as I remembered, rushed in after him.

Dropping the horseshoe, I used my fists again, catching him on his other cheek. He stumbled, and I hit him twice more before he collapsed to the ground with a thud. I waited a second for Barry and when he didn't come, I grabbed the pitchfork and stepped out the door. Seeing me, he hesitated then made a wise decision and turned on his heel and ran.

When I was sure he was gone for good, I stepped back into the stable and checked Pete. He was unconscious but breathing, and I did not want to be around when he woke. Mr. Sheehy was lying on his back, still trying to catch his breath, the horseshoe having caught him just below the ribs.

I knelt beside him, resting my hand on his shoulder. His breath came in labored pants. Hopefully, I thought, I hadn't broken any ribs, only knocked the air from his lungs. He looked up into my eyes, and I could see the shock in his.

"I'm sorry, sir. I didn't mean for any of this to happen."

Eyes filled with pain and still trying to catch his breath, he stared up at me but said nothing.

"I didn't have to come back," I continued. "But I did. I owed it to Tom and to you to tell you what really happened that night."

I never had a chance to explain. I heard shouts outside. *How could Billy have made it here so quickly?* I wondered. I didn't wait to find out. Like I had a year before, I scrambled out the cattle door and fled across the fields.

# Chapter Nine

Like my stepfather, Billy had fought for the British during what later came to be called the Great War. But unlike my stepfather, who had faced the German army's artillery and their poison gas in the trenches in France, Billy had been sent to fight in Mesopotamia. He never told us what he had seen or what he had done, but when he came back he was a different person from the one we thought we knew. To the IRA, always short on experience and supplies, men like Billy, who ironically had trained and fought side-by-side with those who were now our sworn enemy, were a godsend. When our brigade was formed, Billy was made officer-in-charge of our company.

He had led us through drills and taught us to fight, not the conventional way but as guerrillas, using whatever we could get our hands on. We trained in small arms and rifles and learned the tactics for rural ambush as well as those for use in the city. We learned how to make bombs and grenades using whatever materials we could steal. We trained in sabotage and learned how to cut telegraph wires, block roads, and destroy bridges. Late in the evenings, we were trained in intelligence, signaling, and communications—the tools of warfare we needed to know. We trained with wooden rifles because real ones were hard to come by. We drilled on Sundays and Wednesday evenings, our farms and jobs keeping us busy during the week. What we lacked in experience we made up in discipline and a knowledge that our cause was just.

Our first task was to properly equip ourselves, which meant getting our hands on weapons. Initially, we took shotguns and muzzle-loading weapons from farmers we knew and from those we didn't. Some of the muzzle-loading weapons were older than the farmers themselves, but any gun, we reasoned, was better than none. These we passed around so all of our men could become familiar with their workings. When we heard about someone who had weapons we needed, we paid them a visit. Our solicitations weren't always met with cooperation. More than once we had to convince a reluctant farmer that we had a greater need for his gun than he did, and if that didn't succeed, we took it anyway. The British eventually learned of our plans and began a similar program, confiscating guns before they fell into our hands. The game had begun.

Our first raid was against six Peelers who we knew favored a certain pub in the evenings. One night, we lay in wait and, when they left, long after midnight and with each having had a few pints too many, we sprang. With scarves tied around our faces, only our eyes showing, and armed with two shotguns, we surprised them and forced them into an alley. One of the men, a big fellow who we knew to be their sergeant, kept looking over his shoulder, and I knew what was to come. When the shout came from the street, a distraction he was waiting for, he lunged. Billy sensing what was about to happen was prepared, and clubbed him with his gun. There was a loud, sickening sound, the crack of the wooden butt against his head, and he fell like a sack of potatoes. Seeing their leader slumped on the ground, blood pouring from his head, the other five put up no resistance. Moments later, we made off with their revolvers.

Days later, we had our first taste of reprisals, the Peelers seeking their revenge as much for the humiliation of having their guns taken by a bunch of peasant farmers as anything else. They didn't know our names yet or where we lived and so began their intimidation program. They sent out patrols to corner and question anyone whose loyalties were suspect. Being Irish, being Catholic and being a farmer or a tradesman was suspicious enough and, to the British soldiers, suspicion equaled guilt. In the beginning, it was rough treatment: the fist, the club, or the butt of a rifle. They took names and addresses, a young private scribbling furiously, while the sergeant demanded answers. Any hesitation was met with violence. Scare tactics was all it was, and most of it was directed at civilians. Nothing more than a few bloodied noses and a few broken bones, but all that changed one Sunday in April.

There was an RIC barracks about ten miles away. The seven constables were commanded by a sergeant named Murphy who was Irish and Catholic as were many of the Peelers at that time. Unlike other barracks, Murphy's men generally left us alone, more, we suspected, because Murphy's loyalties lay with us and not with the Crown. Our intelligence indicated that they had just received a shipment of rifles—Lee-Enfields that were the standard of the British army. While we had no grudge with Murphy or any of his men, we were sorely in need of those rifles.

What seemed a simple plan quickly unraveled. Immediately before our attack, we cut the telegraph wires to prevent the Peelers from calling in reinforcements from surrounding barracks. As an extra measure of caution, we cut trenches in the roads just outside of town. This would delay any reinforcements if word of our attack somehow managed to reach them. Then we set fire to the building and, with our guns trained on the front door, waited for the Peelers to escape out the back at which point we would rush into the blaze and seize whatever we could. A dangerous plan certainly, but necessity drove us to such extremes.

However, rather than abandon their barracks, Murphy and his men put up a fight. Volley after volley of gunfire was exchanged but, strangely enough, no one was hit on either side. After an hour, our ammunition was running low, but by this time the fire had taken hold and the Peelers were finally forced to flee. Murphy continued to surprise us. Instead of retreating, he tried to encircle us, and a new battle broke out on the street. Ten minutes later, Murphy and another Peeler lay dead, but with our ammunition gone and the fire raging, it was us who were forced to retreat.

Although we failed to seize any rifles, we viewed the operation as a victory nonetheless. It was a brazen attack against the British and, with two Peelers dead and a barracks destroyed, it showed them we meant business. To the citizens of Ireland, who had been living for seven hundred years under the British, it demonstrated that even a group of poorly trained peasants could defeat the well-equipped forces of the Crown.

It was two days later that we first spied the mismatched uniforms of the Black and Tans, and we quickly learned that the British wouldn't be satisfied with merely squashing the latest insurrection—they wanted revenge. The Tans went on a rampage, burning businesses and homes randomly. They arrested scores of people, including one publican who, although he had no connection to the IRA other than serving us a pint now and again, was deemed guilty of sedition. His hands and feet were tied, and he was forced to kneel before he was shot in the back of the head. Despite the rope marks on his hands and ankles and despite the angle of the wound, the court of inquiry determined that he was killed while trying to escape.

An eye for an eye, Billy had told us, and one week after the inquest, we captured a Tan. Like the publican, we tied his hands and ankles and forced him to kneel. Then Billy shot him in the back of the head. We pinned a note to his tunic: *Prisoner of the IRA, killed while trying to escape.*

And like that, the game had changed, the Tans exacting their revenge, and us, led by Billy, exacting ours. As brutal as the Tans were, Billy let them know that we too could play that game.

——

As I ran across the Sheehys' fields, the shouts and voices fading behind me, it was clear that the risks had just increased dramatically. Although there was always the chance that I would run into him, as I nearly had the day I arrived, surely now Billy would come looking for me. If I wanted to see Kathleen again, I had to avoid him.

I found Tim's bicycle where I had left it, a mile from the Sheehys', hidden in the heather behind the stone wall, far enough from the road that it wouldn't be seen. I squatted by it for a moment as I caught my breath. After a minute or two with no sign that anyone was behind me, I dragged the bicycle back to the road. On the bicycle, I was forced to follow the roads but since I was going to Mary's and Billy would be coming from the other direction I thought it would be safe enough.

An hour later, as I made my way over a small rise, there was a clank, and I stumbled on the pedal, barely catching myself before I tumbled over the handlebars. Cursing, I pulled to the side of the road. Glancing behind me, I saw the chain lying broken in the dirt.

A few minutes later, the bicycle hidden again, I pushed my way through the heather past a large oak tree to an open field. It was another ten miles back to Mary's, I figured, maybe less since I would be cutting across the fields. I glanced at the oak, memorizing the spot—I had to come back for the bicycle—then, with the broken chain in my pocket, I set out across the field.

I managed to make it back to Mary's house safely and without arousing any suspicion from the farmers and field hands I had seen along the way. I found them behind the house, Kathleen helping Mary with the laundry. It was a busy day; the bushels and bundles were piled high. Mary had a regular clientele, and it seemed there was no end to the amount of the clothes and linens that the rich could soil. Later in the evening, her son Tim would deliver the freshly washed and folded laundry back to their owners and, in return, collect a few shillings and a new set of dirty linens for Mary to wash.

Kathleen, her sleeves rolled up and her arms plunged into the steaming water, looked up. Mary had just come from the house, another large bundle in her arms. She placed the laundry on the bench.

"And a good day to you, ladies," I said with a smile.

Kathleen's eyes narrowed. She ignored my smile as she pulled her arms from the water and wiped them dry on her apron. Her eyes traveled up and down, to the dirt on my trousers, the rip on my shirt—souvenirs from my scuffle with the Sheehys. She frowned.

"What have you been into?"

I glanced down, certain she wasn't upset at the additional cleaning and mending she would have to do. It was then I noticed that my knuckles were scraped raw, bruises that could only have come from fisticuffs.

Then I noticed the fear in her eyes. For the first time since I had returned—I hadn't told her about my encounter with the British soldiers yet—she was frightened. Mary took two steps toward me and placed her hands on her hips, an angry stance.

"Frank Kelleher, I told you not to go getting involved." Her dark eyes bore into mine. "That's it then," she said, clearly having just made up her mind. "You'll be leaving for Abbeyfeale in the morning."

# Chapter Ten

"You went to the Sheehys and look where that got you! If they'd handed you over to Billy, do you think you'd still be alive now?"

The air was thick, the smoke from the stove and the tension between Kathleen and me filling the room. She was upset at my decision to stay while she went, alone, to Abbeyfeale. She couldn't stay here, I had argued. Now that Billy knew I was back in County Limerick, he was sure to be looking for me. I wasn't certain he would come to Mary's but, if he did, it would be better for Kathleen if she weren't there. I didn't think Billy would be bold enough to do anything to Mary—she was a member of the Women's League, and anything Billy did was sure to anger the *Cumann*. And I didn't think he would harm Kathleen. But would he hold her as prisoner until I turned myself over? It wasn't a chance I felt comfortable taking. I could risk my own life, but I couldn't risk hers.

"But they didn't," I protested.

She shook her head. "You've met with Liam. You've seen the Sheehys. What more do you want?"

"You know I have to see Sinéad. And Sean's mother."

"And tell them what?" She shook her head as if I were daft. "You're wanting to make me a widow and we're not even married yet. At least Dan had the decency to marry Sinéad before he went off and got himself killed!" Then she stormed out of the house, slamming the door in her wake.

Thankfully, Mary had remained silent throughout our argument, but that wouldn't last now, not after seeing how upset Kathleen was. I didn't give her a chance.

"Don't," I said, pointing my finger. Mary glared at me. I left her and went out in search of Kathleen.

I found her by the well. Her mood filled the air, and I stopped several feet away. I wanted to wrap my arms around her, to tell her that everything would be fine, that it was only for a short while. But it would only have angered her more. Instead, I stared back at her as I thought what I could say that would soothe her fears. Arms folded, she stared off into the darkness, seeing nothing but her own anger I was sure.

"I already lost you once, Frank," she said without turning. "That night you came to me, at the Cavanaghs'?" I saw the slight shake of her head. "I never thought I would see you again. I thought I would be forced to have the baby by myself and...and..." She buried her face in her hands; her body was wracked by sobs.

I reached out and put my hand on her shoulder.

"You yourself said it wasn't safe. Now you want to send me away while you stay here. And to do what, Frank? To tell them that you're innocent?" She shook her head. "Ahh, you'll just go and get yourself killed and for what? Just to clear your name?"

"It's all I have Kathleen."

"You have me, Frank Kelleher!" She turned and put her arms around me, her head on my shoulder. "You have me."

"I love you, Kathleen. You know this."

"If you loved me you'd come with me."

"I can't, Kathleen. I need to do this first."

"Then I'll stay here," she pleaded. "With you."

I told her again that I didn't think it was safe. I told her I could protect myself but I wasn't sure I could protect her.

"It'll only be for a few days. I'll come as soon as I can, Kathleen."

"Sure, you say that now, but you won't. After you see Mrs.

Murphy and Sinéad, you'll go and find some other ghost to chase."

The trouble was, she was right.

We went to bed late, neither of us happy.

———

The next morning I found Kathleen at the table, sipping a cup of tea. I had been outside, helping Tim with the horse and cart.

I put my hand on her shoulder and sat in the chair next to hers. I heard Mary behind me, coming from the room she shared with Kathleen.

"It's time," I said softly.

Kathleen nodded and stood. "I'll get my things," she said without looking at me.

While I waited, I could feel the heat from Mary's eyes on my back.

Kathleen was only gone a moment. When she returned, I took her case. She put on her hat. I helped her button her coat, a small gesture, an intimacy I hoped would last us both until I saw her again.

"I'll follow you shortly," I said then kissed her softly on the cheek.

Her face somber, Kathleen nodded but said nothing. Her eyes refused to meet mine.

We stepped outside. I handed Tim Kathleen's case then I helped her up onto the cart. Mary held out a blanket of heavy wool to ward off the chill and the mist in the air. I draped this over Kathleen.

"I'll see you in several days, then," I said again. Then I gave Kathleen another kiss on the cheek and hopped down.

She nodded, her jaw set.

"Mind yourself now," she said, her eyes briefly on mine. Then she turned and faced forward, wanting, I was sure, to get the parting over.

Without a word, Tim flicked the rains. I stood and watched

them for a while, the soft clip-clop of the hooves fading in the dense winter air. Soon they disappeared into the mist. As much as I didn't want her to go, it was for the best.

I turned to find Mary. Her eyes bore into mine.

"It's a dangerous game you're playing, Frank Kelleher," she said, "and one you've no right to, not after what happened."

Ignoring Mary, I turned back and stared off into the mist where Kathleen had gone. She could have taken the train from Limerick, but I thought it would be better to stay away from Limerick. As it was, she would take the train from Patrick's Well, some nine miles away, and would arrive in Abbeyfeale in the afternoon. Mary had arranged by telegraph for her friends the Maloneys to meet Kathleen at the station. Away from Limerick and the people who knew her, Kathleen would be safe for the time being.

"You don't know the half of it," I heard softly behind me. I turned back to Mary.

"What do you mean?"

She took a step closer and shook her finger at me. "Do you know what it's been like for the last year?"

I shook my head.

"She left the Cavanaghs soon after you fled. For six months she saw no one but Tim and me."

Mary's eyes were steady on me, and I suddenly felt embarrassed that I had never asked.

"Every time someone came, Kathleen had to hide. She couldn't let anyone see her, not when she was with child. She was so afraid that Father Lonagan would learn of her condition."

I sighed. Father Lonagan—the priest at St. Patrick's Church, the church I had attended every Sunday since I was a wee lad, sandwiched between my mother and father on the cart as we made the nine-mile trip. If he had learned of Kathleen's condition, I had no doubt he would have insisted she be sent away. Everything we had learned about our faith, about our church, we had learned from

Father Lonagan. He had baptized all three of us, Kathleen, Mary, and me, as he had most of the people I knew. He had heard our confessions and forced his penance on us. Each week he had given us the communion bread, his tireless efforts to save us from the sinful life we each led was nothing less than heroic. Father Lonagan *was* the Church. And the Church that we knew—the Church of Father Lonagan—did not believe in mercy.

"She hasn't been to a mass in over a year." Mary continued. "How could she? Then after the baby died, she was convinced that it was her fault." Mary shook her head. "I certainly couldn't ask for Father Lonagan's help, now could I?"

I shook my head and she continued.

"I've known Father Leahy since we were children. His family's from Rathkeale, but when he became a priest, he was sent to Abbeyfeale. I sent him a telegram, and a week later he came. It took that long for Kathleen to stop crying."

"I'm sorry, Mary. I didn't know."

"Ahh, you didn't know," Mary said, abruptly dismissing me with her hand. "You didn't know and you didn't care."

She turned on her heel and left me there, like the fool I was.

# Chapter Eleven

Although I couldn't have known it at the time, for the next two months, tensions in Limerick would escalate and Ireland would teeter on the brink of civil war. Trouble would begin soon after the British withdrawal, as their forces one by one abandoned the various barracks and garrisons, first in Limerick City and then in the surrounding countryside. We would soon see them parading through our streets in uniforms newly laundered or newly purchased for the occasion. Their march would come with a clipped efficiency and the sounds of the drum, their heads held high and their banners fluttering in the breeze as if they were the true victors. In their wake, Free State and Anti-Treaty forces would rush to secure the abandoned barracks, the nation's fate hinging on which way Limerick would fall.

But as Kathleen disappeared into the mist, that precipice was still weeks away.

Thinking the only thing I had to worry about was Billy, against Mary's advice I set off for Limerick City. I had used the last of the hair dye that morning—it wouldn't fool anyone up close, but from a distance I thought it might. The chemist in Limerick would have what I needed. But more than the dye, I wanted to see for myself if what Mary and Liam had told me was true. I had to find out how bad things were.

It was a nine-mile walk to Limerick, the first few easy as I encountered no one on the road. Farm after farm, I saw men and young boys working the plough, getting the fields ready for the planting. In other fields, cows and goats grazed, and in the hills beyond, collies kept large herds of sheep from wandering. A few men waved and I waved back, knowing I was far enough away that I wouldn't be recognized. The rich scent of the turned soil, the musky smell of animals, and the sweet smell of hay filled the air. It was a peaceful scene, but it was one that I feared wouldn't last.

Occasionally, the growl of a motorcar, the rattle of a cart, or the clop of a horse's hooves would disturb the silence, and I would hide behind the stone walls until the sounds faded. But as I drew closer to Limerick, it became difficult to hide—the lorries and drays too thick to escape. There was nothing I could do but keep walking, hoping no one would pay me any mind.

For the most part they didn't, but still I was on edge. I stiffened at each sound, turning my head slightly away from the road, only breathing again once those that passed me disappeared ahead. When I saw the buildings in the distance, I let out a sigh. Another hour and then I would be able to lose myself in Limerick's crowded streets.

I heard the sound of another motorcar and prayed it would drive by like the others before it. But the sound changed, and I could tell the lorry was slowing. I kept walking, trying not to show I was worried, but still I felt myself stiffen as it pulled alongside.

"A fine day it is!"

I looked up and felt a chill run up my spine as I stared up into the face of a Free State Soldier. He was smiling. My instinct told me running would be foolish. Instead I nodded.

"Aye. T'is a fine day."

He asked me if I was going to Limerick. I nodded again.

"Sure and we're on our way there ourselves anyhow," he said, his friendly tone catching me by surprise. He offered me a lift.

Seeing no alternative, I smiled and thanked him as I climbed on board.

There were six of them, all with the new green uniforms of the Free State Army. Most were lads, younger than me, but the officer was my age. The lorry they were in was British. I tried to piece together what that meant as I fought to hide my nervousness.

"From Limerick, are you?" the officer asked. It wasn't a policeman's question, I realized, just curiosity. Still, I was wary.

"Nay," I said. "My family's from Offaly," I told them, "but I've been to America these last five years." I smiled but offered little more.

I wasn't surprised when they began to ask questions, wanting to know if what they had heard about America was true. It was a welcome diversion. The more I talked about New York, the less likely they were to question what I was doing in Ireland. But still I couldn't resist asking several questions of my own. The officer's name was Mullins, I learned, and they were all from Clare, part of General Michael Brennan's new Free State Forces. I knew Brennan, not by face but by name. After the British had declared martial law in January 1921—just as I was settling in New York—Brennan and his East Clare Flying Column ambushed a Black and Tan patrol at Glenwood, near Sixmilebridge. In the ensuing fight, Brennan's troops killed six Tans and made off with their weapons. That night, in retaliation, the Tans went on the rampage in Clare, burning homes and terrorizing farmers and villagers, most of whom had no connection to the IRA. A fine soldier Brennan was, but now he had thrown his lot in with the Free State.

I wanted to ask what soldiers from the Clare Brigade were doing in Limerick but that wouldn't have been wise. Certainly, I told myself, Mullins and his men had been sent on one errand or another and would soon return to Clare. Besides, these lads hardly seemed hostile. Their eyes were bright and their faces held the hope of new recruits, ones who somehow had managed to avoid the fighting over the last three years.

"Well you're back now and it's a good thing you are," Mullins said as he clapped my shoulder. "We need every Irishman now. There's a lot to do," he said smiling, staring off for a moment, dreaming it seemed. "A lot to do."

I couldn't help but ask. "Do you think there'll be another war? It's all I've heard since I returned."

"Why should we fight?" Mullins answered, "We're all Irishmen; certainly we can put our differences aside now, for the sake of the country."

*If it were only that easy*, I thought.

———

I left them at St. Lawrence Cemetery—paying my respects to a friend I told them—not wanting to be seen driving with Free State soldiers in Limerick. There were sure to be Anti-Treaty soldiers in the city—men I had known and fought with—and they would certainly take notice of a Free State Army patrol. *Who's the well-dressed man wearing glasses, the one riding along with the Free State soldiers in their lorry?* It was a question I didn't want them asking.

I stood by the wrought iron gates of the cemetery and waited until Mullins and his men disappeared up Mulgrave Street. Then I set out up Mulgrave myself. I glanced up at the clock tower as I passed the asylum. I felt a shiver on my spine, remembering a day when Liam and I had gotten too close, only to hear the screams and wails from behind the walls. Set back from the road, the asylum was a dark and foreboding building, its wings stretching out amongst the chestnut trees. It was 11:30 in the morning, the clock told me. I planned to spend a few hours reconnoitering British positions and assessing the mood in the city.

Minutes later I passed the gaol, its stone walls towering over my head, its large imposing green steel door telling everyone that the prisoners on the other side were meant to stay. My spine tingled again. Liam had been held here for a short while before being moved to Kilmainham Gaol in Dublin. I shook the thoughts from my head and continued on. As I passed the Artillery Barracks, a handful of British soldiers stood outside, smoking. Their laughter punctured the air. I kept my pace steady, watching them out of the corner of my eye. Despite my nervousness, they paid me no mind. I made my way up to William Street and the RIC barracks, but no constables were to be seen, Black and Tans or otherwise.

The streets became more crowded and as I walked down Catherine Street, then O'Connell, then Henry Street and finally the Quay, I couldn't shake the feeling that Limerick had changed over the last year. Yet so much was still the same. Men in bowlers and suit coats hurried by while women, dressed in long skirts, coats and hats—some pushing prams, most not—headed back to work or home after their walk. Young boys, dressed in knickers and caps, played with hoops in the street while others sold papers on the corner, oblivious to the sound of horseshoes clacking off the stones and the roar of motorcars racing by. Hundreds of wires crisscrossed overhead, a black web that stretched as far as the eye could see, while puffy black swirls of smoke spewed out of the stacks on top of every building before trailing away in the wind, making the clouds more gray than they already were. All of this was as I left it a year ago.

What was different, I soon realized, was what I didn't see. When I had first joined the IRA, there were five RIC police barracks in Limerick City and at least one in most of the larger towns in the surrounding county. At the time, almost all policemen were Irish and almost all were Catholic. But that had changed over the last three years as our war against the British had taken hold. The RIC—the Peelers—were the front line of Britain's own war efforts and for that reason they became our front line as well. As our raids and attacks grew and our campaign took its toll, Irishmen began to resign their posts, and soon the RIC found it difficult to find others willing to replace them. The British responded by sending in the Tans to replace the Irish Catholics who had resigned and then by closing the more isolated police barracks, some because we had destroyed them, others because they could no longer defend them against our attacks. To us, it was a sign that our campaign was working. Soon, though, it wasn't just the Tans we had to worry about. As we grew more brazen, the British responded by sending their soldiers and their dreaded Auxiliaries, men who were in many ways worse than the Tans. If that wasn't enough, the British Army had strongholds—Strand Barracks, New Barracks, Castle Barracks, and Artillery Barracks in Limerick City—where several battalions and infantry regiments, along with their engineers and artillery, hid behind windows shuttered against the peasants and farmers of the IRA. With additional soldiers stationed in Newcastle, Abbeyfeale, Rathkeale, Kilmallock, and Kilfinane, we were severely outnumbered and outgunned, but still we took our fight to them, undaunted by the odds.

Now though, as I walked through Limerick, the effect of the Treaty was evident. Most of the British military units stayed in their barracks, waiting for orders to prepare for departure and their journey home. The occasional British troops I saw were congregating outside their barracks or casually patrolling, more out of boredom than out of need, waiting, too, it seemed for their chance to go home. The Tans, too, seemed to be less conspicuous, the few Peelers I saw wearing the normal RIC uniform instead of the mismatched one we had come to loathe.

I found the dye I needed but continued to wander the streets, trying to get a sense of what else had changed in the city. At one point, I found myself in front of the Bishop's Palace, across the street from the post office. I studied the building and debated getting my money but, in the end, I decided it wouldn't be worth the risk. When I was last in Limerick, the IRA had men in the post office and, although the troubles with Britain were ending, given the current tensions, I suspected that the men inside were still providing information to the IRA. And that meant to Billy.

By three o'clock, I had seen what I needed. Daily lives, on hold for the last two years, were cautiously returning to normal. I sensed that people were happy that the fighting was over but were still nervous with British soldiers on Irish soil. After seven hundred years—an eternity—it appeared that the British would finally be leaving. But still I felt a tension.

Strangely, other than Mullins and the troops from Clare, I saw little evidence of the IRA, neither the Free State forces nor Anti-Treaty factions. But I felt their presence nonetheless and that made me nervous. Maybe it was what I didn't see. Maybe it was my soldier's eye. And then again maybe it was my own imagination. I wasn't sure what drove the feeling. But in the busy streets, I sensed a widening divide in the IRA, between the groups of men, unseen now but no doubt plotting behind closed doors.

It was in this tenuous peace that I set out to confront another demon that still haunted me.

# Chapter Twelve

"I was wondering if I would ever see you again," my mother said. She was sitting by the fire, a mound of burning embers covering the pot-oven on the hearth. Black soot from the fire stained the whitewashed walls above. Her face was puffy, haggard, full of lines, and her eyes held a sadness I knew all too well. It was something I had seen in many from my mother's generation and from her own mother's as well. Beaten down, she was worn out and old before her time. It was a look of resignation, recognition that the life she knew would never get any better. We Irish had lived for so long under the British, maybe this was now in our blood. But as I stared at my mother, I knew there was something more.

Not waiting for my response, she turned and squatted in front of the fire. Using the hem of her heavy woolen dress so she wouldn't burn her hands, she lifted the cast-iron pot out of the embers and hung it on the hook. Then she lifted the lid to check inside. Steam rose from the pot, and the smell of the sweet cake baking inside filled the air.

My mother lived in Drommore, in the same house my grandfather had built. Some fifteen miles from Mary's, it had taken me four hours of walking, time enough to sort out my thoughts before I arrived. While my mother tended the stove, I looked around the room and was surprised to see that little had changed since I was last there, almost five years before. Two heavy wooden chairs sat by the stove, the finish on both almost black from too many layers of stain and too much soot. I felt a lump in my throat. The chair on the right was the same one my father had sat in each night as he held me in his arms and told me his stories. It belonged now to a different man, I thought sadly. Everything looked exactly as it had when I left, but so much had changed.

"He'll be back shortly," she said, not bothering to turn around. She dropped the lid back on the pot, then lowered it back into the embers. After placing a shovel of smoldering coals on top, she sat again and stared up at me.

I considered her words. Earlier, hiding behind the wall, I had watched my stepfather hitch the horse to the cart. Then, with the plough tied on the back, he steered the dray down the lane. Going to the village, to Patrick's Well, to see the blacksmith, I had thought at the time, to get the plough repaired. But now I wondered. Was he merely returning a borrowed plough to a neighbor? I glanced out the window.

"I'll not be asking what you've done or where you've been," my mother continued. She folded her arms across her chest. Despite what life had done to her, she still had her pride. But then her eyes softened and she turned away, an excuse to check the oven she had checked only seconds before. "You've had no reason for coming back, I know," she said softly over her shoulder.

*No, I hadn't*, I wanted to say. But seeing her now, seeing what life had done to her, the things I had planned to say no longer seemed important.

"I've been to America," I said.

She sat back in her chair then folded her hands in her lap before she nodded. "Aye," she answered as if she already knew. "And how have you been?" She gestured with her head. "You look good." The last part sounded hopeful.

"Aye." I smiled. "America's grand."

She smiled back, and for a brief moment her eyes glistened and I could see the dream they once held. Then she caught herself.

"You have work? You're getting enough to eat?"

I sighed and sat in my father's chair, across from my mother.

"I can't stay, Mam."

"I know." She nodded.

"I only wanted to let you know that I'm fine." Unsure, I reached out and took her hand. "I wanted to see how you were getting on."

She nodded, suddenly unable to speak. After a moment, she looked away and wiped her eyes.

"I thought you should know," I continued, "I have a wife now." It wasn't true—not yet anyway—but I suspected God, if he was watching, would forgive my lie. My mother had lost her hope, for herself at least, years ago. But I sensed that she still held hope for me.

Her hand over her mouth, she let out a small cry. Then she leaned forward, tentatively. I hesitated a moment, unsure myself, then, chasing a life full of memories from my mind, I pulled my mother into my arms.

———

Love and affection weren't common in our home, the mood often matching the clouds and storms that blew outside. Sure, when I was four or five, my father would bounce me on his knee and tell me stories. With his soft voice and dancing eyes, he painted a picture in a way that no one else ever could. I remember struggling to stay awake, warmed by the fire and by his embrace, his stories filling my head and soon turning to dreams when my eyes grew heavy. It was years later when I realized that those very dreams were his own; dreams that would forever remain just that, for life, then death, had other things in mind for him.

Soon it was that the times in front of the fire became but a memory, the chores on the farm and my mother's sharp tongue taking their place. And soon it was when I noticed the change in my father.

The eyes that danced and the voice that carried me away were lost to the worry that now seemed to be always etched into his face. Maybe it was the poor harvest or the price of potatoes or the cow that suddenly stopped giving milk. Then again, maybe it was the sickness that would claim him years later.

As for my mother, it was a rare occasion when I saw her smile—a stern, cold woman she was. But then I thought I knew why. Death seemed to surround her, and if it couldn't have her, it seemed, then it took the ones she loved. She had steeled her heart, preparing herself for the pain that always seemed to be on her threshold.

My parents had three other children before my mother gave birth to me—three older brothers who I never met, all dead before I was born. Two died as infants, my father told me, and one died after falling below the hooves of a horse. Then, when I was two, my mother gave birth again, this time to a little girl. She had been named Ann, after my grandmother. A pretty girl with fair hair and a bright smile, my sister was. She died a year later, falling into the fire while my mother fetched more wood. Watching my sister, seeing her clothes in flames, hearing her screams was one of my first memories and one that to this day invaded my dreams.

After Ann, my mother had no more children. Like my father, she would hold me too, sometimes so tightly I cried. I was never sure if it was from love or from a stubbornness. *You're the only one left*, she seemed to be saying, *and I'll be damned if he'll take you too.* She would hold me on her lap in front of the fire in the evenings. Together we would rock while she hummed. It was always the same tune, a sad melody that made me want to cry.

Both her sisters died when I was young, one in childbirth and one from polio. While my mother did her best to hide her tears, for me death took on a different meaning. I remember the fear and the excitement of the wake, for it was one and both at the same time. My grandfather, when he died, was laid out on the kitchen table. The neighbor women arrived early to help prepare the body and, after that, the food. On the day the wake began, the house filled as people came from long distances to pay their respects. Many stayed for several days, as the wake didn't stop when the sun went down nor did when it rose the next day. While my grandfather lay peacefully on the table—a candle burning nearby, his hands folded around a cross—the best of food was served and the whiskey and stout were poured. While the men drank and told tales, the women keened. The time was filled with stories and games and while an older boy and an unmarried girl might sneak away for some privacy, a few moments away from the chaperone's eyes, the younger boys, myself included, learned how to fight out by the barn. Many a fond memory I had of wakes.

But when my own father died, his wake had been different. He too was lain out on the table, and while the games, the stories, and the drinking took place around me, I couldn't help thinking that nothing would ever be the same again. His dreams would die with him, and soon within me as well, as the burden of the farm—once my father's—now became my own.

I think my mother knew as well that the past was gone, never to be reclaimed. And so while the burden of the farm fell on my shoulders and I lost myself in the toil and sweat of the chores, my mother sat for months inside, by herself, staring at the fire. For her, the wake didn't end, even after we put my father in the ground.

I was surprised then, when one day two years after my father had died, she told me that she was too young to be a widow. Then she announced that she would be getting married again. Somehow, while I was out toiling in the fields, she had managed to find herself another husband.

———

I knew my time was running out, and I think my mother did too. Still she poured my tea.

"Billy's been asking for you."

"Aye," I said, nodding.

Although she suspected that I was involved with the IRA she'd never asked. Which was just as well because there were some things I didn't want to talk about.

I coughed, not quite sure how she would take my next question.

"Is he treating you well?" I asked, although I already knew the answer.

She looked away for a moment. When she looked back, I saw the same tired old woman I had seen when I arrived. She didn't need words to tell me what he had done.

Before I could say anything else, the clip-clop of hooves and the snort of a horse startled us.

"Quick," she said jumping up. "Out the window with you!"

I shook my head as I stood. "I'm not running this time." I took my mother's cup from her hands and gently placed it, with mine, on the table. Then I joined her by the fireplace again and waited. A moment later, the door banged open, and his bulk filled the doorway.

He stopped, seemingly surprised to find me there.

"So you came back, did you, you little shite!" he snarled.

He stepped into the room. I stood my ground. He saw the cups on the table and walked over. He glanced inside, then looked up at my mother. I saw the darkness in his eyes before they fell on me.

"Don't be thinking that you'll be getting anything more from me," he yelled. And with that he swung his arm, knocking both cups off the table. They shattered when they hit the wall, the tea forming little rivers all the way to the floor. My mother cringed, and a small cry escaped her lips.

"You've had your tea," he roared as he stepped toward me. "Now go!"

I could smell the whiskey on him now, and when I didn't move he raised his fist. I was prepared. I hit him once in the stomach and twice in the face. He stumbled, and when he held his hands up to protect his head, as I guessed he would, I hit him again in the stomach. He let out a grunt and, when he doubled over, I slammed my knee into his nose. He crumpled to the floor.

I glanced back at my mother. She was cowering on the other side of the room.

"Mam," I said, waiting until she looked up at me. I nodded. *Everything will be alright*, I wanted to tell her.

She nodded back, seeming to understand, and I turned back to the groaning hulk on the floor. My stepfather rolled to his belly and tried to push himself up. I kicked him in the side and, with an *oof*, he fell back to the floor. When he pulled his arms in, protecting his side, I kicked him between the legs. He let out another *oof* and curled up, groaning and panting on the floor.

I grabbed the iron from the fireplace and waited.

"Turn over," I said softly, but my tone let him know I meant it.

He did but this time with his hands held protectively between his legs. I stared at him, this man I hated, then thrust the hot iron at his face. He cringed, turned his head and let out a yelp, a terrified cry. When he opened his eyes again, I held the iron inches from his eyes.

"I'll be going," I said evenly, each of my words measured. "But if I ever hear of you laying a hand on my mother again"—I paused to make sure he understood—"I will come back, and mark my words"—I shook the iron—"I will kill you."

He flinched. Then I tossed the iron and he flinched again. It banged off the hearth—the clang of metal on stone, his panicked yelp, and my mother's heavy breathing the only sounds in the room.

I helped my mother up and sat her in a chair by the table. I kissed her cheek then, after taking a moment to give my stepfather another warning look, I stepped out the door.

The IRA had taught me well.

# Chapter Thirteen

"The British will be withdrawing soon," Mary said.

"What will happen then?" I asked. I had just returned with an arm full of peat for the stove. I stacked the bricks on the floor.

"They'll hand the barracks over to the IRA."

"And the Tans?" I asked. "The Peelers?"

"Aye," Mary responded. "They'll be leaving too. Lynch is drawing up plans."

Liam Lynch was the chief of staff of the IRA. His exploits were legend. During the war, he had led several successful raids, including the burning of the British Army barracks in Mallow and, later, the killing of thirteen British soldiers near Millstreet. But Lynch did not support the Treaty, or at least he hadn't. *What had changed?* I wondered.

As if she had read my mind, Mary added, "He doesn't want another war."

"So he's throwing his lot in with the Free State, is he?"

A darkness passed over Mary's eyes. "It's a dense one you are, Frank Kelleher," she snapped. "He doesn't want to see any more Irish killed."

Before I could answer, we heard a commotion outside and Tim rushed in.

"Someone's coming!" he gasped for breath. His face was red, and it was clear he'd been running.

I hurried to the door. In the distance, I could just make out the bicycle, far off down the lane, but headed our way. Mary hurried, wiping her hands on her apron, while I slipped out and made my way down to the cow-house. As I hid in the shadows, I realized this must have been exactly what Kathleen had done time and again for the past year.

Peeking out of the small window, my face hidden in the shadows, I saw Mary and Tim waiting in front of the cottage, the rider drawing closer. It was a lad, I could see, not much older than Tim, and he was dressed in a post office uniform. I felt a shiver and wondered for a moment if I had been recognized when I had stood in front of the post office several days before. If I had been, why had Billy waited? I glanced past the boy along the lane then back along the walls and to the fields on each side. I wouldn't put it past Billy to create a diversion to draw my attention away while he and his men crept up on my flank.

The rider stopped and dismounted, leaning his bike against the wall. He nodded at Mary then retrieved an envelope from his sack. I couldn't hear what was being said but, after a second, Mary turned to Tim, and he hurried into the cottage. Tim returned a moment later and handed the delivery boy a coin. He nodded again, tipped his hat, and climbed back on his bicycle. Mary and Tim stood watching as he disappeared up the lane.

Minutes later, I met them inside.

"It's from Kathleen," Mary said as she read the telegram. "She made it safely to Abbeyfeale."

She handed it to me.

*Arrived safely. All is well. Come soon.*

That was it, nothing more. Sure and she sounded fine, but I read it again to be certain. Kathleen, I was relieved to see, had been careful with her words. As with most telegrams, it was vague enough that it wouldn't draw any suspicion. The telegram had been addressed to Mary, not to me, and Kathleen hadn't sent it herself; it had been

sent by Mrs. Maloney, Mary's friend in Abbeyfeale. I smiled, proud
of Kathleen for being cautious and relieved that she had arrived safe.

———

I was torn as to what to do. My heart ached now that Kathleen was
gone, and I tried to convince myself that I had done the right thing.
She was safe with the Maloneys in Abbeyfeale, but I wondered again
if my decision to remain here—to face the demons that continued
to haunt me—had been wise. I had taken a risk going to Limerick,
and before that to the Sheehys'. And the more chances I took, I knew
that one day, soon, my luck would run out. Needing some air, I set
out for a walk, unsure where my steps would take me.

I lost track of time. At some point it had begun to rain, but I
hardly noticed, consumed as I was by my thoughts. In the back of
my mind, I think I knew where I was headed. I told myself it wasn't
wise, that it was another risk that I shouldn't be taking, but once the
rain started and I was absorbed by the mist, I felt safe. I continued
on to Patrick's Well. Some two hours later I glanced up and saw the
church. I made my way around the back, careful to avoid the rectory.

Minutes later, I found myself standing silently—the drops splattering off the wet gray stone of my father's grave before splashing
onto my trousers and my boots—trying the whole while to recite
the prayers. When I couldn't, not with conviction anyway, I stared
down at my father's grave and wondered what he would think of
the life I had made. A young man, just thirty-six when he died, his
hopes and dreams had been left for other men to follow. He had been
a simple man, never wanting much. He was a poet and, like all po-
ets, he had his own way of seeing the world. He found beauty where
others couldn't and often saw the good in people where others, my
mother among them, saw something darker. But when he faced an
injustice, my father was quick to right it, offended as he was by the
audacity of it all.

His dreams he had passed to me, from the stories he told as we

THE DEVIL'S DUE 119

sat by the fire, late into the evening, under my mother's reproachful eye.

"Why do you fill his head with such rubbish?" she had demanded one night, unaware that I was still awake.

"It's our country, Margaret!" he said, the exasperation clear. "What's been happening isn't right."

"And what exactly is it you and your friends intend to do about it, other than getting yourselves killed?" Her voice had risen and I realized years later that it wasn't the first time they had argued about this. "It's a waste of time is what it is!"

Although my eyes had been closed, I felt the sudden tenseness in my father's arms.

"This isn't how God intended us to live, Margaret. Slaves in our own land is what we are!"

"And it's a fine lot of good you'll do this family, off fighting for something you weren't meant to have and while there's work to be done."

There was a shrillness to my mother's voice, something I would forever associate with her. My father didn't respond, not to her anyway, and I felt his arms relax. I can only imagine the change that had come over him, his eyes far away, dreaming again.

"Ahh, you useless shite!"

If he had heard her, he didn't let on.

"One day, Frank," he said softly, "we'll put our differences aside and rise up and claim what's ours. It's our destiny."

It was only when he was dying that I learned the truth. He was a Fenian, having taken the vow of the Brotherhood, joining a handful of men who had agreed, against all odds, to wage a war against British oppression. For years it was a secret war. That had all changed on Easter Monday in 1916. I liked to think that, had he not died, my father would have been in Dublin that day, gun in hand, and for a brief moment he would have tasted how close he had come.

The night he died will be forever etched in my mind. While my mother cried softly in the corner, he called me over, his voice barely above a whisper by then. He told me the stories again, starting at the beginning, knowing that it would be the last time. My mother, God bless her, granted a dying man his wish and said nothing. For my part, I listened. And when it seemed he couldn't find enough air to fill his words, I held the water to his lips, but he waved it away. Then he reached for my hand.

"Frank!" he implored between gasps, "promise me, Frank!"

I had held his hand and stared at his sunken cheeks, at the once wavy dark hair that lay matted and limp against his head. I stared at his face, at the pain that had replaced the dreams that had once danced in his eyes. His body wasted, he hadn't the strength to climb out of the bed, and it was there that death would find him minutes later.

But not before he had my answer.

"Aye, Da," I said as the tears slid down my cheeks. "I promise."

# Chapter Fourteen

I felt better about my decision after the visit to the cemetery in Patrick's Well and seeing my father's grave. *When a thing is wrong,* I could hear him say, *you have to make it right.* My father, I thought, would be smiling, knowing that my decision to stay was the right one even if it meant greater risk to me. Renewed, I set out the following morning to see exactly what I was up against.

From my perch up on the hill, I watched Mick come out of the stable. His cap was perched as it always was, low on his head, his eyes barely visible below the brim. His tweed jacket was worn and threadbare, the years of labor in the fields having taken their toll. He led a horse—a sprightly one-year-old from the looks of it—to the small enclosure. It was surrounded by tall stone walls with a closed gate on one side. Mick led the horse to the center of the ring, the horse tugging at the reins the whole while. Muscles rippled below the flesh, betraying a power waiting to be unleashed. The horse snorted and threw his head from side to side. Mick held the reins firm and, although I couldn't hear him from where I was, I could see his manner: soothing, gentle, whispering softly until the horse quieted. He stepped forward and the horse let him stroke his neck.

The horse snorted again, but this time it was a contented sound, and soon Mick was walking him through paces, circling the ring, starting and stopping again. They did this for a while, Mick speaking softly and the horse listening. After a few minutes, Mick led the

horse to the gate, opened it, whispered something again, and let go
of the reins. The horse cantered for a bit, the muscles rippling, ready
to bolt. Instead he slowed and looked over his shoulder. Mick was
standing in the gate, watching. The horse stopped and turned, regarded Mick for a bit, then trotted off. After a moment, he dropped
his head and bolted, a carefree dash across the field. He could have
easily jumped the outer wall but instead curved and raced along
it. After a minute he slowed and turned with the wall then circled
back to the field just outside the gate. He slowed to a walk and then
stopped and regarded Mick again. After a moment he lowered his
head and began grazing. Even from where I was I could see the smile
on Mick's face. Mick had a way with horses, a far more gentle touch
than I could ever hope to have.

A serious man Mick was, but a dreamer nonetheless. He spent
hours reading, the works of Yeats and Joyce certainly, but Greek
tragedies too. He spoke Irish, rare enough at the time after years of
British suppression, and he was active in the Gaelic League. Like
my own father, Mick wrote poems too, and I remember sitting in
a pub once, with the fire crackling and a pint in front of me, as he
read from his own hand a beautiful poem that captured not only the
pain and the suffering but the beauty and the hope that was Ireland.
Mick also sang, in a tenor voice surprising for a man his size, beautiful ballads which, like his poems, were written by his own hand.

I waited up on the hill and eventually the horse trotted back
through the gate, heading directly to the trough of water. Mick
closed the gate behind him then stepped into the stable for a moment. Seizing the opportunity, I scrambled down from my perch
and made my way over to the wall. Moments later, when Mick came
out, he studied the horse, the same appraising look I had seen before.

"You've always had the gift, Mick," I said softly and he turned
slowly, not wanting to spook the horse I'm sure. The horse glanced up
once, then, deciding I wasn't a threat, stuck his nose back in the water.

"Frank Kelleher," Mick said. I could see the surprise in his face and then something else. He nodded as if he had known all along.

"I heard you were back."

I had expected that. He stepped toward the wall but I didn't move, trusting my instincts.

"I had to come back. To make things right."

He studied me for a moment, his eyes pensive. Then he held up his hands.

"What's done is done. The war's over, at least for me it is. We got what we wanted"—he shook his head—"or mostly for some, but far more than I ever expected we would." He held my gaze. "It's time to let go of the past."

I breathed a sigh of relief, thankful that my instincts had been right. Mick had always been the peacemaker. Like he could with a wild horse, he had always been able to calm the waters, to ease the tension before tempers flared.

"Aye," I said with a nod. "What's done is done. But to know that what people think about me isn't true? That's a hard thing to live with."

He studied me, his eyes pensive again, then he tilted his head, gesturing toward the gate. Without a word, he opened it and I followed him inside.

We sat in the cow-house, on two wooden stools used for milking. I took a deep breath. The familiar odors of hay and animals, of manure and dirt were soothing. Then I told him what had happened, how Dan and Sean and Tom had died. Mick, as expected, nodded now and again but said nothing, letting me tell the story in my own way, waiting for me to finish. When I did, we both sat silently for a while, the only noise the low moans of the cows and the snorts of the horse outside. Then Mick leaned forward, arms resting on his knees, and stared at the dirt between us for a moment. I wondered what he was thinking. Finally, he looked up and nodded again.

"I've known you for most of my life, Frank," he began, looking me in the eye. "I never believed the stories. I told the boys—I told

Billy—that it couldn't be true, that you never would have done such a thing. But he wouldn't hear of it and then you disappeared, gone to London we were told." He sighed and stared off for a moment. "Maybe it was necessary, all of the killing of our own. Maybe it was the only way we could have won."

It took me a moment to realize what he was saying. Informants, real or imagined, were dealt with swiftly and brutally, the only way we knew to enforce loyalty, the only way we knew to prevent the British from learning what we were up to.

"Maybe it was the price we had to pay," he continued, "but I often wonder how many good men died."

He seemed far away for a moment, lost in his own thoughts. Then he sat back, stuck his hand in one pocket then the other, searching until he found what he was after. He pulled out his cigarettes, a pack of Woodbines. He offered me one but I shook my head. I watched as he lit one, the smoke drifting up to the ceiling.

"I heard you went to see the Sheehys," he said.

"Aye, I did." I shook my head but I could see that he already knew. "I think I only made things worse."

He nodded. "And what do you intend to do now?"

I hesitated. "I'm going to see Dan's wife. And the Murphys."

He nodded again as if he had already known. "I suspect you won't find them much different."

"Aye. I know. But I have to go."

He nodded again. "Billy knows you're here," he said, "and he's not one to forget the past."

"Aye. He's not."

He sucked on the cigarette. A moment later he let out a heavy breath, the smoke blowing past me. Mick was silent for a moment, lost in his own thoughts, lost in the smoke.

"They burnt his house down," he said as if he had just remembered.

"Whose house?" I asked. "Billy's?"

He nodded.

I shook my head. I hadn't known that.

"After Argyle Manor, the British wanted revenge. They had Billy's name and some others. They went to his house, and when his mother told them he wasn't there, they forced her out and put their torches to it."

I could picture it in my mind: Mrs. Ryan crying, the Black and Tans cursing and shouting, waving their guns and shoving her to the ground before pouring paraffin inside and throwing their torches in after. It was another reason Billy wanted to put a bullet in me. As if betraying the IRA and Dan, Sean, and Tom wasn't enough, now I was also responsible for what the British had done to his mother.

Mick's sigh interrupted my thoughts.

"I'm afraid that men like Billy will soon have us fighting each other," he said. He took another puff. He seemed lost in thought again, and I waited a moment before I spoke.

"What will you do?" I asked.

He didn't answer right away; instead he took another puff on the cigarette. A moment later, he let the smoke out with a long sigh.

"If it comes to that, I don't know, Frank." He spread his arms. "This is all I ever wanted," he said, gesturing toward the cow-shed.

For Mick, it wasn't just the cow-shed. It was everything that it represented, everything that it was connected to: our history, our culture, our identity. It was a simple life, but it was so much more, especially for a man like Mick who looked at things through a poet's eyes.

He stared at me and his eyes narrowed. "But I know this," he said as he shook his head. "I'll have no part of Irish fighting Irish."

If Mick had said any differently, I would have been surprised. He was right. We *had* achieved far more than most had expected. Still, I couldn't help but think how close we were. How much more would it take to force the British out of Ulster, to achieve a true republic? But to do that, would I be willing to take up a gun against my fellow countrymen first? Would I fight the very government that I had fought so hard to help bring about? And if it came to that, how many more Irishmen would die?

"What about you?" Mick asked. "Will you stay?"

I wasn't sure how to answer. Living in America the last year, watching the turmoil and the conflict from afar, Ireland seemed a different place. There was no question in my mind that if the time came, I would take up my rifle again to fight the British. But betray my own people? That was something I didn't think I could do.

"I don't know, Mick." I shook my head. "I don't know."

He studied me for a moment, took another puff, dropped the cigarette to the floor, and crushed the stub below his boot. He shook his head, and I could see the resignation in his eyes.

"I'm afraid then that there are some dark days ahead for us," he said. Then he reached out, his hand resting gently on my shoulder. He squeezed softly. "Mind yourself now, Frank."

———

It was a strange country we lived in, a bog-land, an unforgiving terrain where the ground spit out rocks like it did the heather, like it did the grain. The clouds and the rain were constant, something we had grown accustomed to over the centuries, but it left a dampness that permeated everything: our cottages, our clothes, our bones, and our souls. Despite the rocks, the soil was rich, good for growing and good for grazing, and the hills held a green that was as constant as the rains. It's hard to picture an Irishman and his land and see them as separate things. Married to the land we were, toiling and farming, seeking our daily sustenance from it, our past, our present, and our future all tied to it in a complex web. We took pride in it, seeing it as we did our own child. We rejoiced over it when the crop was plentiful, when the prices were high. And we wept over it when all it gave us for the hours and the days and the weeks and the months that we had spent devoted to it—coaxing it, loving it—was a mound of rotting potatoes.

We had given it the blood of our dying, so many having fallen over the years to defend it. We had given it the bones of our dead, my own daughter and my father joining countless others who had gone before them, all lying just below its green turf. We were the land, and the land was us. And even though it had been stolen from us centuries before, in our hearts it was still ours.

*What would Mick do?* I wondered. So many had fled already, as generations had before them. For those that had found a plot, some farmland in Australia or Pennsylvania or Massachusetts, where they were able to start over, at one with the land again, life went on. But for those that had traded their identities for jobs—in the factories in New York or Boston or London—something was lost forever. Life for them would never be the same. That was why Mick would never leave, I thought. How could he? The land—Ireland—was in his blood, and he would no sooner cut off his arm or give up his child than he would give up his home.

How he would avoid the bloodshed that was certain to come, I wasn't sure. I wasn't sure how I would either. Kathleen was safe in Abbeyfeale, for now. But with another war looming and with the possibility that Billy was actively searching for me, I wondered again why I hadn't gone with her.

As I made my way back to Mary's, Mick's question continued to nag at me. *If it comes to this, to Irish fighting Irish, what will you do?*

I didn't have an answer for him because I didn't have an answer for myself. I had returned for Kathleen and for my child but, with each day that passed, I realized I would have come back anyway. Sure I was drawn back to right the wrongs of the past. But it was more than that. As I walked down the sodden lane, the stone walls curving with the road and disappearing over the rise, the gray skies over the fields stretched beyond, I could *feel* the land. I could feel its presence, its struggles, our history, our culture. It was the same bond that held Mick. War or no war, Billy or no Billy, I wasn't sure I could leave again.

# Chapter Fifteen

It was late in the evening when I returned to Mary's. As I made my way down the lane, I heard raised voices coming from the cottage. I paused for a moment by the stone wall and listened, the prickle on the back of my neck telling me something was wrong. It was a dark, cold night and I suddenly felt vulnerable, wondering what dangers lurked in the blackness around me. But the night was still, and I crept forward slowly, trying to catch what the commotion was about. I was too far away to make out the words. I only caught bits and pieces—Mary's angry tone and Tim's defiant response—but my instinct told me that somehow it involved me.

Mary and Tim were standing in front of the stove—my fiancé's sister with her hands on her hips and an angry scowl on her face, her son staring at the ground. Tim didn't bother to look up when I stepped into the room. A sullen boy, he had never been the same after his father died. I nodded and said hello, Mary's eyes warning me to say no more. She turned back to Tim.

"We'll talk about this later," she said, but her tone made it clear that it was she who would be doing the talking. She turned and I stepped out of her way as she snatched the wooden bucket from the peg by the door. She scraped her knuckles in the process, cursed under her breath, then stomped outside, slamming the door behind her.

It was as if I wasn't in the room. Tim stared at some unseen spot on the floor. I gave him a moment before I said anything.

"And what's all this about?" I asked softly.

He looked up, and a flash of anger crossed his face.

"Nothing that concerns you," he snapped, then he too stomped out of the cottage.

What had happened I didn't know, but I couldn't shake the feeling that, in some way, it would impact me.

I stepped outside. Tim was nowhere to be seen, but I knew where Mary would be. I followed the well-worn path, barely visible in the darkness, and found her by the well. She was turning the crank on the windlass, lowering the bucket. Her motions betrayed her fury and I stood back, knowing any offer of help would be met with a sharp tongue. A moment later, she reversed direction, raising the bucket until it swung below the windlass. She set the brake, poured the water into the bucket she had carried from the house. Water sloshed over the side, but she didn't seem to notice. Hands resting on the wall, she stared into the well for a moment then turned. Even in the darkness, I could see the glisten in her eyes.

"He's only fifteen!" she said. "The damn fool!"

I waited silently, knowing she would get to it in her own time. With Mary it usually wasn't a long wait.

"He'll be doing no such thing!" she snapped at me.

I nodded.

She let out a breath then shook her head. "Damn that Billy," she said quietly.

"Billy?" I asked, although I was afraid I already knew the answer.

She shot me a look, as if somehow I were the one to blame, then her eyes softened and she nodded.

"Aye, Billy. He's been recruiting men"—she gestured toward the cottage, "and young boys, to join the fight. He's been filling Tim's head full of ideas." A sob escaped her lips. "I'll not be losing him like I lost John."

I stepped forward, putting my arms around her. She leaned into my embrace, cried for a moment, her head on my shoulder. Then as quick as it started, it stopped. She stepped back and wiped her eyes. "The British are beginning to withdraw their forces," she said. "They've turned the Castle Barracks over to the Free State."

"The Free State?" I asked, my mind suddenly spinning at the news. "What happened to Lynch's plan? Where's our lads?"

"I don't know," Mary said. "No one expected that it would happen today."

But clearly the Free State had. I felt a churning in my stomach. The IRA was nothing if not territorial. Boundaries had been established, and divisional and brigade commanders guarded their turf in much the same way that British nobility had guarded their manors for seven hundred years. If you weren't part of the manor, you didn't belong. That Brennan would march his own troops into another's area without permission—even if he did support the Treaty—was unheard of. The fracture in the IRA was now complete.

"And the RIC barracks?" I asked.

"They've turned those over too."

My mind flashed to Sergeant Mullins, the Free State Soldier who had given me a ride only days earlier. Although I hadn't seen any evidence of the two factions during my wanderings in Limerick several days earlier, the Free State government had been prepared for the British withdrawal and had rushed to secure the barracks before Lynch and the Anti-Treaty Republicans could. It was only a matter of time before Lynch responded with his own show of force, and that meant Billy and the boys from my old brigade would soon be facing Brennan's Free State men. Whether there would be fighting or not, I didn't know.

"Would you talk to him, Frank?"

I looked up. Her eyes were still wet, and I understood her fears. If Tim joined Billy and there was fighting, he was sure to be in the thick of it.

"Aye."

Tim was Mary's only child. The birth had been difficult,

Kathleen had told me once—Mary almost dying when the baby came. After Tim was born, Mary was never been able to have another child. I would talk to him, but I wasn't sure what type of reception I would get. Before that, though, I needed to understand what this news meant for me.

"Does Billy know I'm staying here? Did Tim tell him?"

Mary hesitated a moment before she answered. "I don't know. I suspect he does, but Tim wouldn't say." Suddenly she glared at me, her moment of weakness behind her. "But if you had an ounce of brains in that head of yours, after you talk to Tim, you would be on the next train to Abbeyfeale!"

———

I found Tim down by the stream, standing on a large rock that over-hung the water, the same one I remember sitting on with Kathleen what now seemed a long time ago. Tim, Mary told me, often fished from this spot. He glanced up at me but said nothing as he stared out over the water. With no moonlight, the stream looked more like oil than water, a shifting, flowing mass, the rushing, gurgling sounds soft in the night air.

I sat on the rock, my feet dangling over the edge. I uncorked the bottle—an ale Mary had given me—and poured two cups. After a moment, Tim sat down beside me. I handed him a cup. We were quiet for a while, simply sitting and listening to the sound of the water, the wind rustling through the grass. I took a swallow and, out of the corner of my eye, watched Tim do the same. He made a face, held his cup up as if to inspect it, then took a smaller sip and set it to the side. His first drink.

"The first person I killed was a Tan." I spoke softly but my voice or perhaps my admission seemed incredibly loud in the darkness.

Tim turned to me, his eyes suddenly eager, willing me to con-tinue.

"The Peelers had captured a man from Limerick, a man named

Donovan, and after holding him here for several days, they were to transport him to Dublin. We planned to ambush the train at Killonan, hoping to free him. We waited the entire day, hiding along the tracks south of the station. It rained all day, the six of us lying in the grass the whole while. Finally, well after dark, we were told that the plans had been changed and he was to be transported the next day. Wet and tired, we all returned home. The following morning, well before sunrise, we took up our positions again. It rained for fourteen hours straight before we were finally sent home again. On the third morning, we were told that the train was now due to arrive at noon. Our plan was to wait until it stopped at the station. There was supposed to be an IRA man on board, a scout, who would signal us to confirm that Donavan was indeed on the train."

I paused and took a sip from my cup.

"What happened?" Tim asked.

I set my cup back on the rock. "Noon came and went and still there was no train. By this time we were all miserable, tired and wet—this was our third day, mind you—and we were all looking forward to going home. I expected the whole operation to be called off, that we would be ordered to stand down. Then, from the distance, we heard the whistle."

I paused. The image of the tracks, glistening in the pouring rain, and the sound of the approaching train was clear in my mind. When I continued telling Tim my story, I was living it again, the scene playing out in my head.

*We lay still while Billy whispered his instructions.*

*"Check your weapons! Don't fire until I give the order!"*

*We could see the train now, moving slowly into the station, a long cloud of black smoke flowing from its stack. With a screech of metal on metal, the train slowed then, in a hiss of steam, it stopped. A moment later, we heard the shouts, several voices and then the sound of boots. Suddenly, half a dozen Tans were on the platform. That wasn't supposed to happen;*

we had expected Peelers to be guarding Donovan, not the war-hardened Tans. Passengers, those climbing on board and those climbing off, gave the Tans wide berth. We waited, but the signal from the scout never came.

After several minutes, the conductor walked the length of the train, shutting the doors one after another until he got to the Tans. They ignored him while they lit their cigarettes, not concerned about his schedule. The conductor glanced at his watch again then back at the Tans but said nothing. Behind them, a head poked out the window of the second car and the signal came.

Billy improvised and gave each of us a target.

It seemed to happen slowly, me raising my rifle, lining up the sights on the man I had been assigned. He was a big man, older than me by ten years at least. His face was haggard and had the look of dried leather, the creases dirty as if he were a farmer just in from the fields. His eyes spoke both of the atrocities he had seen and those that he himself had committed and likely would again. His tunic was green, the buttons tarnished and the sleeves worn, in need of mending. His pants were black, worn and dirty as well. He held his rifle in one hand, the cigarette in the other, the smoke rising above his head to join the steam from the train.

My world had been reduced to this man before me, his companions somehow fading as if they had never existed. I heard nothing, the sounds of the station somehow fading as well. His chest rose as he took a breath from the cigarette. The whole while I was conscious that my finger was slowly squeezing the trigger, acting on its own.

The gun jumped in my hands and the Tan's eyes flashed wide with shock, a grimace spreading across his face. He staggered, the rifle fell, and his eyes looked up, found mine, as my gun jumped again. He staggered once more when the second bullet struck, but he held my stare, one hand on his chest, the blood seeping through his fingers, the dark stain growing on his tunic. He crumpled slowly, his eyes never leaving mine, one hand still clutching his chest, the other fumbling in the air as if he were trying to catch the cigarette he had dropped.

I stared at the man I had shot. He was someone's son, I suddenly *realized, maybe someone's husband or someone's father. He was lying still on the platform, eyes open and staring now at nothing. Suddenly there was a clap on my back and I was up, scrambling over the wall and running down the tracks. I heard several gunshots and suddenly sounds came rushing back as did my sight. There were several more gunshots, the excited shouts from the men with me, the screams of the passengers and the wailing and moans of the dying. The platform was a scene of chaos, passengers scrambling off the train, tripping over one another, some lying on the ground, hit by bullets or hiding, I didn't know.*

*It was all over in a moment, a brief flash. I stood over the man I had shot, stared down at his lifeless eyes, at the blood bubbling from his lips, at the dark red pool growing on the platform. He was in the middle of a pile of bodies, arms and legs entangled, caps and guns scattered. Billy had a pistol in his hand now and, one by one, put a bullet in the head of any Tan still moaning. Then he was shouting and we hurried to collect the rifles. With two men helping Donovan, who was still wearing shackles, and me and another carrying the guns, we made our escape.*

"We managed to make it back to the house safely," I said, drawing myself back from the memory. "We hid there for three days. We knew the British would come looking for us, seeking their revenge." I shook my head. "For three nights I lay awake. I kept seeing the Tan, the look on his face when I shot him and then him lying on the ground, dead."

Tim's eyes were wide; he was hanging on my every word.

"It won't be the British that you'll be fighting," I told Tim. "It'll be men like you and me. It'll be men who all love Ireland but who have different ideas about what we should do now, with the British leaving." I shook my head. "To kill another Irishman? I don't know, Tim. Killing a Tan is hard enough."

Tim seemed to study me for a while. He took another sip of his stout.

"Did you ever kill an Irishman?"

I was silent for a moment, unsure how to answer, how much to tell him. Finally, I decided that he needed to know. I told him about shooting Brian Conroy, a man who had been forced by the British to choose between his family and the IRA. Because of the choice he made, I didn't have one and had been forced to put a bullet in him and pin a warning to his chest. Then I told him about Argyll Manor and how we had been surprised by the Tans and about the choice I made, to slam my hand onto the plunger, knowing as I did so that any chance Dan, Tom, and Sean might have had would be gone. Sure I had killed three Tans, but I had helped to kill three of our own men too.

I let out a sigh. "I'm not sorry for the Tans and the British soldiers I've killed. But the men like me, men who all loved Ireland but, for one reason or another, had been put in circumstances they couldn't control—their faces will stay with me forever."

Tim nodded then sat back, seemingly lost in thought. It was just as well. Forced to confront memories and images that I'd have preferred remain hidden had suddenly left me depressed. We sat silently for a while, the sound of the stream, the sound of the wind, and our breathing the only noises.

He coughed, glanced up at me, hesitated, and I could see something was on his mind. I knew what he was going to say before he said it.

"Billy knows you're staying here."

# Chapter Sixteen

I left immediately, not knowing where I would go, only that I couldn't stay. Tim, if I were to believe him, had been surprised by Billy's question. When he hadn't answered directly, Billy had kept at him until he had learned what he wanted. Ever since I'd visited the Sheehys, Billy had known that I was back in Ireland. But he hadn't known where I was staying. *Until now*, I thought with a chill.

With Anti-Treaty and Free State troops marching on Limerick, Billy, I hoped, would be too busy to worry about me. But who knew what he would do? I didn't want any trouble for Mary either. Before I left, I had suggested that she and Tim go to Abbeyfeale, that now she was at risk too for putting me up.

"I can handle myself," Mary had replied. "Besides, there's work to be done."

The work, I knew, wasn't just the laundry. The Irish Women's League, much like the IRA, were choosing sides. Mary was a Republican through and through, but the Women's League had sided with the Free State to avoid bloodshed. And now they were working with Michael Collins and the provisional government to put in place the structures Ireland would need to move forward. But with Tim now joining the fight, her conversion was complete. She would do all she could to stop another war.

I wasn't sure if the bloodshed could be stopped. "Michael Collins is a traitor," Mary had said one evening, shortly after I had returned. It was a view I'm sure that she shared with Billy and some of my old comrades. Sure Collins had led us to victory over the British and, after the truce, he had been sent by the new provisional government to negotiate a treaty. Many said the one he returned with—one that would partition the country into north and south and require an oath of allegiance to the King—was the best that we could have hoped for, that the British would accept nothing less. The Free Staters hailed Collins while the Anti-Treaty forces—my old brigade—wanted to see Collins pay for his crime.

I didn't think Collins was a traitor. Sure, when I arrived six weeks ago, I was against the Treaty. Victory, I had felt at the time, was within our grasp and a united Irish Republic, free to manage its own affairs without meddling from others, was the only acceptable road forward. However, I thought of what I saw in Mrs. Sheehy's eyes and in Mr. Sheehy's too and in Liam's and Mick's and my mother's. The country was tired of the war, and I didn't think it could survive another.

I had heard rumors that the Southern Division and the Limerick Brigades didn't have the guns or ammunition to continue fighting. But with Free State forces now in Limerick, if I knew Billy and Lynch, they would find a way. A united Ireland had always been the dream—my father's and now mine—but if it would take a civil war to achieve it, I was no longer certain it would be worth the steep price we would pay, that it would be worth the blood.

I decided to go to Liam's, hoping he would put me up for a day or two. As I made way down darkened roads, I was cautious, not wanting to run into anyone. My hair was black again and, although I wore the glasses, I was nervous. I passed the spot where the Tans had stopped me a month earlier, the lane vacant and quiet now. Even so, with a war looming in Limerick and Billy actively looking for me, I was on edge.

I hoped Tim would take my advice, but I couldn't be certain. Whether he wanted to or not, though, Tim would share my story with Billy. As a precaution, I had told him that I was going to stay with a friend in Tipperary, a priest I knew named Byrne. No such priest existed, or if one did, I wasn't aware of it. Hopefully that would give me time to figure out what to do.

———

The dogs started barking as I walked up the lane. Liam's brother Seamus, stepped out, his eyes guarded, before a grin spread across his face

"Frank Kelleher? Is it yourself?"

I smiled back. I had always liked Seamus. Nine years older than Liam and me, he always had a smile and a joke but was quick with his fists when crossed. More than once he had rescued us from boys twice our size and age, from the fists and the blows against which we had no chance. He had been a Volunteer too, joining the struggle years before Liam and me. He lost two fingers to a British bullet before I joined. Although he could no longer fight—he never learned to shoot a gun with his other hand—he supported the cause in other ways. Seamus was a member of Sínn Féin, whose weapon of choice was the pen and whose battles were fought in the newspapers and within the very halls of the government that held us captive. Sínn Féin hadn't supported the Easter Rising in 1916, preferring a political solution instead of a military one. But in 1918, after Britain tried to force the conscription of Irishmen to join in their fight with Germany, Sínn Féin became our voice. We Irish refused to send our own boys to die in a war that had nothing to do with us and Sínn Féin became our means of protest. Later that year, Sínn Féin won seventy-three seats, representing Ireland in the British parliament. Although the IRA and Sínn Féin didn't always agree, Seamus fought the only way he could.

Two in the morning and he invited me in. I tried to be quiet, not wanting to wake his wife, Tara, or Liam for that matter, but he wouldn't hear of it. He hadn't been here when I'd visited Liam a month ago, off to Dublin as he was for a Sínn Féin meeting. "You've been to America!" he said as he sat across from me, letting out a contented sigh. It was a statement full of hope and dreams and one I certainly couldn't answer with a yes or no. He opened the bottle—an awkward task for a man missing two fingers, but he managed it well enough—and poured two cups. He slid one across the table, anxious to hear my stories.

As I thought of where to start, I heard footsteps and Tara appeared, pulling a shawl across her shoulders. She put several logs on the fire. I apologized for waking her. She nodded and once the fire had caught, she went back to bed.

Not wanting to disappoint Seamus, I told him about New York, careful to avoid the troubling things I had seen. Instead, I focused on the Irish dream of a Golden Door. Like a child, he hung on my every word.

I told him of mile after mile of cobblestone streets, crowded with motorcars, horse carriages, trolleys, and people, all through the day and long into the night. I told him of the trains that ran both above ground and below, full always of well-dressed people with a purpose. The buildings, I said, made Dublin—even London— look like a village. I told him of the Great White Way and the theaters, their signs lit by electric lights, and the grand library nearby. He smiled when I described the Sunday when I walked across the Brooklyn Bridge.

"Hanging from steel wires, is it?" he asked and shook his head as he tried to fathom how such a thing was possible.

Not satisfied with merely going over the water, the Americans, I told him, had gone under too. The tunnels below the Hudson River meant that people and freight in New Jersey didn't have to rely on ferries to complete their journey.

"A tunnel?" he asked. "Below the river?" He shook his head, amazed at the marvel of it all.

I told him of the beef and the fish and the produce that overflowed at the markets, so much food you thought you had died and had gone to heaven. He laughed at the various people I described: the Chinese man who sold fish, the German watchmaker, the Polish bricklayer.

"I knew it!" he said time and again. "I knew it!"

It was a grand picture I painted, for it was the picture he wanted to see.

"It sounds grand, Frank, it truly does!"

Liam had joined us by then, and between the whiskey and the fire, the warmth had finally chased the chill from my bones.

Seamus continued to ask questions while Liam sat silently, sipping his whiskey, a pained look on his face that I attributed to the early hour. Seamus sighed, a smile on his face, as much from my stories as from the whiskey.

"Ah, Frank, I would love to go myself, but Tara would never hear of such a thing."

I nodded. As bad as it had been and as bad as it might soon become, many Irish would never leave the only land they had ever known.

"So, you'll be heading back soon?"

"Aye," I said. I didn't want to disappoint him. "But not before I take care of some business." I hesitated, uncertain how much to tell Seamus. Liam's face was set in stone, but I suspected he already knew what I was going to say.

"I've run into some trouble, Seamus." He knew about the Argyll Manor bombing; what the newspapers and the wanted posters hadn't told him, he had learned from other IRA men as the details of any encounter with the British quickly spread across the brigades.

"I never thought you did what they said." He glanced at Liam then back at me, his face a scowl. Then he laughed and gestured to my cup. "If I did, I would have put a bullet in you myself not poured you a *wee wan.*"

I laughed then wondered for a moment if he was serious.

His eyes narrowed. "So, Billy is after you, is he?"

"Aye," I said and told him about the Sheehys.

Seamus nodded slowly then reached for the bottle again and filled our cups. When he went to fill Liam's, overcome with a fit of coughing, Liam waved him away.

"I need to hide for a while," I said after a moment, breaking the silence. Out of the corner of my eye, I saw Liam wipe his mouth. He had been quiet this whole time but suddenly sat forward.

"Where's Kathleen?" he asked, his voice raspy.

"Visiting friends." I answered. "In Abbeyfeale."

"Does Billy know about her?"

"Aye." I told them what Billy had learned from Tim.

"You can stay here as long as you like," Seamus said.

Liam shook his head, awake now. "No. Billy's sure to come looking."

"That little shite will find nothing here," Seamus said, slamming his fist on the table. "You can stay as long as you want."

I smiled and thanked him but told him no. "Liam's right. I won't be the one to bring trouble into your home."

He seemed about to argue, but Liam waved him off.

"What about the castle?" Liam asked.

I stared at him, unsure what he meant.

He suddenly doubled over, overcome by another fit of coughing. After a moment, he wiped his eyes and sat up. "Ballygowan," he finally said, his voice a whisper.

It took a moment but then I smiled, suddenly remembering a time when we were lads, when our dreams were big and our worries were small.

———

The castle stood on a high bluff on private lands south of Limerick City and further south past Bruff in an area known as Ballygowan. The castle had long been in ruins, much of its jagged, broken walls overgrown. Legend spoke of a fortress under siege hundreds of years earlier in one land war or another as lords of the manor—their names long forgotten—found themselves out of favor with the crown. The place was said to be haunted by the spirits of those who had been killed within its walls. As boys, Liam and I had heard the stories as well as the warnings from the elders to give the castle wide berth. But the warnings only served to fuel our imaginations and our sense of adventure. As Liam told Seamus about the castle, my mind drifted to the first time we had visited, over a dozen years ago:

One Sunday, after mass, Liam and I had set out for Ballygowan, our imaginations having already made the journey long before. Not more than eight years old, we had a grand time, climbing among the weeds and piles of stone, our minds fighting battles as invading armies tried to storm the castle and breech the walls.

We explored the remains of the keep then the circular stump of the tower. Liam had slid down to the base and then crawled over a pile of rubble that had all but filled the arch of a passageway.

"Frank! Come quick!"

I scrambled down from my perch, crawled through the archway and slid down the pile of rubble. I found Liam several feet away, in grass that seemed almost as tall as he was, standing over two large, flat stones. There was a gap of blackness between the two that hinted at something buried below. A grave? A treasure? We didn't know, but we were determined to find it, whatever it was. We struggled for several minutes to move the stones—the muscles straining in our young bodies—and when we finally did, we stared, wide-eyed, at what appeared to be a series of stone steps disappearing into the darkness below. This, we told each other, in whispers as much filled with excitement as they were with fear, was the entrance to some secret passageway, one that had remained hidden for centuries.

We didn't hesitate. Chasing the spirits and banshees from our minds, we climbed down into the dark, narrow shaft. Some fifteen or twenty steps later, the stairs ended and we stood in several inches of water. After a few steps, we found solid, dry ground. In the faint light from the entrance above, we began to explore. We were soon swallowed up by the darkness, our hands held in front as we blindly moved forward. Ten steps then twenty and then, despite my hands, I stumbled and fell forward onto a pile of stones.

"Are you alright, Frank?" Liam called from behind me.

I told him I was, nothing more than a few cuts and scrapes on my hands and shins, a few more to join those that had come from moving the stones above. I heard him rustling and then a scrape and suddenly the tunnel was bathed in a soft, flickering light. Liam was holding a match.

"I stole two cigarettes from my Da," he said, the light dancing along his grinning face.

"How many matches do you have?" I asked then turned back to study the pile of rubble before me as I waited for his answer. The pile of stones, several as big as me, had filled the passageway. The ceiling had collapsed, likely centuries ago.

"A dozen. No more."

The match went out and Liam lit another. We talked excitedly, our heads filled with dungeons and knights and secret torture rooms.

"We can't move these," I said, pointing. "And if we could, what would we do with them?"

Liam nodded. "Sure and it might not be safe beyond," he responded, a rare sound bit of reasoning from two boys drunk with adventure. "But, still," he continued, "what do you suppose is on the other side?"

The match went out, and Liam lit a third. We talked excitedly, making plans to return, better prepared for the next time. Then, knowing it was time to leave, before someone discovered what we had done, we turned around and began to make our way back to the shaft of light. Suddenly I stopped. In the wall to my right was a dark, narrow recess. I stuck my hand in and grinned, knowing I had discovered another passageway, one that was partially hidden and visible only from this direction. This passage was much narrower than the main tunnel, and we had to turn sideways to slip though the opening. We saved our matches, using our hands as our eyes instead, and a moment later, we could sense that the walls had suddenly disappeared. Although pitch black, our excited voices sounded different, and we realized that we had entered a chamber. The air was musty and dry with the faint smell of peat. Liam lit another match, one of the few he had left, and the soft light filled the cave, chasing shadows across the walls. A pile of stones was arranged in a circle on the floor, but the corners of the chamber were lost, fading into dark recesses. The match flickered out, and we were plunged once again into darkness. We only stayed for a few moments, Liam striking another match as soon as the one before it went out. Then, with only one match remaining and with little else discovered, we had no other choice but to leave. Back on the surface, we carefully slid the two stones back in place, concealing the opening. We grinned at each other, both knowing that nothing would keep us from coming back.

It was several weeks before we were able to return, school and our farm chores keeping us both busy. But the castle stayed with us, filling our heads and every conversation. We were careful though not to speak of our adventure with the adults. Even then, we knew the strength of their fears and the penalty for our transgression. This didn't stop us from finding out everything we could, which was little. Then one night at Liam's house, the seanachie—the storyteller—paid a visit. An old man, blind by then, he reminded me of the hawthorn tree. As if he too had been forced to battle the wind his whole life, his body was bent and his face weathered and gnarled. As he puffed on his pipe, the sweet smell of his tobacco filling the room, he told us the stories, the ones never committed to paper but passed from generation to generation by men like him. We were spellbound, Liam and I, as he spun tales, but by none more so than when he spoke of secret tunnels below some long-lost castle, the nobles using them to escape when the fortress was overrun.

That Sunday, after mass, Liam and I stole away again, this time with two spades and a strip of cloth soaked in paraffin. Wrapped around a stick, we fashioned this into a torch. With light this time, we climbed down into the tunnel again, the glow of the torch filling the passage. Reaching the cave-in, we turned back again and slipped into the passageway that led to the chamber.

Liam moved the torch from side to side; the crackle of the flame and our excited breathing the only sounds echoing off the walls. It was a large chamber, bigger than we had remembered. A few loose stones had been arranged in the middle as if for a fire, with three larger stones arranged around as benches. There was nothing else, but to Liam and me, it felt as if we were the first to set foot inside the chamber since the days when nobles had ruled and knights had patrolled. In the light, the dark recesses we had seen in the corners during our last visit turned into additional passageways. Long gone were our parents' warnings as we slipped into the first.

Our excitement, however, soon turned to disappointment when, after two tight turns, the passage led to another cave-in, another pile of stones blocking our way. Frustrated, we turned back. The second passageway led to another chamber, this one with barely enough room for the two of us. Unsure what its purpose was but knowing there had to be more, we turned to leave when my boot hit something. I drew back as Liam moved the light.

"Oh, Jesus, Frank! Would you look at that?"

At our feet, partially covered by dirt, was the handle of a sword, the blade broken off just past the guard. The hilt and pommel, although long since tarnished, shimmered in the light. I picked it up and, as we examined it, we talked in excited whispers about knights and sieges and long battles, inventing our own stories for how the broken sword had come to be.

"If we found this," I said, waving it in front of Liam's face, "where's the rest?"

He had a gleam in his eye, one to match my own I'm sure, and we set off in search of the missing blade.

We carried the hilt back to the first chamber, leaving it on one of the stone benches to be picked up later. Without hesitation, we slid into the final passageway, crawling forward below the low ceiling until we came upon a third chamber. Standing, Liam held the light high and let out a gasp. We found the broken sword blade all right, sticking up from a pile of bones.

We never went back to the castle. My mother, when she found the handle—poorly hidden in the barn—was after me until I told her the truth. Angered and fearful of the grave consequences that were sure to come from disturbing the spirits, she took the strap to the both of us. Then she told Liam's father, who, for good measure, did the same.

———

If Liam was right, and I thought he was, the stones we had slid back some dozen years earlier likely hadn't been touched since. We talked through the night, Liam, Seamus, and I, discussing the castle. Seamus had never seen it, having been warned away by the punishment that Liam and I had suffered. But, like Liam, he thought it might be safe for one night, maybe two, until we figured out what to do. He had said we, I noticed, finding comfort that both he and Liam would help me.

Before I knew it, the sun was rising. Seamus and Liam wouldn't hear of me leaving until after breakfast. As Tara slid a plate of boiled potatoes in front of me, Seamus looked up.

"I'll be speaking to Billy."

I shook my head. "It'll do you no good," I said, explaining that Billy was an enemy that he didn't need.

Seamus seemed ready to argue, but after Liam shook his head, he said no more. His frown told me he didn't agree. Knowing Seamus, he was likely to ignore my request.

After finishing my tea, I stood to leave. I thanked Tara for her hospitality then stepped outside with Liam and Seamus.

"Would you send a telegram to Kathleen?" I asked Liam before I made my farewell. "Would you tell her I'm fine? Tell her I'll be there soon?"

Liam nodded. I hadn't yet responded to the telegram Kathleen had sent, and she was sure to be worrying.

Seamus had disappeared around the side of the cottage, and a moment later he returned, pushing a bicycle.

"You'll be taking this," he said, nodding to the bicycle. I thanked him again but he waved his hand as if it didn't matter. Then he stuck a small package, something heavy wrapped in butcher's paper, in my hand.

"Take this too," he said, his brow furrowed. "You'll be *wanting* the bicycle but you might be *needing* that."

I stared at him for a moment, his face that of a soldier's once again. I unwrapped the package to find a German Luger and six bullets.

"It still works," he continued as he nodded toward the gun, "but I've no more ammunition than that."

Although grateful, as I stuffed the gun in my pocket, I had a bad feeling that I would soon be forced to use it.

# Chapter Seventeen

I wasn't going to Ballygowan, not yet anyway, and not unless I had to. Despite what I had told Liam and Seamus, I had no intention of simply hiding until Billy lost interest in me. Certainly, if I had no other choice, I would take refuge in the tunnels and chambers. But in the meantime, I had things to do and, with Seamus's Luger weighing heavy in my pocket, I set off. Being caught with a gun could only lead to trouble, and I was half tempted to hide it somewhere along the way.

"Damn that Brennan!" Seamus's words still rang in my ear. "It's a traitor, he is!"

Seamus had told me that troops from Cork and Tipperary—Anti-Treaty Republicans—were on their way to Limerick. Free State troops—more men from Brennan's Clare Brigades—were likely on their way as well. I had no desire to run into either, and being caught with a gun would make me suspicious to both.

I hadn't told Liam or Seamus what I had in mind because they wouldn't approve, certainly not Liam anyway. Disguised as Desmond Condon again, I set out for the Sheehys. It was over thirty miles from Seamus's farm, but with Seamus's bicycle, I reached the Sheehys' cottage late in the afternoon. I settled myself in on the hillside and watched the farm below. The men were nowhere to be seen, off in the fields I suspected. But the women were busy. Angela fetched water from the well while Colleen shook out quilts, one by one, then carried them back to the house. Every now and then I saw Mrs. Sheehy in the doorway, issuing one instruction or another to the girls. The draught horse was grazing in front of the stables.

A few hours later, several dark shapes appeared in the distance, coming up the hill behind the stable—Mr. Sheehy and the boys were returning for the day. As they drew closer, I could see that it had been a successful day. Barry carried a leather tie, two rabbits dangling on the end. Pete and Mr. Sheehy walked beside a second horse, the empty rock sled dragging behind. Seeing the rabbits made me hungry and, while the Sheehys prepared themselves for the evening, I sat back and ate the potatoes and bread that Tara had packed for me. It was my first meal since sunup.

Soon I could see the soft flicker of yellow light from the lanterns in the widows, the smell of the grilled rabbits strong in the air. It grew dark as night settled in and the temperature dropped. Thankfully it wasn't raining, but still I shivered as I kept an eye on the cottage.

Sometime later, the door opened and Mr. Sheehy stepped out, silhouetted by the light from behind. He stood there for a moment and soon was joined by Pete and Barry. While Mr. Sheehy shuffled to the outhouse, Pete and Barry trudged over, one to the stable, the other to the cow-house, the night's chores to do. Tall shadows raced back and forth from the lantern that swung by Barry's side. A short while later, the door of the outhouse banged open and Mr. Sheehy joined his boys in their chores.

It was some thirty minutes later when I saw them again. Pete closed the gate to the cow-house—the goats and the cow settled in for the night—while Mr. Sheehy and Barry stood in front of the stable. Pete joined them, and all three stood for a moment in the soft glow of the lantern. I couldn't hear what was being said—not that it mattered—then Pete and Barry turned back to the cottage, the light chasing the shadows to and fro, until the shadows, like the two boys, disappeared inside.

I saw a flash of light as Mr. Sheehy lit a cigarette. He stood there for some time, outside the barn, the glow of his cigarette flaring then dimming then flaring again. It wouldn't do to speak to him now, not with Barry and Pete so close by. As if he too agreed, Mr. Sheehy tossed his cigarette to the side. A moment later, the door to the cottage banged shut behind him. I settled in to wait and it was several hours before the lights in the cottage finally went out.

Cautiously, I made my way down, giving the cottage wide berth. Behind the stable, I stood still for a moment, listening to the sounds of the night. There was a rustle and a cackle from the fowl-house followed by low moans from the cow and the soft, high-pitched whinnies of the horses. The animals could sense I was near. Thankfully, the one sound I didn't hear was the growl of the Sheehys' collie. I hadn't seen Fergus the last time I was here and I hadn't see him today. He must have died, I suspected. That the Sheehys hadn't another dog surprised me.

I whispered softly and, after a moment, the animals quieted. The cattle door was closed but not locked and the cow and goats stirred again when I slipped inside. I calmed the animals one by one, letting them smell me then stroking their necks, all the while with the soothing sound of my voice in their ears. As for the horses and the hens, they were in their own sheds and there was little I could do but wait. My whispered words must have worked or, more likely, the cow finally decided a man as small as me couldn't possibly be a threat. She regarded me for a moment then folded her legs below herself and lay down. Soon the cow-house was quiet and a moment later the hen-house and the stables went quiet as well. I found a corner, away from the stalls and settled down into the hay.

I slept fitfully, my dreams leaving me anxious, and I woke well before dawn. Quietly, I slipped out of the barn and made my way back up the hill. In the chilly darkness, I settled in to wait. It wasn't long before I heard noises from the cottage. They were soon followed by the creak of the door, loud in the stillness of the morning. Three shadows slipped outside. They stood quietly for a moment, stretching and a yawning, chasing the sleep away. Then each went off in different directions, Barry and Pete to tend the animals and Angela to the well. In the windows of the cottage, I saw the flicker of light as, one by one, the lanterns were lit. Soon I could smell the peat from the fire again.

The day's work began early, as it always did on a farm. The cow was milked, buckets of water were fetched from the well, the animals watered and fed. The few eggs were collected from the roost, and soon I could smell the breakfast on the stove mixed with the sweet odors of burning peat. My stomach grumbled. I hadn't eaten since yesterday, the potatoes and bread that Tara had given me long gone now.

At first light, Barry stepped outside again, Caroline by his side. A sack draped over each of their shoulders, they set out down the lane. The school was eleven miles away, and they wouldn't return until afternoon. Pete came next, letting the cow and the goats out before disappearing inside; cleaning the stalls I was sure. As daylight grew, he stepped outside and then began loading straw from the hayricks into the handcart to replace the straw in the stalls. Mr. Sheehy had joined him by the time he finished and together they brought a load of peat to the house for the fire.

I shifted my position, trying to ease legs stiff from sitting. Moments later, Pete led the horse to the cart, and I hoped my long wait would soon be over. After hitching the horse, Pete and his father talked quietly before Pete climbed up. With a gentle flick of the reins, he drove the cart out onto the lane. Although I was a fair distance from the road, I lay flat, hidden by the heather as he passed by.

Mrs. Sheehy and Angela were doing the laundry, a steaming bucket of water set on the bench outside. Mr. Sheehy said a few words to them then stepped into the barn. Minutes later he appeared again, two draught horses in tow. I watched as he led them around the barn, across the field, soon disappearing over the hill. As I left my perch, careful to avoid being seen by the women, I had a feeling I knew where Mr. Sheehy was headed.

I found him again, some thirty minutes later, struggling to hold the plough steady, as the horses pulled the heavy blade through the stubble of last year's crop. Newly furrowed ground, rich and black in the winter light, trailed behind. Hidden behind the stalks, I watched for a while, waiting for him to take a rest as I knew he eventually would. Finally, he let the reins go slack and the horses stopped and, after a moment, began nibbling at the dried stubble at their feet. Mr. Sheehy took off his cap, wiped his sleeve across his brow, then knelt and picked up a handful of soil—inspecting it, I knew, for any clue as to what the ground would yield come harvest time.

Pushing that thought from my mind—I hadn't come here to discuss farming—I crept forward. Desmond's glasses were stuffed in my pocket, but there was nothing I could do about my hair. I tugged my cap low, hoping it covered most of my head and that Mr. Sheehy wouldn't notice the little black that stuck out.

I walked up behind him, as quiet as I could, stopping about ten feet away. He was on his knees, still inspecting the soil. Suddenly he stiffened, then his head spun around. There was a brief moment of alarm in his eyes before they darkened. He jumped up, something I hadn't expected from a man his age. His fists were balled at his sides. His eyes flicked back and forth and there was another flash across his face as he suddenly realized he and I were alone. The horses behind him startled and lunged forward. Without Mr. Sheehy to hold it steady, the plough flipped over and dragged behind. After several paces the horses slowed then stopped but they continued to regard me warily. Mr. Sheehy ignored them, his eyes boring into mine. Lucky for me, he didn't have the fork with him this time.

I had my hands up, my palms out.

"Sir," I began, "it's only a daft man who would come back."

"Then it's a daft man you are, you little shite!"

"Sir," I pleaded, "I promise I'll not waste your time or your patience. I only ask that you listen to me."

"And why should I?" he snarled. "You killed my son!"

I let out a breath. "I did, sir, but he was dead already."

He flinched at my words, his eyes narrowing. He was confused, I could see.

"I'm not a traitor, Mr. Sheehy," I continued, not giving him a chance to respond. "I'm not an informant. It was only by luck that I was outside when the British burst in."

He stared at me, dazed it seemed by my words, but his body remained tense, ready to fight.

"You know me, Mr. Sheehy. You have since I was a wee lad. Tom was my friend."

He flinched again. It was subtle, but I caught it. Still, he said nothing.

"I've no reason to come back," I continued, shaking my head. "Not now. Not with the threat of another war and not with Billy after me. But I had to, sir. I had to tell you what happened that night because the story you know isn't true."

He let out a small sigh, and I saw the doubt creeping into his eyes.

"Tom was a hero, Mr. Sheehy. He did his part for Ireland. He did, sir, just as Dan did and just as Sean did." I paused and took a breath myself. "I did my part too, sir, and not a day goes by that I don't wish it were me instead of them that had been killed."

A single tear ran down his cheek, and his shoulders sank as he slouched forward. He suddenly looked old and frail. It was then I noticed his hands: the fists he held before, the angry hands that wanted their revenge, were gone. Now they were what they had always been, the gnarled hands of a farmer. Yet they were more: they were old and tired, the hands of a man who had buried his son.

He sank to the ground, worn out from the anger and the pain he had been carrying. I heard a small cry and watched as Mr. Sheehy, with his head in his hands, began to weep.

# Chapter Eighteen

I wasn't certain if Mr. Sheehy believed all of what I told him, but whatever anger he had in him was gone by the time I left. He asked a few questions, wanting to know more about that night, about how Tom had died. I told him what I knew, about hearing the shouts and the gunfire, about seeing Tom and Dan on the floor, one screaming, the other certainly dead. I told him that Sean had no escape, wounded as he was and trapped upstairs with little ammunition left. When I hit the plunger, I admitted, I had saved myself. But I had killed the Tans too, and I had prevented Tom and Sean from facing a worse fate in the hands of the British. They were dead one way or another. If I hadn't done what I had, the British would have killed them all, if not that night, then after a rushed inquest—a mere formality, the outcome well known in advance. The firing squad would have been issued their orders before the inquest began.

I left Mr. Sheehy in the field, overburdened by the weight of what I had told him. He hadn't asked me where I was going, and I hadn't told him. His son was gone and the emptiness he had been running from came rushing back, filling his head. It was a burden he would bear for the rest of his life.

I thought of my own daughter, alive only a few days, and wondered what Mr. Sheehy would do. Would he get up from the field, find a bottle, and lose himself in the drink, growing numb with the whiskey until he could feel no more? Or would he lie awake at night, wondering for the ten thousandth time what he could have done to prevent what had happened that night? Or, as I had hoped, would he finally sleep, perhaps for the first time in a year, knowing that his son had died in battle, that Tom had died a hero and not at the hands of a traitor?

I had no intention of going to see Dan's wife when I left Mr. Sheehy. The Sheehys lived in Carrig, nineteen miles south of Mary's. Sinéad Buckley lived in Charleville, in County Tipperary, farther south still. I soon found myself at the crossroads and, impulsively, I turned. Something compelled me, and I headed south toward Charleville, the Galtee Mountains that were visible on a summer day now lost in the mist. It was a quiet day, and as I pedaled down the lane, across a landscape dotted with whitewashed cottages, recently turned fields, and grazing cows, dark clouds began to roll in over the hills. Lost with my own thoughts, I hardly noticed. It was a chance I was taking, but I didn't think it was foolhardy. Sure, now that he knew I was back, Billy would know that I was likely to visit Sinéad Buckley and the Murphys as well. But Billy would be in Limerick, preparing for the battle that was looming.

Besides, I told myself, I had come back to Ireland to set things right, and I couldn't leave until I did.

———

I hadn't seen Sinéad since the wedding. She and Dan were married in September 1920, three months before Argyll Manor. We all knew that we could be captured or killed anytime and, for Dan, if that was to be his fate, he wanted to be married when death finally found him. Such was the thinking of many a Volunteer, myself included. But Dan couldn't have known that death would come for him so soon after his wedding day.

It was a grand affair, the wedding was. After the service, as was custom, Dan and Sinéad walked together to the house, taking a different route this time than the one they had followed earlier to the church. People were lined along the lane and threw rice and gifts in front of them—pots and pans, a horseshoe—the things Sinéad would need to make a home.

We positioned two companies of men, scouts and lookouts, on the roads leading to the church and to the quiet lane leading to the house. More men were in the fields surrounding both. Of course, we all had our guns with us, prepared as we always were for the British. But our luck held, and we didn't need them that day.

There were formalities, and one was the photograph. Liam and I poked fun as Dan and Sinéad sat, Billy and Carol standing behind. Sinéad wore lace, the very dress her own mother had worn, and Dan was in his uniform, a rifle held across his lap. Billy was wearing his uniform too, and carried a revolver on his hip. Carol, dressed in lace, could have been the bride herself, a longstanding practice to confuse the fairies, lest they steal the real bride away.

The formalities done, we had a grand celebration, a break from the war. To the sounds of the fiddles and hornpipes, we danced as if we hadn't a care in the world. There was plenty of food and honey mead and soon the dancing turned to song. We sang of love and courtship and of bonnets and roses. We sang of the girls that haunted our dreams and the ones that had broken our hearts. We sang of the rivers and the green hills that graced our land. As the night wore on, our songs turned to our struggles and the ballads became those of our fathers—songs that, like my own father's stories, filled our souls with a longing and fortified our resolve to fight for what was ours. We sang songs of rebellion, of rising up and claiming our birthright; we sang of bold Fenian men bravely fighting to build an Irish nation once again.

It was one of the few times I remember seeing Billy smile.

———

"So, you're back," Sinéad said when she saw me, her words high-pitched and clipped.

Without waiting for my response she turned back to the churn. Bent over, she raised the handle then plunged it back into the cream, quickly falling into a rhythm. Up and down, up and down, again and again, as if I wasn't there.

I noticed the basket behind Sinéad and felt a lump in my throat. Swaddled and asleep inside was the baby, the daughter that had come eight months after Dan's death, just a month after Margaret. Like me, Dan never had a chance to meet his own daughter. I shook my head and turned away for a moment, telling myself I hadn't come for that. Steeling myself, I turned back to Sinéad.

She was a pretty woman with fair skin and a shock of red hair. But there was a hardness to her now. The lines in her face and the coldness in her eyes spoke of the pain in her heart and the struggles of the past year. She glanced my way, checking to see if I was still there or perhaps wishing me away, I wasn't sure. A moment later, still churning, she looked again, briefly at me then up at the sky. The dark clouds continued to roll in over the hills.

"And what is it you want, Frank Kelleher?" she demanded.

"A word with you, Sinéad. That's all and then I'll be gone."

"Who's that?" I heard from the cottage. An old man, stooped and held up by a cane, poked his head out the door. I didn't recognize Sinéad's father right away. I remembered him dancing at Sinéad and Dan's wedding. Now, old and bent, he stared at me with tired eyes.

"He's leaving, Da," Sinéad said evenly, her eyes not leaving mine.

"What does he want?"

Sinéad turned to her father. "Nothing, Da," she said softly. "Nothing. Now go back inside and let me finish my work. We'll have tea soon."

The old man's eyes flicked back and forth between us before he turned, mumbling something as he dismissed us with his hand before disappearing back into the cottage.

Sinéad began plunging again and I watched silently for a moment. Suddenly she slammed the plunger back into the barrel, then glared at me, hands on her hips.

"Oh, it's a fine one you are, Frank Kelleher, wanting to talk and with me trying to put up the butter before it rains."

The baby began to cry and Sinéad shot me a look. I felt the flash of heat as my face turned red; I reached for the stave.

"I'll finish the butter," I offered. "You see to the baby."

She seemed about to argue then, without a word, turned, picked up the baby, and disappeared into the cottage.

I began to churn, glancing up at the sky, at the clouds racing overhead. It was something I hadn't done since I was a lad and soon my arms began to tire, a burning creeping down from my shoulders. I stopped once or twice, lifting the lid to see if the butter was setting, as I had seen my mother do. Finally, when the dash stood on top without sinking, I wiped the sweat from my brow then glanced over my shoulder, wondering what I should do next.

It was only five minutes that I waited but it felt much longer. Sinéad returned and, without a word, lifted the lid. She studied the butter for a moment, her eye far better at these things than mine. I must have done it right; she closed the lid and turned to me.

"You can talk," she said, her voice still cold, "but that's all it is and it won't make a grand bit of difference to a widow with a baby and a father to care for."

She had every right to be bitter. When she and Dan were wed, it was a happy life Sinéad had dreamed of, not of putting her husband in a box three months later.

As I helped her put up the butter—rinsing and salting and then filling the jars—I told her what I had come to say. Sleeves rolled up, hard at her task, she barely glanced my way, but I could see her face soften. We were interrupted once, the young lad she had hired to help tend the farm coming to tell her that the cow would have a calf by spring.

When the last of the jars were filled and put away, I cleaned the churn then joined Sinéad by the cottage. She stood silently for a moment, staring off into the distance. The clouds were black and heavy, rolling with a fury now as the sky rumbled overhead. The wind began to rustle through the field, scattering the dead stalks from last year's harvest.

"It'll do no good, standing here," she said then turned away.

I wasn't sure if it was an invitation but I followed her inside anyway, the wind blowing at my back, whistling through the thatch on the roof as I shut the door. Her father was sitting in front of the stove, snoring softly. I pulled the shutters on the windows, catching a glimpse of the scene outside. The horse pranced nervously, skittish, as the farm boy led it back to the barn, one hand on the reins, the other on his cap to keep it from flying away.

The drops were large at first, splattering on the stone. In the distance, I could see the waves of rain racing across the field. Then with a howl it was upon us, lashing with a fury, a cascade slanted by the wind. As I secured the last shutter, there was a flash in the sky and, a moment later, the crack of thunder.

The storm raged outside, but the baby and Sinéad's father both slept soundly, the baby stirring only as her mother tucked the swaddling around her once more. Then Sinéad filled a kettle, the pot clanging then hissing as she placed it on the stove. Despite the howls of the wind, the rain lashing at the roof, our silence seemed loud in the small room. I wished she would say something, anything. More than that, I wished for the storm to end so I could leave.

The kettle banged and Sinéad turned. I could see the tears in her eyes.

I took a breath, the sound of my sigh lost in the wind.

"I'm sorry, Sinéad." It was all I could think to say.

She stared at me for a moment. "You visited the Sheehys," she stated as if she hadn't heard what I said.

"Aye."

"And I suppose you'll be seeing Mrs. Murphy too."

"Aye."

She seemed to consider this for a moment.

"This last year has been hard," she continued then paused a moment, looking down as if unsure what she wanted to say. When she looked back up, the confusion was gone. "I'm angry, Frank," she said, shaking her finger at me. "So don't be expecting to be forgiven. You'll have to see the priest for that." She let out a breath, her voice catching in her throat. She turned away for a moment, wiping her eyes. When she turned back, she shook her finger again "I'm angry at all of you," she said. "I'm angry at you and at Billy and at Sean and at Tom." She let out a sob. "Oh, God! I'm angry at Dan! How could he leave me like this? What kind of man goes to meet his death when there's a family left behind?"

The baby began to cry and, crying herself now, Sinéad picked her up and carried her to the chair by the stove, across from her father. He woke, confused for a moment it seemed, his eyes darting between Sinéad and me. Sinéad rocked back and forth hugging the baby, her chest heaving with great sobs, her own wails and those of the baby somehow sounding all the more terrible with the howling of the wind outside. Quietly, I slipped outside.

As for Sinéad's question, I had no answer for her. It was the same question Kathleen and Mary had asked of me.

——

The rain had stopped, almost as quickly as it had started, the storm blowing past, leaving a gray sky and a heavy fog in its wake. The air was much colder now, and I turned up my collar and held my jacket tight below my chin. My breaths, like the smoke drifting from the chimneys of the cottages across the fields, twisted in the wind and I wondered again if it would snow.

Sinéad hadn't been surprised to see me. She had been warned, no doubt by Billy, told that I had already visited the Sheehys. *Would she tell him that I'd been to see her?* I wondered. She had no loyalty to me, that was certain, but I didn't think she would say anything, unless she was asked. Somehow, though, I knew Billy would.

I found the bicycle where I had left it, leaning against the stone wall at the end of Sinéad's lane. I climbed on before I noticed that the tire was flat. Cursing, I climbed off and began pushing the bicycle, careful to avoid the puddles that filled the muddy lane. It was almost ten miles to Ballygowan and the castle and, in these conditions, it would take me almost four hours.

The conversation with Sinéad and seeing her baby left me wanting to see Kathleen, more so than I already did. I decided to pay Mrs. Murphy a visit in the morning. She lived in Rathkeale. The train to Abbeyfeale would stop at Rathkeale at noon. I planned to be on it.

Lost in my own thoughts, I didn't hear the dray until it was upon me, the clop of the horse's hooves and the splash of wheels in the puddles causing me to jump. In a panic, I almost dropped the bicycle as I fumbled for my glasses, remembering that I had stuck them in my pocket before speaking with Sinéad. I slipped them on and, as the dray drew up next to me, I tugged at the brim of my cap, a friendly gesture but one that I hoped would hide my face. Suddenly the cart slowed and I caught a glimpse of two men inside.

"A soft old day it is!" One called down.

I didn't recognize either of them, still I was wary. The one who spoke was older than me, the other my age. They looked to be a father and son and, although their smiles seemed friendly, I was wary but I did my best to not let it show. I nodded back.

"Aye. A day for a fire," I replied. The weather in Ireland was miserable more often than not, but in our own peculiar way we spoke of it fondly.

"And it looks like you've had a bit of bad luck, have you?"

"Aye." Sinéad might have had a pump but, given the way I had left her, I thought it best not to ask.

"Well, toss it on back. We're headed to Limerick."

Sensing they meant me no harm and not wanting to insult them, I accepted. A moment later, I was sitting next to the son as the father flicked the reins.

Their name was McGrath, I soon learned, and they were on their way from Kilmallock to Limerick City to pick up a new set of harrows for their farm. I introduced myself as Michael O'Sullivan, my long-dead friend from childhood.

"O'Sullivan?" Mr. McGrath asked. "From Limerick City?"

"Nay," I shook my head. Did they know the O'Sullivan clan? Suddenly I wished I hadn't accepted their offer. "My family's from Offaly, but I live in America now."

"Americay!" Mr. McGrath said, pronouncing it as my own father had. He stared off for a moment, dreams of another life—one he would never see himself, I was sure—filling his head. After a moment, the wistful smile vanished.

"Sure and more Irish will be joining you in Americay soon." He shook his head. "The British are finally leaving, but now we'll be fighting each other."

I asked him what he had heard.

"O'Malley's troops are marching on Limerick," he continued.

I wasn't surprised. O'Malley was Commander of Second Southern Division and was responsible for all IRA operations, not just in Limerick, but in County Kilkenny and County Tipperary too. He had been captured by the British, I had heard, while I was making my way to Cobh just over a year ago. Badly beaten and awaiting execution, somehow he had managed to escape. That he was now marching on Limerick wasn't a surprise. Even when we were all fighting on the same side, he would never have permitted Brennan's troops to occupy Limerick. Such was the tenuous pact that was the IRA.

The McGraths hoped to pick up their harrows and be well away from Limerick before the fighting started. Like Mick and many an

Irishman, Mr. McGrath wanted nothing more than to tend his farm. He welcomed the truce and the Treaty, his own aspirations not going beyond the holding he toiled over daily in Kilmallock.

We crested a hill and, in the mist ahead, I could see the crossroads. The turn would take me to Ballygowan and the castle, and it was there I would say farewell to my new companions.

"Americay sounds grand," Mr. McGrath said as the cart slowed. Suddenly, his eyes seemed far off. "But we've lost so many."

It took me a moment to understand what he meant. So many had left Ireland over the last sixty, seventy years—all seeking a life better than what Ireland could give, most never to return.

"It's a dangerous time for Ireland now," he continued. "I wonder what will happen to us all."

His words continued to ring in my ears as the McGraths drove off into the mist. The sound of horse's hooves began to fade and soon they were swallowed up by the fog. I turned, cinched my coat up around my throat. *I wonder what will happen to us all.*

———

Shaking Mr. McGrath's words from my head, I focused on the night ahead. I hadn't been looking forward to finding my way through the ruins in the dark and now, thanks to the lift from the McGraths, I wouldn't have to. The castle was only a mile away. The wind gusted and I shivered. Ignoring the cold, I thought of the castle and hoped things were as Liam and I had left them years ago. My clothes were damp and, although the tunnels and chambers would be dry, or mostly anyway, it would be a cold night. To make matters worse, I hadn't eaten since the day before. I could survive one more night without food but being cold on top of the hunger would make for a miserable night.

I caught a glimpse of the field beside me and suddenly stopped, staring out over the wall. Remembering something from when I was a lad, I studied the sloping hill covered in heather. *This might be the right spot*, I told myself, *or if not it's close*. I leaned the bicycle against the wall then clambered over and made my way down the slope through the heather. Twenty minutes later I found what I was looking for: a low-lying marshy area, several long trenches stretching into the distance, grassy clumps piled to the side. The cut peat was stacked in heaps, most as tall as I was. I picked up a brick. Despite the rain, it was hard. This was last year's crop, having spent a season drying in the wind and the sun. I was alone in the field and with no one around to stop me, I helped myself. Laden down with an armful of peat, I made my way back up the hill to the lane. It wouldn't last all night, but it would be enough for several hours of sleep.

Back at the wall I was about to stack the peat on top and climb over when I heard the sound of a motorcar. I dropped the peat and slid to the ground, not wanting to be seen, especially not when I was in possession of someone else's peat. Cautiously, I peered over the top of the wall. The growl of the engine grew and, a moment later, a motorcar suddenly appeared out of the fog. My face hidden by the heather, I watched as it approached. A sudden chill run up my spine. Billy was driving and Kevin, another from our old brigade, was with him. There was a third man, one I didn't recognize, in the rumble seat in back. I ducked my head behind the wall, cursing my luck. Pulling the revolver from my pocket, I prayed I wouldn't have to use it.

The sound grew louder, then the growl of the engine suddenly dropped and I heard the squeal of the brakes. Fighting the panic growing inside me, I crawled along the wall, hoping to put a few feet between myself and the spot where they might have seen me. It was then that I remembered the bicycle and, cursing, I frantically crawled farther until I heard their voices. I froze. Memories of IRA raids came flooding back and, with them, the fear I had always felt before a battle. I thought of jumping up and unloading my revolver on them. If I caught them by surprise, I would have the advantage. But if they had seen me, surely they would have their own guns out.

I couldn't make out the words and I realized they were farther away than I expected. But the little I did hear didn't sound like the frantic shouts of men in battle. Cautiously, I peered over the wall only to see Kevin lifting the bicycle—Seamus's bicycle—into the rumble seat in back. Their companion, the man I didn't recognize, held it somewhat awkwardly as Kevin climbed back in. Then the engine growled and there was a high pitched grinding of gears. It wasn't long before the sound of the motor and the car itself were both lost in the mist. In the eerie silence that followed, the only thing I heard was the soft rustle of the heather in the breeze and my own heart hammering in my chest.

———

It had taken some time to find the opening, hidden as it was in the grass and the weeds and the stones not where I remembered. Finally, settled safely in the chamber that Liam and I had explored a dozen years earlier, I got the fire going. I watched the smoke rise, twisting and turning then finally disappearing into hidden channels and gaps above my head. It took a while before I felt warm again. My stomach ached, but I did my best to ignore it. Was it only a coincidence, I wondered, that Billy was in Ballygowan? He should be with Ernie O'Malley's troops, marching on Limerick. What business did he have out here? There was no evidence that he had discovered the tunnels; the stones that Liam and I had placed over the opening all those years ago had been difficult to find in the fading light, covered as they were with years of vegetation. It was clear that he hadn't been here. But then what had he been up to?

Seeing Billy had left me shaken. The crooked nose that sat over the square jaw, the dark, hooded eyes—the eyes of a hunter—Billy's face was stuck in my head. My mind tumbled over what he could have been up to, out here, so far from the battle that was looming in Limerick City.

I realized he thought the bicycle must have been abandoned,

the rider having grown tired of pushing it. And Billy had comman-deered it. By tomorrow it would be repaired and put into use by the IRA. The bicycle, though, was the least of my worries. From what Liam had told me, the brigade had maintained a level of military discipline with weekly drills and meetings and no company more so than the one Billy commanded. While most residents went about their daily business, happy now that the British were leaving, the IRA in Limerick had continued to operate as if war might resume at any moment. And when it did, it would start in Limerick. So what was Billy doing out here, miles from the city? Surely he hadn't been out looking for abandoned bicycles.

Recruiting was the only reason I could fathom, or perhaps meeting with the advance party of troops coming to support the Limerick IRA. A coincidence that I had seen him, I told myself, nothing more. Still as I stared at the soft flames of the fire, I couldn't shake the feeling that it was something more.

# Chapter Nineteen

I heard the men long before I saw them. Crouched behind a stone wall, well back from the crossroads, I watched the column marching towards Limerick. They were making no attempts to conceal themselves and, although their march was casual—rifles held loosely by their sides—they had the look of experienced soldiers. They weren't wearing the new Free State uniform. I studied them as they passed, looking for faces.

Fifteen minutes later, I was still crouched behind the wall as the column faded in the distance. I had recognized some two dozen faces, men I knew and some I had fought with. They were part of O'Malley's forces, true Republicans, men who had no love for the Treaty—what some had taken to calling *Irregulars*—come to chase Brennan's Free Staters from Limerick. Tense as I was, I couldn't help feeling proud as they marched by.

I waited another ten minutes, hidden behind the wall, all the while my ear strained for more troops. Finally I stood, climbed over, and continued on my way.

———

It was because of Billy that I found myself in church two hours later, long after the morning mass was over. Cautiously, I made my way toward the altar. My footsteps echoed off the stone floor, the sound loud in the silence of the church. Knowing what I was doing was a sin, one more to add to the many that I had committed over my life, I shook my head, trying but failing to chase the dark thoughts from my mind. Twenty years of hearing there was no salvation for the likes of me had left its mark.

I took a breath again, trying to forget Father Lonagan and his eyes that were more often filled with scorn than with compassion and his voice more often filled with reproach than with understanding. I tried not to think about the hand that was quick to mete out a punishment for sins that couldn't be forgiven by mere penance alone. Shaking my head, I tried to focus on the task at hand. What I wanted was in the small sacristy in back.

"And what do you think you're doing here?"

I jumped at the sound, the deep voice thundering off the walls. Spinning around, my hands held up ready to fight, I saw Father Lonagan hidden in the shadows in the back. He stepped into the light, his eyes dark, his steps slow but full of menace nonetheless.

"I asked you what you're doing here!" his voice boomed again as he came toward me.

Halfway down the aisle, he stopped. His face contorted, disbelief mixed with rage.

"Frank Kelleher," he said, his voice now a low hiss. "The nerve you have to defile God's house with your presence! Get out!" He pointed toward the door, his voice rising. "Get out of my church!"

He continued to yell until I took a step forward. Then suddenly he went quiet, something flashing in his eyes. The indignation was gone, replaced by something else. *Confusion?*

I continued toward him, stopping only when I was five feet away. His eyes darted around, suddenly nervous. He wasn't much taller than I was—four or five inches at most—although that wasn't how I remembered him as a child.

"All God's children, Father, is that it?" I asked, my own rage rising. "All created in his image, are we?" I stared at him a moment, but he said nothing, "Yet somehow we're sinners all and because of that there's no escaping our fate." I paused, not bothering to hide my own fury. "Did I learn that correctly?" I took a step forward and he backed up. "And supposedly, according to the shite you've been preaching for God knows how long," I said, jerking my thumb toward the man hanging on the cross behind me—the one I had been taught to avert my eyes from because I wasn't worthy, "because of his sacrifice, all is forgiven." I took another step. "But here's the thing, Father," I continued as he backed up against the pew, "there's something I don't understand. Despite all of that, for some reason you've never explained, lads such as me are denied that salvation. Despite the masses every Sunday and never missing a holy day even when the fever was raging, despite the thousands of rosaries I said in penance ever since I was a wee lad"—I jerked my thumb up at the cross—"you have the nerve to tell me that this is denied me?"

His eyes darted to the side, looking for an escape.

"And despite what you've done yourself, despite your own sins, you have the nerve to judge me?" He flinched. I shook my head and, in the silence that followed, I could see the panic in his eyes.

"The British only terrorized us for seven hundred years, Father," I said, pointing my finger at him. "How long will the Catholic Church?"

He shrank backwards but there was nowhere to go.

"You useless shite," I hissed then stomped out of the church, leaving him in stunned silence.

———

I walked with a vengeance, my hurried steps a poor attempt to ease my rage. If anyone was a traitor, it was Lonagan and the men like him, men who had created their own holy doctrine, keeping a nation locked in a cage of guilt and self-loathing. It would have been nice to think that the abuses of the church—by popes who loved power more than they did their own God, by *holy* men who sanctioned the slaughter of millions during the crusades, by popes and bishops who built their own private armies and willingly used them against their enemies and who had amassed fortunes by stealing and selling indulgences all while they committed the gravest of sins themselves—were a product of the middle ages, practices that had died out long ago. Many did, but the totalitarian, authoritarian rule of the Church—one that controlled people through guilt and kept them ignorant of the truth and ignorant of the Church's own hypoc-risy—continued, and nowhere more so than in Ireland. The church hadn't changed; the sermons of forgiveness directed outward some-how falling on the deaf ears of the men who spoke the very words. Maybe it was too much to expect.

Had it not been for Father Lonagan, I would have found what I was after. He left me with little choice. I would be forced to dye my hair again and wear the glasses—pretending I was Desmond Condon—until I found some other disguise. I crossed the bridge, then left the road, the church disappearing behind me. I wasn't sure where I was headed but, needing time to think, I followed the stream, hugging the bank that twisted and turned along with the water. The tall grass grabbed at my legs, the thick mud clinging to my boots, but I hardly noticed. It was a half hour later, my boots swollen and heavy with muck and my trousers wet, that I stopped by a wide area, a calm pool that I remembered swimming in with Liam years ago.

I picked up a handful of small stones and threw them one by one into the water. The ripples marched out in all directions, row after row. It wasn't five months ago that I had visited a church and then it was in New York; the same church—Catholic—but it couldn't have been more different. Still it brought back memories of all that I had left behind and I had no intentions of setting foot inside a church again. Not until today. And even then, it hadn't been salvation I had been after.

I sighed as I tossed another stone into the stream. The encounter with Father Lonagan had left me tired, the anger gone now, replaced by a weariness. Try as I might, I couldn't shake the image of Liam, his seven year-old face crestfallen and his eyes full of tears.

———

I was only seven myself at the time but I had already learned how to fear. As I stood outside the door, I looked down at my hands, at the marks on my palms that never seemed to go away. I could already feel the sting that was to come. My chin began to quiver but I fought it. I dropped my hands—it wouldn't do to torture myself—and let out a sigh. This time, I promised myself, I wouldn't cry.

I heard the sharp slap of the leather, the howl from inside. I pushed it out of my mind and thought of what I would do that afternoon. Another slap, the howl louder this time. Sunday and there were no chores to do, not until after supper. I would go fishing with Liam, perhaps. A slap and then sobs behind the closed door. It was idle thinking, something to distract me. Liam wouldn't go with me. Not now. Still I tried to fool myself, thinking he would.

The door banged open, startling me. Liam stepped out, his shoulders hunched and his hands balled in fists, held protectively across his chest. Tears streamed down his face. His eyes avoided mine, only seeing the floor as he passed me. My chin began to quiver again.

"Kelleher!" the voice boomed from within.

I took another breath, wiped my own eyes and stepped inside.

Father Lonagan stood by the desk, the handle of the leather strap in one hand, the frayed ends I had come to fear in the other.

He stared at me for a moment, his eyes penetrating, seeing, I knew, what I couldn't see myself.

"What did you see, Kelleher?" he demanded. His face was red, his eyes dark and menacing like the clouds outside.

"I don't know, Father," I stammered. "There was you and Liam..."

"And?" he demanded.

"And...," I began, not sure if he wanted the truth, but somehow knowing it would be worse to lie. "I...you..." I shook my head, unsure what I had seen. I had come back to the church, the cast-iron pot dangling, a meal for the Father. I had stopped outside the office, confused by the noises within. I opened the door—even now I'm not sure why—and there was Liam and Father Lonagan. But where were their trousers?

I shook my head as I stared up through the tears at Father Lonagan. What had I seen?

"It was like the sheep, Father..."

"What did you say?" he thundered as he stepped toward me. The flash in his eyes told me I had made a mistake.

I stepped back as his hand came down, the leather slapping loudly against the desk.

"What did you say?"

I shook my head, my chin quivering again. The answer caught in my throat. "I don't know, Father."

"How dare you lie to me!" he bellowed.

The leather crashed into the desk, the ceramic figure smashing to the floor. I stared down at the pieces, at Mary, broken on the stone below.

"Now look what you've done!" he screamed.

The leather strap rose then flew down, the sharp slaps and the pain like fire raging in my hand, shooting up my arm. Choking my sobs, I watched it rise again. I remember the strain on his face, the sweat on his lip as he swung his arm high and brought it crashing down again. And then again. And again. I don't know how many times, a dozen, likely more; I lost count.

"How can you tell such lies with Mary and Joseph looking down at you?" he screamed, the strap held high in the air again. "And Jesus, right up there," he said, out of breath, pointing to the crucifix on the wall.

I was blubbering by now and he lowered the strap, taking deep breaths himself.

"It's a sinner you are, Frank Kelleher," he said, his voice softer now, the rage gone but his eyes full of disappointment. "It's the devil, for sure, filling your head." He shook his own sadly. "I don't know how God will ever forgive you." He grabbed me by the shoulders, shaking hard. "But you must beg for his mercy and maybe he'll listen." He knelt on the floor, pulling me down. "You must pray. Kneel and I'll pray with you."

We prayed, Father Lonagan said the words while I choked on my own tears. He begged God to spare my soul, claiming I didn't understand what I had done. My mind spun and, by the time we had finished the Hail Marys, the Our Fathers, by the time we finished the Rosary, I wasn't sure what I had seen anymore.

Confused and with the weight of eternal damnation crushing me, I left, his final words ringing in my ears.

"You must never repeat any of these lies," he said, each word measured. "To anyone. Do you understand?"

I looked for Liam outside, but he was gone and it was just as well.

When I got home and my mother saw my hands, my wrists, my arms—bloodied and blistered now—she took her own strap to me, certain that my sin must have been grave. Thankfully it was to the back of my legs and not my hands.

Neither Liam nor I ever spoke of that day.

———

I threw one last stone in the water and watched one ripple after another march across the surface—such a small thing but the impact continued long after the stone disappeared into the darkness below.

# Chapter Twenty

"Can you make them for me?"

"Sure and you don't need me." Mary scowled. "There's a store in Limerick that sells them." She folded her arms across her chest, her eyes narrow, disapproving.

I waited. She knew I couldn't go to Limerick. Not now.

After a moment, I saw her chest rise and she let out a heavy breath. "I'll go tomorrow."

I thanked her, but she waved her hand, the discussion done.

"You haven't been to Abbeyfeale." It was a statement not a question.

I shook my head. "Nay. I'll be going soon, but I'll need the vestments first."

She nodded, already aware that I hadn't gone. She studied me in silence, her eyes searching for something.

"Have you found what you're after?" she asked. The disapproval was gone, or mostly; her eyes were curious.

*Have you found what you're after?* I didn't know how to answer.

"It'll do you no good, all this trouble you're stirring up." It was a reproach, but at the same time it wasn't. No clipped words, no commanding tone, just a statement. "Not for you. Not for anyone."

"Aye, Mary." I sighed. "But I have to try."

She nodded as if she had known my answer all along. "Come back tomorrow, in the evening," she said as she turned away.

I studied her back for a moment. Something was wrong.

"And Tim?" I asked.

She reached for the table. Her shoulders began to shake, and I realized what a fool I had been thinking the only troubles in the world were my own.

"He's gone," she said softly, still facing away.

"Billy?" I asked.

When she turned back, her cheeks were wet. She nodded.

"Aye. He left last night."

She buried her face in her hands, a sob escaping. I stepped forward, taking my wife's sister in my arms. She heaved, great shudders wracking her body as her tears spilled on my shoulder.

"I'll find him." I said softly.

"No!" Mary pushed away, striking my chest with her hands. "You'll only get yourself killed!" I grabbed her wrists gently and leaned forward. I wrapped my arms around her once more.

"I'll find him," I said again. "And I'll bring him back."

She sobbed again and I suddenly saw her for what she was. Not as the older sister who had raised my wife, not as the head of the Irish Women's League, not as the woman with iron in her spine. She was a mother, worried over her child that had fled.

She pushed away, gently this time. "I know," she said, wiping her eyes. "I know."

———

Tim was fifteen, already a man, and yet he wasn't. Sure he would fight when given the order. But he had no fight in him. It had been different for me. The knowledge that our cause was just, the dream that burned from within, these are the things that made me a soldier, as they had the men I fought with. Knowing there was something greater for this godforsaken country of ours, whose soil was forever below our nails and in our blood, we had been willing to die for Ireland. No such fire burned inside Tim. His fight would come from fear alone, but the uncertainty within his heart would kill him in the end. The battlefield was littered with the bodies of men who had no conviction, men who—deafened and frozen by the bombs that tossed up great clods of dirt and panicked by the bullets that chipped away at the stones they hid behind—had hesitated for a brief moment, glancing down at the rifle in their hands, and wondering what had put them there, with death marching closer and the screams growing louder, and for what?

Tim would never survive. I had to find him before it was too late. I wondered if one of my old comrades—one of the men from my brigade who, like Mick, no longer had any loyalty to Billy—could tell me where he was.

Padraig was a boot maker, or was before the war. I had known him as a child, when he had gone by the name Patrick. Along with adopting the Irish form of his name—something he had done when he joined the Volunteers—he insisted that he was a boot maker, not a cobbler. *I don't cobble*, I remember him insisting once, holding up a pair of boots, pointing to the stitching, explaining the unique pattern he crafted into every shoe he made. *A shoe like that*, he said with no small amount of pride as he spun the half-finished form for me, *is a shoe that will last*.

Padraig had been wounded a month after I left—this I had learned from Liam—and now walked with a wooden leg. Although he and Billy had been friends at one time I wasn't certain they were anymore. Both Liam and Mick had hinted that something had come between them, something related to the raid where Padraig had been shot. Padraig wouldn't be fighting anymore, not with the leg, but something told me that he still might be able to help me find my nephew.

I hoped I would find him in his shop or, if not, that his father would know where he was.

After visiting Margaret's grave and saying a prayer for my daughter, I set out for Ballygowan where I spent the night in the castle. With candles and a blanket from Mary and the bit of food she had given me, I was comfortable, or as comfortable as I could be. Still, sleep eluded me, and the little I finally got hadn't been peaceful at all. My dreams had been filled with scenes and the sounds of the war: the Crossly Tenders full of soldiers, the explosions and the fire, the cracks of the rifles, and then the screams of men who had been wounded—Irish or British, it sounded the same. I saw the faces of the men I had killed, both those I had intended to and those I hadn't. They floated past, looking as they had when they had died, some with their eyes wide, surprised at the bullet that had found them, others their faces contorted in pain, their eyes squeezed shut as if to hide from the death that had finally come. And then there were those with their mouths open, their screams silent but filling my head as the flames consumed them.

Tired and haunted, I set out at first light.

——

Padraig lived in Kilteely, nine miles from Ballygowan and five miles from Lough Gur, or at least he had when I'd last known him. Gray clouds filled the sky, but thankfully it wasn't raining. Other than a few men in the fields, I saw no one on my journey. The roads were dry and two and a half hours later, I found myself outside Padraig's shop.

I heard the rhythmic tap of the hammer, and I peeked through the window. Padraig was sitting on a stool, an awl in hand. The leather that would become a shoe was stretched over the wooden *last*. I watched as Padraig slipped the awl through, then first pushed then pulled the needles, drawing the thread tight. When he finished, he tapped the hammer along the seam, spinning the *last* as he did. Thankfully, there was no one else in the shop.

I glanced in both directions and, seeing no one on the street, I slipped inside, careful to make no sounds. The smell of leather and oil was strong as was the smell of peat from the stove in the corner.

"It's a fine boot you make, Padraig," I said softly.

He spun on his stool, wide-eyed.

"Frank Kelleher!"

I felt a moment of pride, having surprised him—the IRA had taught me well. My skills hadn't left me, on the run as I had been for the last year. But Padraig had settled back into a boot maker's life, his days as a soldier and the skills that Billy had taught us soon forgotten.

"Is it yourself, Frank?" Padraig smiled and shook his head. "Jesus, it's good to see you!"

He dropped his hammer on the bench, slid off the stool and hobbled over, an awkward gait with one leg dragging behind him, never quite able to catch up. I sensed he meant me no harm, and I stepped forward to meet him.

"Ah, Jesus," he said as he threw his arms around me, "I was afraid they'd killed you."

There was a noise outside, and I felt him stiffen. He let me go and pushed past me, moving faster than I thought possible with his leg.

"They still might," he said over his shoulder, "if you're not careful." He bolted the door then closed the shutters on the window. He came back, slower now, and I could see the pain on his face.

Seeing my reaction, he forced a smile. "Ah now, Frank. There's many worse off than me." He pulled another stool over. "Here. Come," he said, patting the seat. "Sit with me."

I did.

We talked, sharing our journeys over the last year. He told me how he had been wounded, the Crossley Tender, the military vehicle favored by British soldiers, coming on them by surprise. When the machine gun roared, they were defenseless. With no bombs and no machine gun of their own—theirs was hidden in the weapons dump, the ammunition exhausted weeks prior—there was nothing they could do but duck below the wall and pray.

Padraig had told Billy and the men to make their escape, to slide along behind the wall until they were clear. He told them he would stay and provide cover fire.

"They began crawling off, Billy and the others, while I slid the other way, hoping for an opportunity to take a shot." He shook his head slowly, his eyes suddenly far off, back on that lonely rain-soaked road. "I don't know how I was hit, behind the wall like that. Glanced off the stones, the bullets must've, but I was hit twice in the leg." He tapped below his knee, the sound of knuckles on wood. He was silent for a moment, his face becoming dark. "He left me like that, Billy did." He shook his head and I could see the pain in his eyes, pain that came from the memory and not from the wounds to the flesh.

But as quickly as the darkness had come, it was gone. He waved the memory away and smiled again.

"Ah now, Frank. You didn't come all this way to hear about my troubles."

I smiled back and answered his questions, most of them any-way. I spoke mostly of America but little of what I had done since I returned. He had been Billy's friend long before he had been mine and, despite his story, I was wary.

"America's grand, sure, but with the war over, I had to come back."

"What are you on about, Frank?" he asked as he shook his head. "It's a fine time you've picked, coming home now and another war certain."

"Aye, I know."

He smiled again, but the question lingered in his eyes. *Why had I come back?* I had come back for Kathleen and our child, but I wasn't about to tell him that. The real question was: *why had I stayed?* I wasn't sure how to answer, how much to tell him.

"What happened that night?" he asked softly. There was no malice in the question, no judgment, just curiosity.

I took a breath and told him about the raid on Argyll Manor,
how I had been outside when the British, who must have been hiding somewhere inside, had opened fire. I told him that with Dan,
Tom, and Sean all wounded, I had no choice but to hit the plunger.

"They knew we were there, the British did," I said. "There was
an informant alright, but it wasn't me."

He nodded slowly. "I know."

I stared back, not certain I heard him right.

"Sure, I thought it was you at first. We all did." He waved the
thought away, as if it never mattered. "Do you remember the lookout?"

"The lookout?" I asked, confused. "That was the problem, we
didn't have any." As soon as I said it, I realized I was wrong. An hour
before the raid, we had been hiding in the heather, waiting for the
scout, a boy of sixteen named Rory Conklin. He finally came, and
while Sean, Tom, and I provided cover, Dan went out to meet him.
The road was clear, he told Dan. The British patrol that had been
sighted an hour earlier were now miles away.

"Rory?" I asked, not believing my own question. He seemed a
good lad, I thought, and would make a fine soldier one day.

Padraig nodded. "I went to see Billy the next night. I had heard
what had happened, and I was sure he was going to ask me to do the
job." He sighed as his eyes drifted off again.

*Do the job.* He was to be the one who would put the bullet in
my head.

"Rory was there," Padraig continued. "He was crying, and Billy
was shaking him, hitting him. '*You don't know what you've done,*'
Billy said over and over." Padraig's eyes found mine again. "Rory
disappeared that night. Put on a boat to Canada, I heard later."

"Rory was the informant?" I asked as my mind tried to put together the pieces. "Billy knew?"

"Aye. Billy knew."

"And he still tried to kill me?"

Padraig nodded slowly. The color had drained from his face. "I wish I had done something. I told him it was wrong, that he'd already lost three men and here he was sacrificing another and an innocent one at that." Staring at the ground now, he shook his head, not meeting my eyes. When he looked up I could see the tears. "I didn't think he would do it, Frank. I swear on my mother's grave, I didn't." He shook his head again. "By the time I heard about it, you had already escaped and Liam had been captured."

He sighed, his breath loud in the silence between us.

"Something had changed in him," he continued after a moment, his eyes far away again. "I never trusted him after that. And then when I was shot..." His voice trailed off.

"Why did he let Rory go?" I asked, confused. "Why did he blame me?"

"You don't know?" Padraig stared at me for a second then shook his head. "Of course you don't. How could you? Rory," he continued as his eyes narrowed, "Rory is Billy's nephew, his sister's child."

I felt a hollowness spreading in my stomach as it all became clear. Someone—Rory—had informed the British, and Billy needed to make an example. Spies and informants were dealt with swiftly and brutally. But he couldn't sacrifice his own nephew so he chose me instead. Me, the only one left alive, and with no other witnesses, I was guilty.

# Chapter Twenty-one

By the time I left Padraig, my anger was slow, simmering. The injustice of what Billy had done—sacrificing me to cover for the sins of his nephew—left me wanting more than what I had returned to Ireland for. I wanted vengeance. A bounty on my head, placed there by the British, was expected, something that likely would have happened anyway, if not for Argyll Manor then for crimes I had already committed or those I soon would. But to have my own men turn against me and all for a lie? I crossed over the now-empty fields, leaning into a heavy wind as dark clouds roiled overhead.

It was a harsh land we lived in, and I often thought that's what made Billy who he was. Cold and calculating, he was loyal when it suited his purpose. He could brutally inflict pain and punishment on his friends one day and then defend them until he was bleeding the next.

I never understood why Billy had taken up his rifle against the Ottomans, nearly spilling his own blood in a far off land against an enemy he didn't know as he fought side by side with another. But then what else could a man like Billy have done? With war raging across Europe and beyond, he must have jumped at the chance. And when he returned, how different the country must have looked through eyes that had seen what his had in Basra and Bagdad. And how much it must have looked the same. Maybe for the first time he saw Ireland for what it was. But I suspected that he had always known.

Billy joined the IRA not because the cause burned in his heart, but because he still had enough fight left in him when he came home. He joined because there was nothing left for him to do. And now that men were choosing sides, some joining the Free State and others staying true to our oath, it had always been clear, I suppose, which side Billy would choose. An end to the war was something he couldn't fathom. And if the Republicans ever decided to lay down their arms, he would find a new war, in Ireland or elsewhere, it didn't matter. As for the men he had fought side by side with, I wondered how he saw us. Were we nothing more than cannon fodder for a war that only he understood?

Maybe this was how I saw Billy now, but the signs had always been there.

——

I was nine at the time. We were playing in the churchyard, Sunday mass long over and no chores to do until the evening. Liam placed a small stone—his duck—on a large flat rock near the wall that surrounded the cemetery. Sean, Tom, Dan, Billy, and I stood ten paces away, our own stones held ready. One by one we took aim, trying to knock Liam's off. Billy had the same aim then as he would later with a rifle. As Liam's stone skittered away, we scrambled after it, our own version of Duckstone.

Billy ploughed ahead of us, the first one to hit Liam, with shoulder and head down like he would do on a football pitch years later. In the tumble of arms and legs, somehow, small as I was, I got my hands on the duck. Never one to lose, Billy tried to wrest it away. We tumbled and rolled on the ground, oblivious to the pain from the elbows to the ribs and the sharp rocks that found our shins.

It wasn't surprising that I found myself on my back, Billy on top jeering at me. Not surprising but it had filled me with shame nonetheless. Billy sat on my chest, pinning my arms below me, the duck held triumphantly over his head. He was twice my size then,

and there was little I could do to push him off. That didn't stop me
from trying.

"Get off!" I screamed.

That only seemed to amuse him. He began taunting me, bouncing up and down on my chest. His grin spread, his eyes dancing
with malice as I struggled to breathe, thrashing all the while below
his weight.

"Get off me, you shite!" I screamed again, or tried to, but with
not enough air for any of the words, it came out as a grunt.

I heard the laughing and jeering from the lads, all except Liam
who I saw out of the corner of my eye. Blood was streaming from
his mouth.

"Get off!" I screamed again, or maybe it was Liam.

It's a terrible feeling, not being able to breathe, and I began
to panic, feeling trapped and helpless. That only seemed to excite
Billy more, and he began to bounce harder. No sooner could I suck
in a mouthful of air when it shot out with an *ooomf* as Billy came
crushing down again. My vision began to blur and, as the tears slid
down my cheeks, the laughing seemed to grow louder, a crescendo
flooding my ears.

"Get off!" I heard again, or maybe I imagined it. Darkness began to creep across the edges of my vision, and suddenly I welcomed
it. Oh, how I wanted an end to the helpless feeling, to the panic.

Suddenly the darkness receded and Liam was kneeling beside
me, brushing my tears away. Gasping and sputtering, I sucked in
a lungful of air, fueling the wails and screams and anguish that
had been trapped inside. My small body shook with sobs. Through
the tears, I saw Billy, hands over his own face, the blood streaming
through his fingers as Dan led him away.

Liam would pay dearly for that later.

———

It wouldn't do to confront Billy, not now, not while I was filled with anger, and not until I could figure out how to gain an advantage. Still, I felt as if I was being drawn to him, the confrontation inevitable as he sought to exact a punishment he had no right to and I sought to right the wrongs of the past. And now with Tim missing—likely run off with Billy, his head filled with the romance of war—our clash would come sooner rather than later.

Padraig didn't know where Tim was, but the little he told me was enough. Billy, he had heard, had been drilling the men twice a week, six miles east of Limerick in a godforsaken, rock-strewn, heather-covered stretch of land near Mullin's Cross, good for neither planting nor grazing. I remembered it from my own training. I would have to wait until Wednesday, though, to do some reconnaissance.

Meanwhile soldiers continued to march on Limerick, and the country continued to edge closer to war.

———

I stopped by Mary's later in the evening, but she hadn't been able to get what I needed. A wheel on the trap had broken and, by the time Mary had arranged for a neighbor to fix it, dusk was at hand. She only just made it back to the cottage before me.

Still she brought me news. Limerick City, she told me, was filling with soldiers.

"Brennan's forces have the Castle Barracks," she said. "And the Strand as well." They had also commandeered the RIC police posts on Williams Street and Mary Street, she added.

"And the Republicans?" I asked.

"Just the local men," she responded.

*Where were the troops I had seen yesterday?* I wondered. They must have billeted somewhere outside of the city. Why were they waiting? Had they sent in scouts? Or had they sent in one or two men to negotiate, keeping the rest out of the city to avoid fighting? As it was, since I had returned to Ireland, I had more questions than I had answers.

Mary promised to try again tomorrow. She offered to put me up for the night, but still nervous about Billy, I declined. Still she provided some bread and potatoes and, after I stole some more peat, I spent another night in the castle. The conversation with Padraig swirled in my head; it was a long while before I fell asleep. I woke well before sunrise and, while it was still dark, I set out to find Mrs. Murphy.

———

Sean's mother was a widow, his father's death coming the same month I joined the IRA. Sean was a soldier by then, a source of pride for his father and one of worry for his mother. When his father died unexpectedly—his heart, everyone said—Mrs. Murphy was suddenly left to deal with her loss and the silence of an empty house. Sean was the youngest, the only boy out of six children, and by then, he was spending more time on IRA business than he was at home.

Mrs. Murphy's worries were not unfounded. A year and a half after her husband died, Sean joined him, dying in the flames of Argyll Manor. Bad luck never comes alone. The Tans, not satisfied with Sean's death, took their revenge on Mrs. Murphy as they had on Billy's mother. As neighbors held her back, Mrs. Murphy cursed and screeched as the Tans set fire to her house, the flames leaping into the dark night.

When Sean died, Mrs. Murphy was left without a husband, without a son, and without a home. Sean's sister, Siobhan, two years older and married and living not ten miles away in Croom, took her in.

Mrs. Murphy lived above the pub, Mick had told me. While her son-in-law, Martin, stood behind the bar—in the same spot as his own father had and his grandfather before him—Mrs. Murphy helped Siobhan prepare the stew and the bread, something for the men to wash down with their pints. The Tans didn't know it, Mick said, but they had done Mrs. Murphy a favor, forcing her out of an empty house into one full of children and with a pub downstairs that needed minding.

I avoided the lanes and roads, tramping instead across fields, under a black sky. Two and a half hours later, as I crested a hill and clambered over a wall, I knew Mick's cottage was only half a mile away. I thought about stopping in but, given the hour, I continued on. A half hour later, I heard the soft rush of the River Maigue and soon saw the outline of buildings in the mist ahead. Although the last two days had been dry, the clouds on the horizon told me the rain was coming. I approached cautiously, stopping by a chestnut tree on the edge of a field to survey the village. Other than the river, there wasn't a sound. The houses were dark, silent. I checked the windows one by one, thankful to find them still shuttered. Seeing no one, I took my chance and sprinted across the last field, some hundred yards to the stone wall that edged the road. Crouching behind, I peered over and found Martin's pub several buildings down across the way. The houses were quiet, sleepy, the soft baying of animals from the fields beyond and the smell of burning peat carried by the wind. From my position behind the wall, I had a view of the road, disappearing in both directions. I couldn't see the river but could smell it now, its dampness filling my nose. It was early still, and I settled down in the tall grass behind the wall to wait, keeping an eye on the dark clouds overhead the whole while.

Over the next thirty minutes, I caught the soft glow of light peeking out from the shutters as, one by one, lanterns were lit in the homes that lined the road. Above the pub, the curtains fluttered occasionally as shadows passed by, young children to mind and morning chores to do. I waited. The wind swept across the field, stirring the grass at my side, and I glanced up again at the clouds building above my head. I heard the clank of a stove, the bang of a door, followed soon by another. A few people came and went, leaning into the wind and the day's work ahead of them. Soon, a soft rain began to fall, and I turned up my collar and pulled my cap low, all the while watching as the occasional horse and cart or bicycle passed by.

As the morning wore on, the rain slowed—for a while any-way—and soon there were two old men standing by the pub, backs bent and held up by their canes. I glanced at my father's watch; it was ten o'clock. It wouldn't be much longer.

I assumed it was Martin who opened the door and welcomed the two men inside for their first pint. I had never met him; during Mr. Murphy's funeral he had been home in bed with the fever. I stood and brushed as much of the dirt off my trousers as I could. Now that the pub was open, I wondered whether Mrs. Murphy was already inside.

———

"A fine day it is," I said when I entered. The pub was dark, lit by several oil lanterns, the soft light flickering across the dark tables and even darker walls as I closed the door. I felt the heat from the stove in the corner, a comfort after my hours behind the wall.

Martin looked up, not surprised to see a stranger, or if he was he didn't let on. He nodded then glanced down at the cups he was washing. The two old men, their faces gaunt, their cheeks sunken, gave me toothless smiles as they sipped from their pints, the smoke from their cigarettes drifting up to the ceiling. The place smelled like a pub should, of old men and smoke, of bacon and stale beer.

Martin dropped his rag and stood up straight as I stepped up to the bar. My age or close to it, he was half a foot taller than me, but he had the shoulders and arms of a man who spent time in the field as a boy and still did by the looks of it. He gave me a smile, a cautious one reserved for a stranger.

"Aye, a soft one at that," he said as he studied me for a second. Something flashed across his eyes and then it was gone.

I felt a tingle in my spine but still I smiled. Martin glanced over at his two customers.

"You're set for the moment, lads?" he asked, although it was clear he didn't expect an answer.

They both nodded anyway, giving Martin the same toothless smile they had given me and then turned back to their pints,
hunched over with their cigarettes and their silence. Martin stared
at me for a moment then motioned for me to follow. Hiding my surprise, I glanced at the two old men then at the door before my eyes
settled on Martin again. *What was this?* I wondered. I glanced back
at the door once more, half expecting Billy to burst in, wondering
if I had made a mistake. There was a moment of silence, Martin and
I standing there, the only sound the two old men wheezing as they
sucked on their cigarettes.

Martin nodded again, toward the door behind the bar. I studied
his eyes, seeing only a question, nothing more. I pushed myself away
from the bar, brushing my hand along my coat, feeling the reassuring weight of the Luger in my pocket.

He led me into the back room, one with several empty casks
lining one wall, an empty table pushed up against another, and a bin
full of turf for the stove. A broom, a dustbin, and two spades stood
in the corner. He left the door open as he stepped inside. Wary, I
stopped at the threshold. He left me there, a foolish thing to do if
he meant me harm.

"I know who you are," he said. His arms were folded across his
chest, but there was no tension in his face, no violence in his eyes.
Only a question.

I raised my eyebrows, an amused look, but said nothing. I
slipped my hand in in my pocket, finding the gun.

"You're Frank Kelleher."

It was a statement, not an accusation; still I felt a tingle in my
spine. My hand tightened around the gun. There weren't any weapons in the room except, I noted, for the spades. I wondered if he had
a gun himself, or maybe a knife.

I glanced at the two old men, content in their silence, and then
at the door.

"Aye," I answered, my eyes narrowing, waiting to see what he would do, wondering again why he had brought me here. If he had meant to trap me, he had trapped himself instead.

"I never served," he said. "Still, I took care of the lads when I could."

I nodded but said nothing. He had provided food and shelter, possibly billeting men from time to time as they hid from the British. He supported the IRA, or had at one point, but that meant nothing to me. Not now, not with Billy after me.

"Mick told me you would be coming," he continued.

I hadn't expected that. "Mick?" I said softly as I studied him. "Are you sure it's not Billy you mean?"

He nodded. "Aye. And Billy too."

I waited but he said no more. "And what did they tell you?"

He shook his head and let out a sigh. "Mick said you didn't do the things Billy said you did. And as for Billy..." He never finished the sentence and didn't have to.

"And what do you believe?"

He stared at me for a moment. "I'm a man that makes up his own mind," he said. Then he nodded to the floor above. "It's Mrs. Murphy you're here to see, is it?"

"Aye," I nodded, relaxing a little. Despite that, I kept my hand on the gun. "Might I have a word with her?"

————

If Martin had sent word for Billy, it would be several hours before he came. Still, I checked the window every few minutes. Finding nothing, I sipped my tea and looked at Mrs. Murphy.

"Sean was upstairs then?"

"Aye. He was spreading the paraffin."

She sat back, heavily it seemed, weighed down by the story I told her. She was an older woman, sixty I guessed, but with the Irish it was difficult to know. The harsh life we lived left many looking old by the time they were forty. Like the men in the pub, her cheeks were puffy below her eyes but sunk in sharply around her mouth where her teeth had once been. Her eyes were set back in her head and had a haunted look, unable to let go of the suffering that had followed her. She had lost her husband and one of her children and, like my own mother, she still wore the widow's black.

She looked at me again, her eyes returning to the present. "Was he brave, my Sean?" It came out so soft, I almost didn't hear it.

"Aye." I nodded. "Sean was brave."

She nodded slowly and her eyes drifted off again. In the flickering light from the lamp, I could see they were wet. I left certain details out, not wanting to upset her. Sean had died bravely and that was enough. I pictured him as I had last seen him

———

"Jesus! And what is it you have there, Frank? A baby?"

I grinned, nervous. "The sooner we can get out of here, the better I'll be," I muttered below my breath as I placed the crate gently on the floor and began checking the wires.

"It's a proud father you are," Sean said as he clapped my shoulder. He must have leaned over, his mouth right next to my ear. "Boom!"

I jumped, my breath escaping in a hiss.

"Jesus, Sean! What the fuck are you on about?" I shook my head.

"Sean, Frank." I heard Dan's hiss. "Just do your jobs."

Sean grinned once more at me then went off to spread the paraffin. I looked back at the crate and sighed. How the hell had I been chosen to be the bomb man?

Sean was full of stories, always looking for a laugh. I looked at Mrs. Murphy. *Maybe he took after his father*, I thought. I could see nothing of Sean in her tired eyes. For Sean, unlike his mother, life was too painful to take seriously. I remembered once, in the middle of a battle as my own heart hammered in my chest, Sean's eyes full of mischief as he taunted the British, his laughing voice ringing over the sound of the guns.

"It's the mighty British Army is it? The forces of the Crown?"

Sean elbowed me in the ribs, his eyes twinkling with laughter as bullets chipped the stones above our heads.

"God love you, lads, but you're fucked." Another elbow, another laugh. "Today's your lucky day, lads. You'll be going home. Of course you'll be full of lead and in a box. But still"—he laughed again—"you'll be going home!"

Sean and I crawled to the side, chips of stone raining down on our heads. The British had more ammunition than we had, and Sean's taunting helped to even the odds. He poked his rifle up above the wall.

"It's no wonder you're losing the war! You can't shoot for shite! I'm over here, lads, over here."

We crawled on as the British fire swung to where we were. Meanwhile Billy sent a flanking party to the side.

Sean and I crouched again. "Ahh, Frank," he said softly, "did I ever tell you about the lass I met in Dublin?"

———

"He did his part?" Mrs. Murphy asked, dragging me back along with her to the present.

"Aye. He did," I said. "Even as he died, he cursed the British."

"Come and get me you daft bastards!" I had heard Sean taunting as the guns blazed, the Tans at the foot of the stairs, Sean somewhere above. Suddenly there was a scream, and I realized he had been hit.

There was a moment when the gunfire stopped, the only sound the crackle of the fire. Then I heard him again.

"Frank!" he screamed. "The baby, Frank!"

One Tan spun on his heel, searching before he spotted me by the door. I dove to the side.

"The baby, Frank! The baby!"

I slammed my hand into the plunger.

# Chapter Twenty-two

It was midafternoon two days later when I lay down next to a large rock, hidden in the heather near Mullin's Cross. From where I was, I would be able to see the men drilling. It was unlikely, though, that they would see me and not unless Billy sent out scouts, something I didn't think likely. If what Padraig had told me was true, it would be another hour at least before any of the men arrived. As I settled into wait, my eyes darted around, searching for movement while my ears tried to sort out the rustle of the wind through the heather from the more ominous sounds of soldiers slipping forward. All my senses told me I was alone, but still I wondered if Billy knew I was coming. *Had Padraig betrayed me? Or Martin?* I shook my head at the thought as I had done a dozen times before. The pain in Padraig's eyes had been real. He himself had been betrayed and his allegiance to Billy broken. As for Martin, I didn't know. But he would have no way of knowing that I would be here today. Still, the doubt nagged at me.

I had done what I had come back to do. Whether the families believed me or not, I wasn't sure, but there was little more I could do to ease their pain. Now, though, instead of setting out for Abbeyfeale, away from Limerick and Billy as I should have, my promise to Mary and Mrs. Murphy's last words only pushed me closer.

"I'm an old woman but still I hear things." Mrs. Murphy had said, her eyes steady on mine. She shook her head. "The men in the pub, the young lads, they talk." She paused and her eyes had narrowed. "There'll be another war, for sure."

"Aye." As much as I didn't want to see it, I thought so too.

"Good," she had said, catching me by surprise. "Sean didn't die just to see Ireland split in two." She had grabbed my wrist, her eyes suddenly intense. "Finish it, Frank. You owe it to Sean. Make his death mean something!"

I sighed. That I had an obligation to Mary, I couldn't deny. But did I have an obligation to Mrs. Murphy too? Did I have an obligation to Sean to finish a war he no longer could? I sighed again as I tried to shake the questions from my head. I couldn't afford to be distracted by such thoughts.

Yesterday, after meeting with Mrs. Murphy, I had stopped by Mary's on the way back. She had the things I needed, wrapped in another blanket, along with some more potatoes and bread. I told her what I had learned, about Billy's weekly drills and what I planned to do. Her eyes were red, and the swelling below them told me she hadn't slept well. When I was leaving, she reached out and grabbed my arm, staring at me for a second as her eyes brimmed with tears.

"Find him, Frank," she pleaded. "Please find him."

I had spent another night in the castle, my own sleep troubled as the faces of the people I knew haunted my dreams. The eyes troubled me the most: Liam's, old before their time; Father Lonagan's, filled with the arrogance of the Church; my own father's, no longer capable of dancing or dreaming; and my mother's, cold and hardened against the death that constantly chased her. As I twisted and turned on the hard stone floor, Mrs. Murphy's eyes begged me to fight, a free Ireland the only price for her son's death, while Mary's eyes, already full of grief for her lost husband, were now filled with anguish at the thought of losing her only son. I saw the bitterness and anger in the Sheehys' eyes and the destroyed hopes reflected in Sinéad's.

And then there was Kathleen, waiting for me in Abbeyfeale.

Her eyes reminded me of the promise I had made, the one I had failed to keep. They were angry and scared.

——

It was 4:30 before I spotted two men walking up the long road from a direction I hadn't expected, coming from Tipperary. Their rifles were slung over their shoulders, their bulky trench coats pulled by the wind. Ten minutes later, I saw more, then the columns, two lines of men marching, rifles slung over their shoulders, a military precision to their step. I was too far away to recognize faces, but their movements were those of soldiers, not the hesitancy of fifteen-year-old boys. There were over a hundred, more than I had seen the day before.

At five o'clock, a motorcar crested the hill and, as it drew closer to the waiting men, I strained to see who was in it. I didn't think it was Billy. Three men climbed out, and I squinted in the fading light, trying to see their faces. Too far away to see clearly, I decided to get closer. I wondered again about scouts but pushed the thought from my mind. I had lain, hidden in the heather for hours, long before any troops had arrived, and I hadn't seen anyone.

It took me twenty minutes to slide forward on my belly to a point where I could finally see. I heard the voice, the sharp order carried to me with the wind, as the men were called to muster. I watched the lone figure, pacing back and forth in front of the men. I couldn't see the face well enough, but with the bushy hair and the unlit pipe he carried in the palm of his hand, it could only have been Ernie O'Malley. And that he was here now, assembling troops mere miles from Limerick City could only mean that the fighting was just days away.

Realizing Tim wouldn't be here—not amongst the war-hardened soldiers I saw below me—I was just beginning to turn, preparing for the long crawl away from the mustered men, when I heard the sound of another motorcar. It bounced and slipped its way down the lane as the driver navigated the ruts and mud. Moments later, I watched as Billy and Kevin hopped out. Billy shook hands with O'Malley. I couldn't hear the words but could only watch as Billy pointed down the road and then across the fields. O'Malley nodded and, as Billy climbed back into the motorcar, the men were called to parade formation.

Then, with Billy and Kevin in one car, O'Malley and his officers in another, the men were paraded down the road. With less than an hour of light remaining, I thought I knew where they were going. When it was safe, I slipped out of the heather and followed from a distance, the whole while worrying about Tim. O'Malley's presence meant war was looming. Tim would never survive once the shooting started.

I cut across the field, running where I could, knowing I had to get there before they did. Fifteen minutes later, I took up a position across the field from O'Shea's barn. The temperature dropped as the light faded, and the lanterns flickered in the windows as the men filed inside. It was too dangerous to get any closer, and I wondered for a moment if they were planning on marching into Limerick tonight. *Not likely*, I told myself, but still I waited to see what they would do.

An hour later, I spotted the silhouette of a lone bicycle coming down O'Shea's lane. The rider stopped, leaned the bicycle against the wall, and approached several men outside. I was too far away and the light that spilled out of the barn was too dim to tell who it was. But something about the shadow I saw sent a prickle up my spine.

Several minutes later, the rider left with three other men, pushing his bicycle now as he walked with them. The rest, it appeared, were staying at O'Shea's for the night, or at least I hoped they would be. I wasn't certain the rider was Tim, but his size and hesitant gait told me it probably was. They disappeared into to the darkness of O'Shea's lane. Suspecting that they would be going to town, I slipped out of my position and set out across the field again, staying well clear of the road.

Some thirty minutes later, I lay in wait by the crossroads. I heard the squeak and rattle of the bicycle and the sounds of hushed voices before I saw them. Suddenly three men appeared flanked by a boy pushing a bicycle.

One look at the face and my heart sank. It wasn't Tim.

———

It was after midnight when I reached the castle. With IRA men all over the county, my journey had been slow as I avoided the lanes and fields where other units might be. After stopping to steal more peat, I slid the stones back and climbed down the steps and into the ancient chambers where I prepared to settle in for the night.

In the glow of the fire, I struggled with the forces that tugged at me, each in a different direction, and with the decision I had to make. Caught in currents no man could control, Ireland edged closer to war—one Mrs. Murphy so desperately sought but one that would surely kill Tim. I had given Mary my word that no harm would come to her son, and the thought of failure weighed heavy on my shoulders. And although I had made no such commitment to Mrs. Murphy, her plea to take up a rifle again—the only comfort for her grief a united Ireland—troubled me more than I had expected. And then there was Kathleen, waiting for me in Abbeyfeale, reminding me of the promise I failed to keep.

In the middle of it all was Billy.

Shaking the thoughts from my head, or trying to anyway, I opened the bundle Mary had given me the day before. As I ran my hand along the cloth, I made my decision.

# Chapter Twenty-three

"Might I have a word with you, Father?"

I stopped and turned. The man was hesitant, his troubles etched into his face.

"I've only a minute," I said, gesturing toward the tracks. The train was due into Patrick's Well junction, and I intended to be on it. He nodded, unsure. I offered a brief smile, knowing I had no choice. He glanced over his shoulder. We were alone at the end of the platform. My attempt to avoid people had failed, and now that he was standing before me, I had to play the part.

"What's troubling you, son?"

He took a deep breath, unsure, it seemed, how to start. "I'm a soldier, Father," he said softly. He paused again, unsure now how to continue.

"The IRA?" I asked, suddenly nervous. But when I saw the pain in his eyes, my worry faded. I did my best to appear empathetic. If I was going to play the part, it certainly wouldn't be as Father Lonagan.

He nodded again.

"You're not from Limerick," I said, hoping I was right about his accent.

"No," he admitted. "Clare."

"With Brennan?" I asked.

"Aye." He shifted on his feet. "I know what I've done is wrong…"

he began again. He shook his head. "Some of the men weren't even British."

I thought of the men I had killed, some Irish like me who for one reason or another found themselves working with the British, as Peelers or informants. But this was his story, I reminded myself, not mine. Even so, I knew his plight. He was here with Brennan's Free State forces, and he was troubled by the thought of fighting other Irish men, men like himself.

I nodded as he continued. Why he had thought to approach me, I didn't know. Surely his own priest had shunned him. Why did he think I would be any different? He couldn't know that my faith, like his tenuous beliefs, had finally been stolen one Sunday, just over a year before.

It was in December 1920, just days before the Argyll Manor bombing, when Father Lonagan read a pronouncement from the Bishop during mass.

"Anyone who takes part in an ambush or in a kidnapping shall be guilty of murder, or attempt at murder, and shall incur by that very fact the censure of excommunication."

I sat in silence, not quite believing what I'd heard. Our own church was turning its back on us. A stunned hush came over the congregation. The mass continued and when the communion procession began, I quietly stood and slipped out the door, vowing I wouldn't set foot in a church again.

And here it was, a year later, the war over and the British leaving, and the Church had chosen sides once again. Many of the very men they had condemned a year ago were now forming the new government. Ever mindful of the shifts in power, the bishops had sided with the Free State. I wondered how long it would be before threats of excommunication were directed at the Anti-Treaty faction.

I nodded to the man before me, a lad not much older than myself. While he might have been able to justify his actions as part of the war, as I had tried to justify mine, the guilt still plagued him.

"Our choices aren't always easy, my son," I said as I laid my hand on his shoulder. "Especially during a war."

He nodded, his head bowed.

"Killing is a sin, but sometimes God knows that we have no other choice." I squeezed his shoulder as I continued. "I know some disagree with me, but I believe our God is a forgiving God. His own son died so that our sins might be forgiven." Then the words spilled out of my mouth, the absolution, the instructions for penance, the blessing. It was the same thing I had heard countless times myself while kneeling in a confessional.

He let out a breath and nodded. "Thank you, Father," he said.

I heard the whistle and glanced down the track as the train approached, black smoke trailing from its stack, steam billowing from the wheels.

"Surely God wants Ireland to be free," I said, "and if your heart is right, surely God forgives you."

He nodded.

"Now you must forgive yourself."

He smiled for the first time and shook my hand, the burden he had been carrying not quite as heavy anymore. I bid him farewell.

As I climbed onto the train, I glanced back. He nodded and smiled again and I wondered. Was it a sin to help a man find peace? Was it a sin to tell him the same things I had been telling myself for the last year? I was already going to hell—did one more sin matter?

———

"Frank!" Kathleen shouted, then she threw her arms around me.

I held her tight but suddenly she pushed me away and slapped my face.

"It's a fine one you are, Frank Kelleher, leaving me to worry, not knowing if you're dead or alive!"

I frowned. Liam hadn't sent the telegram as he had promised. I apologized and reached for her, but she pushed me away again.

I grinned, hoping to soften her mood. "Ah, Kathleen. It's good to see you. Truly it is."

She stared at me a moment, her eyes dark before she turned and stomped away. I followed her, toward the cottage in the distance. I had made a wise decision earlier, I realized, when I stopped to change behind a wall. Kathleen was already angry and turning up dressed as a priest would only have made it worse. The vestments were now in a bundle slung over my shoulder.

"It's a good thing for you I was here," Kathleen snapped without looking back. I followed silently, knowing it wouldn't do to say anything.

"The Maloneys went into town, but I was feeling ill this morning and didn't go."

We stopped by the wall, the path continuing on to the Maloneys' home. The cottage looked like thousands of others in Ireland: white-washed stone with a thatched roof and smoke curling up from the chimney.

"Are you…" I began.

"I went for a walk," she said, cutting me off, "hoping that would help." She turned, arms folded across her chest. Her eyes were dark but rimmed with red. "Where have you been?" she demanded.

I told her about my visit with my mam and with Mick, but before I could say any more, she cut me off with a wave of her hand.

"And what is it you intend to do now, Frank Kelleher?" she demanded, her voice shrill, her hands on her hips, like she'd seen her own sister do. I never had a chance to answer. "Oh, the likes of you. Off in Limerick, chasing demons, while I'm stuck here, filled with worry." She poked me in the chest. "It's a fool you are. When you should be taking me to America, away from the fighting, you're traipsing around Limerick where there's nothing but an early death waiting for you!" The pale light cast dark shadows on her face. Her eyes narrowed, her jaw was set, she wanted to fight.

I held my hands up. "Tim's missing," I said.

"What are you on about?" she demanded, not ready to give up her anger. Then her face softened and I saw the confusion.

I told her what Mary and I suspected, that Tim had joined Billy's forces.

"I promised Mary I would find him."

Kathleen dropped her arms. "Oh, poor Mary."

She stepped toward me. I reached for her hand, and a moment later she was in my arms, her head on my shoulder.

———

Cousins of Mary's dead husband John, the Maloneys had welcomed me into their home. When Mr. Maloney learned that I had fought with the IRA, he shared his own stories of his time with the Brotherhood.

"We were prepared to march to Dublin," he said as he described the confusion in the days before the Easter Rising six years earlier. "There were too many people who thought they were in charge." He ticked them off on his fingers: "The Hibernians, Sínn Féin, the Brotherhood, the Citizen's Army, the Volunteers. They all had their own ideas, and no one agreed on anything." He shook his head. "At the last moment, we were told to stand down. And then we read in the papers what had happened and, in the days that followed, were frustrated that we hadn't been given a chance."

The men in Dublin had held out for six days before they were forced to surrender. Ultimately the Rising was doomed as the battles for control within the various factions created confusion. The lack of men and guns, despite the fact that units around the country were ready and willing to join the fight, left the men in Dublin to fend for themselves. In the days that followed, the leaders had been rounded up and sixteen had been executed. But while Britain had exacted its revenge, they had unwittingly turned the Rising's leaders into martyrs; their executions and then the arrest and harsh treatment of thousands of others finally serving to bring the factions together.

"In a way," Mr. Maloney said, "it was a success." He shook his head and smiled wistfully. "I only wished I could have joined you lads." His right arm rested on his lap—a stub where his hand should have been—and he slapped my knee with the only hand he had left. An accident on the farm, he told me, the cut had become infected and the doctor had no choice but to take his hand. While he could no longer fight, Mr. Maloney and his wife had provided food and shelter to men on the run—men like me—and in their own way had done their part for Ireland.

The Maloneys were gracious hosts, and we sat by the fire till late in the evening discussing what the next few years held for us. There would be another war, Mr. Maloney insisted. With the British gone, the coalition that had held us together would dissolve as each faction sought a different path for our young country's future. I couldn't argue for I believed the same.

I stole a glance at Kathleen. Her brow was furrowed, filled with worry as images of the future she wanted to escape played in her mind.

———

I took a deep breath, taking in the sweet, pungent smells of the manure spread across the fields before the planting, and with it the newly turned soil, rich and fertile. The wind shifted and carried with it the burning peat from the Maloneys' fire. The moon hung low in the sky, a rare sight during an Irish winter, the pale light fighting its way through the clouds.

Kathleen and I continued on, an evening stroll and a chance to talk in private.

"I met with Father Leahy," Kathleen said.

"Aye."

"He wants to meet with you."

"Just me?" I asked.

"Yes. He wants a private meeting."

"And will he allow us to wed?" I asked. "Will he give Margaret a proper burial?"

Kathleen nodded then bit her lip. "That's why he wants to meet," she said hesitantly.

"Does he have concerns?" It was a stupid question I knew but one I had to ask anyway. A friend of Mary's, Father Leahy had agreed to bury Margaret in the church cemetery, in consecrated ground, despite the fact that she had never been baptized. Surely the bishop, if he learned of this, would never permit it.

"I don't know," Kathleen said. "I think it's only a formality. What priest could marry a man or bury his child without meeting him first?"

I nodded but said nothing. I wondered what Father Leahy wanted in return.

"He told me we can't hold the child responsible," Kathleen continued. "It's what's in our hearts that matters."

"Aye," I said. Father Leahy wanted to assure himself that I was a Catholic and a pious one at that. While I too believed that an unbaptized baby was innocent—what kind of God would punish a child for dying before the priest could bless her with holy water?—Father Leahy's plan was unusual, though I suppose he had the right given the risk he was taking.

"I'll meet with him," I said. While I wasn't sure of my own convictions, I wouldn't take a chance with my only child.

Kathleen squeezed my hand. "He said he has to baptize her, then register her."

"But she's already..." I began then caught myself as I realized there was more to this than I had thought. Father Leahy hadn't agreed to baptize Margaret just to please Kathleen and Mary. He had no other choice. Margaret couldn't be buried in the churchyard without recording her birth and death in the parish records. And she couldn't be buried unless she had been baptized first. The parish records had to match.

I nodded as the picture became clear. This was Father Leahy's price. He wanted to ensure that Kathleen and I were wed. I also suspected that he was concerned about the dates on all of the documents. Would they show that Kathleen and I were wed, then Margaret was born, then she was baptized and then she died, in that order? I suspected that was what he wanted. It would allow Margaret to take my last name and the stone marker to reflect Kelleher instead of Coffey. Without that, it was likely to invite questions from the curious, and that Father Leahy couldn't permit. It was likely to invite questions anyway since Kathleen and I weren't members of his parish. How Father Leahy planned on handling that I didn't know.

"You'll have to go to confession," Kathleen continued, interrupting my thoughts.

I frowned but said nothing. I had already confessed my sins, to Liam, to the Sheehys, to Sinéad, to Mrs. Murphy. What good would it do to tell a priest? Still it was a small price to pay to ease Kathleen's worry.

"I need to go back," I said. "Tomorrow. I have to find Tim first."

Kathleen nodded. We stopped walking. She turned and held my hands. "But you'll come back? And you'll meet with Father Leahy?"

"I will, Kathleen," I promised.

# Chapter Twenty-Four

My trip back to Patrick's Well was uneventful; the scowl on my own face warning people that the priest they saw had his own worries and couldn't be bothered with theirs. Mr. Maloney had wanted to take me to the station but I had refused, walking the four miles instead.

"It'll be no bother at all," Mr. Maloney had insisted.

"Aye," I had told him. "Thank you. But I'll not be putting you out any more than I already have."

Kathleen had given me a strange look, unsure why I would decline Mr. Maloney's kindness. But I had to change back into the priest's vestments before the station. Mr. Maloney would probably have understood, but Kathleen wouldn't. And if he had given me a lift on his cart, she was sure to have come along.

I found Mary coming out of the fowl-house. She glanced up at my approach and wiped her hands dry on her apron. Her look was hopeful. I shook my head and her face dropped. I told her about my visit to Kathleen and she nodded, understanding that I had my own worries. But I had returned, this time with Kathleen's reluctant blessing, to find Tim.

"Are you sure he left with Billy?" I asked.

She nodded again. "Aye. I saw them talking by the well, and later that evening Tim was gone." She let out a breath. "O'Malley's forces marched to Limerick yesterday." She told me that both sides were now entrenched, each in their own strongholds but, as of yet, no shots had been fired. Still, more troops, Free State and Anti-Treaty alike, continued to march toward the city.

Too tired to make it back to the castle, I decided to spend the night at Mary's. She had done enough for me and I didn't want to put her in any more danger than I already had so I spent the night in the cow-house. The fowl-house was close by, and Mary's chickens were the best sentries. They were sure to wake me if anyone approached. I didn't think Billy would come for me, not tonight—he would be preoccupied with what was happening in Limerick City. Still, I thought, he had surprised me before. Hopefully the events in Limerick were enough to ensure my safety for one more night.

Despite that, as I settled into the hay, I knew that Billy would never give up his search for me. He wanted the past and his own lies to stay buried. And when I fled Ireland a year ago I had unwittingly helped him; unable as I was to tell anyone what had happened in Argyll Manor. But when I returned, Billy had no choice but to try and stop me before I could tell the truth. By now, I was sure, he had learned that I had spoken to the Sheehys again and to Sinéad and to Mrs. Murphy. What would he do? Would he tell them that *I* was the *bréagadóir*—the liar—insisting again that I had betrayed my own men for British gold? Would he tell them that I had only come back to seek amnesty? He would, because he had no choice. If he didn't, his own betrayal would be laid bare. By hiding his nephew's sins, he had committed his own. He had betrayed Tom, Dan, and Sean, and he had betrayed me. He had betrayed the IRA.

Had Rory been anyone other than Billy's nephew, his body would have been found on the side of a lonely, rain-soaked boreen, a note pinned to his chest warning others that the price paid by a traitor was death. And had the Volunteers discovered what Billy had done, sacrificing me to save his nephew, it would have been his own body found in a ditch.

It was a dangerous game. To find Tim, I had to find Billy. When I returned to Ireland, I had given him wide berth, knowing I had little chance of convincing him of my innocence. Yet he had known all along, and I realized now that a confrontation with Billy was something I could no longer avoid. My only hope was to choose the time and the place. Only then would I stand a chance to free Tim and to set things right.

I had inherited more than dreams from my father. I had inherited his sense of justice. *When a thing is wrong, you have to make it right.* Telling the Sheehys, Sinéad, and Mrs. Murphy wasn't enough. I had to make this right.

My burdens and the dreams that came with them had kept sleep at bay for a few weeks, and that night was no different. It was a while before I finally drifted off and an even longer while before I woke.

The bang of a door startled me and I jumped up, instantly reaching for the revolver. With my heart banging in my chest, I saw Mary standing over me. I lowered the gun and waited for the lecture. Instead, she stared at me for a moment.

"I've made breakfast and your tea's waiting," she said softly then turned and stepped outside. I shielded my eyes against the light—a gray Irish winter light but bright nonetheless. I checked my watch. It was 8:30—dawn had come and gone. Tired as I was, I had slept through the cry of the rooster and the clucks of the hens. As I glanced around I saw the cows were gone. No doubt Mary had let them out hours earlier. Weary and with the aches of an old man in my back, I stood and stretched, trying to chase away the stiffness.

I stumbled out of the barn to the shrill of the chickens. They scattered before me but quickly regrouped after I passed. They were drawn together, finding safety, but were wary of outsiders. Still rubbing sleep from my eyes, I paused and stared back at the birds as the thought struck me: Could that be what had happened to Tim?

The troops I had seen two nights earlier had fought together before. They were experienced soldiers, part of several brigades sent to take Limerick back from Brennan's forces. These war-hardened men would never trust Tim, a sullen fifteen-year-old boy with no fight in him. *So where was he?*

———

I visited my daughter's grave and, when I returned, I found the bicycle leaning against the side of the cottage. I wheeled it around to the front where I found Mary.

"And how did this get back here?" I asked her. I had left it hidden in the heather, some ten miles away, on the road to Croom after my first visit to the Sheehys.

"Tim found it," she answered. "Right where you left it."

"Tim found it?" I asked, confused. I remembered Tim and I discussing taking the cart to retrieve it. But we never did. I was surprised that he had gone alone for it.

"It was John's," Mary said, as if she had read my thoughts.

I nodded, then shook my head when I realized that it was probably here the last time I had visited and could have saved me a lot of walking. I inspected it, running my hand along the chain. I stood and wiped my hand on my trousers. *He even fixed that*, I thought with a grin.

Dressed as a priest, I made it to Liam's safely. The people I saw nodded politely, but no one bothered the young priest as he passed by on his bicycle. I found Seamus outside hitching a horse to the cart.

"Ah, Frank," he grinned when he saw how I was dressed. "You're up to your old tricks again, are you?"

I offered him a thin smile as I leaned the bicycle against the wall and helped him with the harness. "Many a man on the run before me hid behind the cloak of a priest," I responded.

"That they have," Seamus answered. "That they have." He paused as he studied me, trying, I was sure, to find the answer in my eyes. "Have you had much luck?" he finally asked.

I shook my head then told him of what I had done since we last spoke. His eyes darkened when I told him about Rory and what Billy had done after the bombing.

"That little shite." His voice was a hiss. "I never trusted that one." He paused. "And now Tim's with him? Do you know what that means?"

I nodded, but he continued to stare at me as if he were still waiting for my answer. His eyes, dark and full of worry, told me I had missed something. Suddenly, it became clear, and I felt a hollow pain in my stomach. Tim was in more danger than I had thought. Billy had no loyalty to the men he fought with. He had abandoned Padraig after he was wounded, and he had willingly sacrificed me to save his nephew. Tim and the other new recruits, untrained as they were and untrusted by the IRA men who had already tasted war, would be used as fodder—a diversion—while the more experienced men flanked the enemy. It would be a slaughter.

"I have to find him, Seamus," I said, a lump forming in my throat. "Before the fighting starts."

Seamus nodded. He started to say something, but the door banged open and Liam stumbled outside. Tara was on his heels, her voice sharp, frustration and worry etched into her face. I glanced from Tara to Liam. Something was wrong. Liam was pale, and the glistening in his eyes told me he had a fever. His shoulders sagged as if he hadn't the strength to hold himself up.

"He should be in bed," Tara said, her anger, it seemed, directed at both Liam and her husband. "But he doesn't listen." *He*, I suspected, could have been either Liam or Seamus.

Liam began coughing, a deep hacking sound. He swayed and began to sag. Both Seamus and I rushed forward to catch him before he fell. His hands and one sleeve were bloody, and when I lifted his chin, I saw more blood on it and his lips besides.

"How long has he been like this?" I asked, as a hollow pit settled in my stomach.

"Since you left," Tara answered.

My hands below his arms, I led Liam back to the house. Now I knew why he hadn't sent a telegram to Kathleen. Gently I wiped the blood from Liam's hands and face and we put him back in bed. He lay there listless, his head damp from sweat, his breathing ragged. Tara handed me a damp cloth and, as I held it to my friend's forehead, I tried to chase the image from my mind. I had done the same thing to my father.

"We have to take him to Limerick," I said, glancing up at Seamus.

Seamus nodded, his eyes wide. Tara frowned as she looked down at her brother-in-law then back at me.

"Consumption?"

"Aye," I said. Once again I pictured my father—his eyes filled with pain, his hair lying matted and limp on a forehead damp from fever, his once strong body skin and bones, his coughing threatening to shake apart what little was left. That's how he was right before he died.

# Chapter Twenty-five

Two nuns guided Liam to a bed while the doctor frowned. He shook his head and sighed, resentful, it seemed, that another patient had been brought into his ward. As if it took tremendous effort, he sighed again and began to check Liam's eyes and nose. He asked several questions and Seamus answered. The nuns glanced back at me several times. I felt a prickle on my neck, fearful they could see through my disguise.

The doctor placed a black cup over Liam's chest; two tubes extended from it, and he stuck the ends in his own ears. He was listening to Liam's heart or lungs or maybe both, I didn't know. After a long while, he finally pulled the cup away. He stood and said something to one of the nuns. Liam moaned softly while the other nun wiped his head with a damp cloth. The doctor turned and, as if he were just seeing us for the first time, sighed again.

"He has tuberculosis," he said. "Consumption," he added with a dismissive wave of his hand. "He'll need to stay here, but..." his words trailed off as he caught my eye. *Surely*, his eyes seemed to say, *you understand*. The lump in my throat made it hard to swallow. The doctor continued to stare at me then raised his eyebrows in question. I stared back, confused for a moment as the hollow ache in my belly grew. I shook my head. He, like the nuns I now realized, seemed to think Liam needed a priest more than he needed a doctor.

"I've nothing with me, no oils, no bible…" I said. "There wasn't time."

One of the nuns frowned, but the doctor nodded and waved his hand again as if it didn't matter.

"There are others here who can see to him."

I let out a breath as a rush of thoughts swirled in my head. For the last two hours, as I'd held Liam in my arms in the back of the cart on our journey into Limerick, I had been hopeful that there was something the doctor might be able do. And if the possibility that Liam might die wasn't bad enough, here I was dressed as a priest. Playing a priest was hard enough as it was and, while I knew the words, I was certain that the nuns would recognize me for what I was: a fraud.

I stared at Liam, watched the bed linens rise with a wheeze and then settle again as the air rattled in his chest. My friend had suffered greatly because of me, falling into the hands of the British all while I made my escape. And even though I told myself I wasn't responsible for the sickness that raged in his blood, I felt guilty. The nuns and the doctor backed away as I stepped over to the bed. I bowed my head and closed my eyes and said a prayer—a silent one—but I prayed nonetheless. *He's suffered enough, hasn't he?* I pleaded, hoping someone was listening. When I was done I looked up and, as I had seen Father Lonagan do countless times, I raised my hand and made a sign of the cross over my friend, the eyes of the nuns, the doctor, and Seamus on me all the while.

———

The Limerick Workhouse was on Selbourne Road, across Sarsfield Bridge, and only blocks from the Strand Barracks where, Mary had told me, Free State forces had mustered. Built in the middle of the last century, after Britain passed the Poor Laws, the workhouse was more a prison than a dispensary. It was there the destitute traded their freedom and labor for a filthy bed in crowded quarters and rations barely enough to keep a dog alive. As a result of the *great hunger*, the workhouse swelled during the second half of the last century. And it wasn't long before the poor were joined by the widows, the elderly, the unwed mothers and the orphans—*wretched souls* the British called them, unable to care for themselves. That their plight had been caused by centuries of living under Britain's rule was never mentioned. Ever benevolent, the British built the workhouse—the *poor house*—a half-hearted attempt to help those in need. It wasn't until the Sisters of Mercy came to the workhouse hospital late in the last century that conditions improved. Since then, the nuns had been responsible for the hospital, serving both as administrators and as nurses.

It was there that Seamus and I had brought Liam.

Seamus insisted on staying, not wanting to leave his brother's side. The doctor argued with him, but he wouldn't budge. Finally, the doctor threw his hands up. He pointed a finger at Seamus.

"You'll be the next one in that bed," he said with a huff then turned and stomped off. One of the nuns dragged a chair over by the bed. Seamus ignored them both as he held his brother's hand.

———

As adamant as Seamus was about staying, he was just as adamant that I leave before it was discovered that I wasn't the priest I pretended to be, or worse, before I was discovered by someone from my past. I told him I would return the following day, but now I had a new worry. When I did, there would be no excuse for not having my priest's vestments with me.

Outside, I untied the horse, nodding silently to the occasional greetings—*Good Day, Father*—as I thought about what to do. I couldn't stay in Limerick. On our journey to the hospital, Seamus and I had seen signs of the war to come: Free State troops and Anti-Treaty forces marching, the military precision clear in their step, while Crossley Tenders, armored cars, and lorries raced through the city. Free State or Republican, both sides would see me as a traitor, the stain of Argyll Manor difficult to hide. It had been a tense journey into the city, my worries of being recognized and my heartache for my friend filling me with a sense of dread. But with Liam's frail body cradled in my arms, no one had bothered to stop us. They had more important matters to attend to than the priest and his sick friend making their way through the tense streets to the hospital.

As I climbed up on the cart now, the low rumble of a motorcar startled me, and I turned to see the lorry coming up the block. I studied the soldiers—Free Staters—their faces stern, their rifles held ready; another patrol in a city bracing for war. I felt the prickle in my spine again, and I searched their faces one by one before settling on the officer riding in front. Quickly, I spun away as the lorry approached. I stroked the horse's neck as I adjusted the bridle. The whole while I could feel the officer's eyes on me. I prayed he wouldn't recognize the man he saw—the priest with the dark hair and a pair of glasses perched on his nose—as the same man he had given a lift to only weeks before.

Even with my head down, I could still see him out of the corner of my eye. The smile he had given me when we had discussed Ireland's future was gone, and the eyes that had been full of hope were now dark. Lieutenant Mullins now wore the face of a soldier.

My disguise must have worked; he turned away as the lorry raced up the street. Several blocks later, I lost sight of it and, in the silence that followed, I could hear my heart pounding in my chest. Thankfully, Mullins and the Free State Troops he commanded were more concerned with the Anti-Treaty forces flooding the city than they were the priest outside the workhouse.

I flicked the reins and, as the old mare began to plod forward, I considered my options. There was nothing I could do for Liam at the moment, but Tim was still in danger. If he was anywhere, I realized, he was here in Limerick. O'Malley would have ordered all available men, experienced or otherwise, to defend the city.

With the few hours of dull gray light remaining before darkness, I set out in search of the things I would need, and to see if I could learn where Tim might be.

———

I didn't find Tim, but I was able to see for myself how tenuous the situation had become. As I guided the mare back across Sarsfield Bridge, a column of Free State soldiers in their new uniforms, rifles slung over their shoulders, was forming in front of the Strand Barracks. Coming or going, I wasn't sure but I didn't wait to find out. I continued on William Street, and as I passed by the RIC Post, a handful of Free State soldiers was standing guard out front while the barrels of rifles held by others poked out between the steel shutters above. I couldn't help but notice the tricolour flag flapping in the breeze. The provisional government had taken this symbol—the same green, white, and orange banner that had been hoisted above the General Post Office in Dublin six years ago when we had declared our independence—as a symbol of the Free State.

I continued down William Street then Mulgrave, passing the Artillery Barracks where the remaining British soldiers were stationed, waiting for orders to ship home. Several soldiers stood outside while the Union Jack fluttered high above the walls. Unlike the British soldiers I had seen two weeks earlier, these carried rifles, the excitement of returning to England gone and their eyes now filled with tension.

Then, moments later, as I approached the gaol, I spied the first Republican soldiers in front of St. Joseph's Asylum. Ernie O'Malley's men I was certain; the soldiers I had seen at O'Shea's barn had finally marched into the city. I pulled back on the reins, and the horse stopped by the prison's gates.

A dozen men stood out front of the asylum—in their trench coats and caps, rifles slung over their shoulders—with a half-dozen motorcars and lorries behind them. Beyond, there were at least a hundred men in groups below the chestnut trees, waiting, it seemed, for O'Malley's orders. Although most were sitting, smoking and talking, their darting eyes and cautious glances told me they too were tense.

O'Malley was sure to have sent scouts to reconnoiter the Free State troops, assessing their strength and positions. If what Mary had told me was true—and the Free State soldiers I had seen in front of the Strand and the Police Barracks told me it was—the Free Staters had seized the advantage. The fortified barracks they controlled would be difficult to attack. My heart sank as I estimated the number of men O'Malley had with him. If that's all there were, they were outnumbered. Images of medieval sieges and bodies left wounded and dying in the dirt filled my head.

If Tim was anywhere, I told myself, trying to chase the scene from my head, he would be there, with the Republican forces mustering at the asylum. And if he was, Billy and Kevin were too. But, priest or no priest, I couldn't risk getting any closer.

I watched for several minutes before I turned the cart around. I should have left then, set out for Seamus's house—Tara was sure to be worrying and waiting for my news. Instead, I headed back into Limerick.

There was one more thing I needed to do.

————

It was after dark when I heard the slam of a door. The priest, Father Reagan, I remembered, turned, pulled the collar of his coat up below his chin, and set off at a brisk pace up the street. A moment later he turned the corner. From my perch on the cart, I watched the rectory for another few minutes before I climbed down and made my way across the street. I rang the bell, waited a moment, then rang again. A few seconds later, an old woman answered. When she saw me, she bowed her head in the same submissive greeting I myself had given since I was a wee lad.

"Is Father Reagan in?" My tone, far from friendly or inviting, was laced with the impatience of a man used to dealing with servants and one whose authority came from the collar he wore.

"No, Father," she said shaking her head, refusing to meet my eyes. "He won't be back until nine."

I let out a loud sigh. "I haven't the time," I said as I stepped forward. "Show me to the sacristy."

She hesitated, briefly glancing up at me before bowing her head again and opening the door.

"Yes, Father," she said as I stepped inside.

Ten minutes later, a small black leather burse slung across my shoulder, I left. The burse seemed to grow heavier as I walked back to the waiting cart; the feeling of pending doom was difficult to shake. I hoped I wouldn't have to use what was inside but couldn't escape the feeling that I would.

# Chapter Twenty-six

"Will he...?" Tara asked, unable to finish. Her eyes were red. It was clear she'd been crying.

"I don't know." I sighed heavily, not wanting to tell her the truth. Consumption had killed scores of Irish men and women, including my father, but children were the favored prey. However, surviving childhood was no guarantee that death wouldn't find you later. I wiped my own eyes at the thought. That Liam had survived all he had in his life, from the priest who had stolen his childhood to the atrocities at the hands of the British, only to fall victim to the consumption was too much to bear.

"And Seamus?" she asked. The muscles were stretched tight across Tara's face. Her worries weren't only for Liam but what might happen to her husband too.

"He insisted on staying," I said. Her eyes went wide, and I realized she had assumed her husband was outside tending the horse. "I'm going back tomorrow."

She nodded then dropped her head and stared silently at the table, lost in her worries.

"Has he been sick before?" I asked.

Tara looked up. "Aye," she answered. "He was sick in the gaol. I think that's why the British let him go. For two weeks, he hadn't the energy to so much as climb out of bed." She shook her head. "He's never been the same since."

I sighed. Liam's sickness had come from prison. I couldn't help but think that he never would have been captured by the British— and never would have gotten sick—had it not been for me. But it was more than that—it was a chain of events that all started with Billy.

————

Once again, sleep was a long time in coming. What happened during the day only added to the weight of the worries I carried with me. My friend Liam was dying, and there was little I could do to help him. And I still hadn't found Tim. I sighed. In the silence that followed, I heard the ticking of my father's watch on the stand beside me. I reached for it. Seeking the comfort it had always provided, I held it over my heart, feeling the rhythmic *tick-tock* in my chest. I had wound it earlier. Now taut, the springs would turn the gears, and the hands would march forward, nothing to stop them until the tension was gone. *Is Ireland any different?* I wondered. As if the springs had been wound, the fragile pact that had once held us together was unable to stop the gears from turning and, minute by minute, Ireland marched closer to war.

As I had finally seen for myself, a tense game of positioning was taking place in the streets of Limerick, the Free State on one side, Anti-Treaty forces on the other, with the British caught in the middle. Limerick was vital to the provisional government's hold on power. Staunchly Republican, staunchly Anti-Treaty, Limerick was the key. Without it, the Free State government would never gain control of all twenty-six counties. While Dublin, Belfast, Cork, and Donegal watched, the fate of the fledgling nation hung in balance in the streets and lanes of Limerick.

Men who had fought side by side against the British, in a time when we were bound by a camaraderie and a shared sense of the justness of our cause, now regarded each other warily. Even as the Treaty was being signed, now two months ago, negotiations had continued

in Dublin and in cities around Ireland to bring the two sides together. The negotiations, I now saw, were doomed from the start.

The IRA as an organization had come together at a crucial time
for Ireland when men of different backgrounds and political beliefs
joined forces against a common enemy. Young and naive, I hadn't
realized this when I joined, thinking that our differing political
views were minor and could be sorted out. Many a night I had sat
and listened to the debates, the heated arguments that would last
till the wee hours and which more than once nearly ended in fisticuffs. Organizations like Sínn Féin, the Citizen's Army, the Irish
Volunteers, the Irish Republican Brotherhood, and even the trade
unions and athletic leagues all had different visions for the future
and different thoughts on how we should battle the British.

Now that the war with the British was over—and before the
Crown could withdraw their forces—old ideologies and old rivalries
had surfaced again and threatened to shatter the tenuous peace that
had settled over the country.

These thoughts and images of Liam filled my head, and sleep, as
it had for weeks now, refused to come until just before dawn.

——

I woke early to the smell of the turf in the stove and realized that
Tara was already up. I lingered for a moment, sorting through the
jumble of thoughts in my head. Unable to make sense of any of it, I
finally rose and dressed quickly, anxious to escape the thoughts that
plagued me. After a cup of tea and a piece of ham, I patted Tara on
the arm and stepped out into the gray mist of the early morning.
Thirty minutes later, after feeding and watering the horse, I hitched
her to the cart and set out for Limerick.

It was but a short while later when I pulled back on the reins,
slowing for the flock of sheep in the road. An old man—a shepherd—walked in the center, the flock moving with him, the bleats
comforting in the stillness of the morning. A collie darted back and

forth, keeping the strays from wandering too far. I sighed, finding solace in the moment. This old man and his dog tending their flock, as countless generations had before them, reminded me why I had joined the IRA. It was as much for the old man that I had taken up a gun as it was for myself. And now, having finally succeeded in throwing off the shackles of British oppression, we were free to be Irish once again. I nodded and bade the old man good day as I passed, feeling a little more optimistic than I had the night before.

My mood continued to brighten when, a short while later, there was a break in the clouds. I felt a warmth on my neck and soon on my back. Glancing behind me, I saw the sun rising low over the Galtee Mountains in the distance. A rare thing to see, the Irish winter sun—I hoped it, like the old man and his sheep, was a sign of good fortune.

I passed the road to Ballyneety and, a short while later, I came upon a young lad, a boy no more than twelve, standing in the ditch, waiting, it seemed, for me to pass. His eyes were downcast and he wore the look of a man, his own troubles as well as those of his country evident in the droop of his shoulders. He had a bundle slung over one. He reminded me of Liam. Knowing I shouldn't, I slowed then stopped beside him.

"A fine day it is," I called down.

He startled, looking up cautiously, wary of the priest that had stopped to speak to him.

"Aye, Father. A fine day." He looked down again, hoping, I was sure, that I would be on my way.

"And where might a lad such as yourself be off to on such a fine day?"

His head jerked up, uncertain. "My brother, Father." He paused. "He left to join the army."

I nodded, hiding my surprise. "The IRA?" I asked.

"Aye," he nodded then shook his head. "But not the traitors in

Dublin," he added with a hiss. Then, realizing what he had done, he bowed his head again. "Sorry, Father."

"He's not for the Treaty, is he?"

The lad hesitated then shook his head.

"Neither am I," I announced.

He looked up in surprise.

"Where's your brother?" I asked.

"In Limerick," he responded. He held up the bundle. "Me mam sent me with this."

I nodded as I pictured the worried mother, sending food to her son. I couldn't help but think of Mary. I studied the boy for a moment, knowing I shouldn't but also knowing I had no other choice.

"I'm going to Limerick," I said then offered him a lift. After a moment's hesitation he climbed on board.

"I'm Father Byrne," I said as I stuck out my hand. Surprised again, he shook it and offered me a thin smile.

His name was Andrew, he told me, and his brother, Diarmuid, had joined the IRA, Billy's Anti-Treaty brigade. Diarmuid, he said, was sixteen and had been sent to the Royal George Hotel, on O'Connell and Roches Streets. I had passed it yesterday but hadn't noticed anything unusual—certainly nothing that told me it had been commandeered by the IRA. *What else had I missed?* I wondered. I agreed to drop Andrew off. If Diarmuid had been sent there, maybe Tim had been as well.

As the city drew closer, Andrew grew quiet.

"A lad I know joined too," I said, then told him about Tim. "His mother doesn't know where he is. She's asked me to find him."

He nodded but said nothing.

"He's only fifteen," I said, describing Tim. "Tall and thin like a willow and with curly black hair." I described the scar on Tim's chin. I paused and searched Andrew's eyes. "Would you look for him?" I asked. "At the hotel?"

He considered it for a moment then nodded. Whether it was

because he thought I was a priest or because his own worries filled his head, he never questioned why I had asked him to do something I should have been able to do myself.

I thanked him, feeling a small sliver of hope that Tim might be at the Royal George.

"Father?"

I glanced back at Andrew. In his eyes, I saw Mary and Kathleen and his own mother. There I saw the worry and fear that someone his age shouldn't know.

"Will there be another war, Father?"

"I don't know, son." I shook my head, not wanting to lie but also not wanting to tell him the truth. "I don't know."

————

Liam had been moved to a special ward for people with consumption. I found Seamus where I had left him, by Liam's side. Liam's bed was by an open window. The other beds in the room were full, nine other men all struggling, like Liam, to breathe. Seamus nodded when he saw me but said nothing. His heavy eyes told me he hadn't slept or if he had it hadn't been for long. Liam was the same: a scratchy whine as his chest rose slightly followed by a ragged wheeze as it settled uneasily once again. He continued to cough up blood, a sure sign of consumption, the doctor had told us yesterday. He was asleep, and the shine on his forehead told me that he still had the fever.

"You can't stay here," I said softly. "There's nothing you can do."

Seamus looked up at me but said nothing.

"Tara needs you at home."

Finally, he nodded but turned back to his brother as if he had no intent to leave. At least not yet.

I decided to give him some more time.

I found the doctor in the hallway, chastising a young lass with a mop and bucket. Her head hung low; she cringed at his sharp hiss. I couldn't help but picture Father Lonagan but quickly put the thought out of my head. I had more battles than I could handle at the moment and didn't need another. The doctor turned and sighed heavily when he saw me. His look let me know that, priest or no priest, with the beds full, he had little time for someone as healthy as me.

"How is he?" I asked.

The doctor shrugged. "Only time will tell," he said. He went on to explain that the best treatment for consumption was fresh air. The windows in the ward were kept open as often as possible and, once a day, most patients were moved outside to a covered veranda. Some benefited from surgery to the lungs but, for most, it was the fresh air. Still, many didn't survive, he continued, and Liam was quite sick.

"Although," he added, his tone offering a glimmer of hope, "his condition has improved slightly since yesterday."

What the doctor had seen, he never explained, and, before I could ask, he hurried off.

Returning to Liam's side I felt the nuns' eyes on me once again. I looked down at my friend and sighed, knowing what was expected of me. I opened the burse I had stolen from Father Reagan's sacristy. I ignored Seamus's frown as I placed the two small vials—one for oil and one for holy water—on the table. This was followed by a small, gold container—the pyx, I think Father Lonagan had called it—that held the communion wafers. As I placed the bible on the table, I took a deep breath, knowing I couldn't avoid what came next.

"In nomine Patris, et Filii, et Spiritus Sancti." The Latin spilled out of my mouth as I anointed Liam's eyes with the oil, pardoning his sins as I had seen Father Lonagan do to my own father. I did the same with Liam's ears, and then his nose, his lips, his hands, and his feet. The whole while I could feel the nuns' eyes on me, or maybe they weren't the nuns' at all, I thought, as I tried to avoid looking up at the cross on the wall.

———

"Surely you know Father Reagan," one of the nuns said as Seamus and I stepped out into the hall. "He's in the next ward."

"Aye," I nodded but said no more as I grabbed Seamus's arm and steered him down the hall. I had no desire to meet Father Reagan or any other priest, knowing for certain they would recognize my lie immediately. It wasn't until several minutes later when we stepped outside into the sun that I let out the breath I had been holding.

As we readied the horse, I explained to Seamus what we needed to do. He was weary and needed sleep. There was nothing he could do for Liam, but maybe helping Tim would bring him some relief. This is what I told myself, but I knew it was a lie. The real reason was that I couldn't do it alone. Shaking the thought from my head, I pulled the cart around, and we made our way down Shelbourne Road.

Ten minutes later, I pulled back on the reins and the horse slowed. Seamus, who had been dozing next to me, looked up. I nodded in the distance. A column of soldiers was turning onto Sarsfield Bridge. Their new green uniforms told me they were Free Staters. Other than Officer Mullins and a few other men I had soldiered with over the years, the Free Staters, most from Dublin and County Clare, I was told, wouldn't know me. I repeated this to myself as I edged the cart closer. Rifles slung over their shoulders, they marched with a precision.

Seamus sat up.

"They're reinforcing their positions," he said at once, his soldier's eye not missing anything. His eyes darted around then settled back onto the column. I realized he was right. Troops from Clare had mustered at the Strand Barracks first before crossing the Shannon. The Castle Barracks, on King's Island, was across the Shannon from the Strand. By occupying both, Brennan's Free State Troops now controlled the bridges, denying Anti-Treaty forces the opportunity to reinforce from the north. They would also reinforce their positions in the RIC Barracks on William Street and Mary Street. They had quickly seized the advantage.

"Fucking Brennan," Seamus cursed under his breath. Arms still folded across his chest, he stared at the column of men.

We watched silently as the end of the column turned onto the bridge. Despite their disciplined march, several of the soldiers were only lads, I noticed, no more than fifteen or sixteen—perhaps even younger by the looks of them. Three rows from the rear, a lad with red hair spilling out below his cap glanced our way and caught my eye. Despite his uniform and rifle, his eyes held the fear of a child—one who wanted no part of the war that was coming. I felt a lump in my throat as I thought of Tim. I glanced at Seamus, but his eyes were on the soldiers on horseback bringing up the rear.

We waited for the column before we crossed. The whole while, I wore a scowl on my face, a displeased glare to further my disguise. With all that had happened, feigning my own worries wasn't difficult. Minutes later, I pulled the reins gently and we turned onto O'Connell Street. A Crossley Tender raced by, and I suspected it was more Free State soldiers heading to one of their barracks. Despite the chess game being played out in the surrounding streets, Cannock's department store was busy. Several women were entering as we passed, seemingly unaware of the two sides fortifying their positions around them. Several blocks away I spotted a group of men and lorries in front of the Royal George Hotel and let the reins go slack. We edged closer as both Seamus and I assessed the situation. As far as I could determine, this was one of two Anti-Treaty positions in Limerick. A block away, I pulled the cart to the side of the road, far enough from the hotel where the men in front wouldn't see me clearly. And if they could, the dray in front of us would block their view.

The men were dressed in trench coats and caps, their bandoliers and rifles clearly visible. I couldn't tell for certain, but they looked to be the same ones I had seen earlier, when I had dropped Andrew off in the morning. Two men were struggling with a bureau, building a barricade in front of the hotel with furniture taken from inside. Above, I saw rifles poking out of the windows and the shadows of the men behind them. Two more men were on the roof, their rifles held ready. I stole a glance at Seamus. He was silent, his eyes darting back and forth, taking it all in.

I glanced back at the door. *Where was Andrew?* I wondered. We had agreed to meet here. Sure we were late, but where would he go? I scanned the street, wondering if he was in one of the shops or if something had gone wrong. Tired of waiting on me, had he decided to walk home?

After fifteen long minutes, I was ready to leave. If we stayed any longer, I feared, we would draw attention to ourselves. I reached for the reins, but Seamus grabbed my arm.

"I'll go," he said.

Without waiting for my reply, he climbed down. As he made his way down the curb, I glanced back at the men in front of the hotel. Caps pulled low over their faces, their eyes scanned the street, finally settling on Seamus. My eyes flicked from them to nearby buildings. Across the street, several women pushing prams glanced nervously at the soldiers as they hurried by. They weren't alone. But many, it seemed, ignored the IRA men and their guns. As we had seen at Cannock's, the shops along O'Connell Street were busy, drays and lorries continued to make their deliveries, and old men still whiled away the hours in the pubs.

I pulled my father's watch from my pocket and made a show of fussing with it, keeping Seamus in the corner of my eye. He approached the hotel, and I could see him speaking with three men— soldiers I likely had fought with at one time or another. One of the men shook his head and I sighed, frustrated. They talked a moment more, and the man shook his head again. Seamus nodded and turned, heading back up the street toward me, the men watching him the whole while. Head down, Seamus didn't glance up until he was just feet away and then he shook his own head, telling me what I already knew. I let out another sigh as he climbed back onto the cart.

"Andrew left an hour ago," he said.

I frowned. "And Tim?"

"Not there," he said with a shake of his head. "According to that lot anyway."

"What did you say?" I asked.

"That I was looking for the son of a friend. That his mother was sick."

"Did you have any problems?"

"No," he said. He hadn't recognized any of the men, he added.

"Do they have any idea where we might look?"

He shook his head again.

Sighing, I flicked the reins and turned the cart. The three men were still watching us and, although I was too far away to see their faces clearly, I didn't want to get any closer and let them see mine.

There had to be other Anti-Treaty strongholds, I told myself, besides the asylum and the Royal George. I was tempted to reconnoiter the streets again, looking for what I had missed yesterday but after glancing at Seamus, I decided it was best to set out for home. He was asleep within minutes, oblivious to the shaking and bouncing of the cart and to the commotion in the streets around him as the city prepared for war.

With a sigh, I flicked the reins and turned the cart. Next to me, Seamus's chin had fallen to his chest. The lack of sleep and the worry over his brother weighed heavily on him. But it was more than that. I sensed something else: a weariness of the days to come.

# Chapter Twenty-seven

I fought back the tears as I held Liam's limp hand. His breathing was raspy, coming in quick, shallow pants. His cheeks were sunken, and his hair lay matted on his head. His sheets were stained from his coughing, and blood seeped out of the corner of his mouth. The fever was back, and every now and then Seamus wiped Liam's forehead with the damp cloth. Seamus looked across the bed at me, his own eyes wet.

Earlier, when we arrived, the doctor only shook his head, his eyes telling us what his words couldn't. The nuns didn't argue this time when Seamus and I refused to leave Liam's side. Their eyes, like the doctor's, told us it was time. There Seamus and I sat, one on each side of Liam's bed as we had since early morning, oblivious to the chill in the breeze from the open window.

I heard a gasp, and Liam's frail body shuddered. The lump in my throat grew but, after a moment, his body settled and his raspy pants continued. Wiping away my tears, I closed my eyes, praying for my friend as I had been since we had arrived.

"Frank." Liam's raspy voice, barely a whisper, startled me. His eyes were glassy, full of pain.

I wiped my own eyes, not from the shame of crying, but wanting to spare my friend the lack of hope my tears held.

"Aye, Liam. I'm here." I said softly. "Seamus is too."

Liam's eyes shifted, found his brother, and I couldn't stop the tears now as they stared into each other's eyes. Without words, Liam and Seamus were talking, sharing one final time a lifetime of pain and sorrow and joy and hope and their bond as brothers. The tears rolled down Seamus's cheeks as he nodded.

"Frank?"

Liam's eyes found mine again.

"Aye, Liam."

"Did we win?"

"Aye, Liam," I said, nodding and wiping my eyes again. "We won."

His lips curled, a faint smile. "Ah, that's grand, Frank. That's grand."

Then my friend closed his eyes for the last time. A moment later, he shuddered again, a choking sound in his throat this time, and then he was gone.

———

Liam left the hospital the same way he had arrived, in the back of a cart, his head cradled in my lap.

"We're taking him home," Seamus had told the nun, his voice barely above a whisper.

"You can't," the nun scolded. "Not until…" Her voice trailed away under Seamus's glare. She looked at me. There were forms, there were procedures—surely I would understand, her eyes seemed to say. My own glare matched Seamus's and she backed away.

I stood back as Seamus carefully tucked the blanket around his brother. With his hand, he gently brushed Liam's hair, stepped back then, after a moment's hesitation, folded Liam's hands across his chest. He looked up at me and nodded. Together, we wheeled the bed out of the room, ignoring the reproachful looks from the nuns. A moment later, we wheeled the bed out of the hospital, into the harsh gray light of a city preparing for war.

———

Liam was waked at his parents' house in Drommore, a stone's throw from my mam's cottage. Like my own father had once, Liam's father raised pigs and made his life from the land. Tara, one of Liam's cousins, and my own mother had prepared the body. Liam was laid out on the table, the white sheets, ones that had never covered the living but were reserved for the dead, tucked neatly around him. A crucifix lay on his chest, and the beads of the rosary were laced through his fingers. On the table beside him, the candle flickered. Seamus, as he had done right up till the end, took his seat next to his brother. His parents—Liam's mother and father—sat beside him. I knelt by my friend and said a prayer. When I finished, I stood and turned to Liam's mother.

"Ah, he looks good, Missus Ahern." I said as I patted her arm.

She glanced up at me and nodded. Her dark eyes were set above puffy, round cheeks that sank inward by her mouth, and the skin hung loose on her jaw. She looked much older now—I hadn't seen her since the day I had fled my own house years ago—but in only a day the death of her child had surely aged her in a way that no years could. The tears, I could see, would not be long in coming.

"Tara did a fine job laying him out," I said, the first of many who would tell her the same in the hours to come.

She nodded again then thanked me. Her eyes held mine for a moment before she let out a sob and grasped my hands.

"Look what they did to him, Frank," she pleaded. "Look what they did to my Liam."

I held her hand for a long moment, fighting back my own tears. Empty chairs were arranged around the room and in the next as well. The first of many mourners, and Liam's friend since we were lads, I was expected to sit with the family throughout the day and the night as well, eventually joining the men in the kitchen for a *wee wan* when the bottle was passed.

"I can't stay, ma'am."

"I know," she said, patting my hand now, and I wondered how much Liam and Seamus had told her. I turned to Liam's father.

"I'm sorry for your troubles, sir."

Mr. Ahern looked up and nodded.

"Thank you," he said quietly before his eyes settled again on the empty chairs across the room. Staring straight ahead, hands folded neatly on his lap and his spine stiff with Irish resolve, he would remain there for hours throughout the endless procession of neighbors and friends all come to mourn his son. People would soon fill the cottage, and the haunting sounds of the keening would soon fill the air.

I left quietly before it did.

———

Word of Liam's death had traveled quickly, as news of a death usually did, and within days, those who needed to know were told. Telegrams and telephones weren't needed, nor would they have done any good, as the people who knew Liam had little use for either.

By the time I reached Mary's, it was late afternoon. I found her outside, hitching the horse to the cart. She watched as I climbed off of the bicycle and leaned it against the wall.

I shook my head, a silent answer to the question in her eyes. I told her what I had done since I had last seen her, of my search in Limerick for her son. She nodded, her eyes wet. I knew it wasn't only for Liam. She nervously smoothed the wrinkles off of the black lace dress that I had only seen her wear to funerals. Today she wore it for Liam but I sensed she was filled with dread that she would soon be wearing it for her own son. We stared at each other in silence for a moment.

"What will you do now?" she asked.

"Go back to Limerick," I said.

"Tonight?"

I thought about it for a moment. "Tomorrow. I'll stay at the castle tonight."

"You'll do no such thing," she scolded gently. "You'll stay here."

I opened my mouth to protest but never got a chance.

"Billy's sure to be in Limerick," she reasoned. "And if he isn't, he'll be paying his respects to the Aherns. He certainly won't be coming around here."

I didn't think Billy was capable of showing such compassion, but I understood what she meant. Billy had other worries at the moment and wouldn't be looking for me. A moment later, Mary flicked the reins on the cart. I watched as she disappeared into the mist. I stuck my hand in my pocket and found my father's watch. I felt the ticking, but this time I wasn't able to find any solace in the rhythm. Instead, it only reminded me that Tim was still missing and I had little time left to find him.

# Chapter Twenty-eight

In the darkness before dawn, I set out on the bicycle following the same roads I had the last few days. The shepherd I had seen days before was nowhere to be seen that morning, nor was the sun. It was raining, a slanting hail that forced me to duck my head, barely able to see the road before me.

I wiped the rain from my eyes and pedaled on in silence, sloshing through the mud and puddles, lost in my own thoughts. The rain matched my dark mood and allowed me to pass the carts, motorcars, and people I saw along the way with nothing more than a nod. The darkness of the night had given way to a cold, wet, gray morning. My trench coat cinched tight, hiding my priest's collar, I was just another Irishman with neither the sense nor the choice but to be out in the rain.

I had set out with the intention of going to Limerick. After only a few miles, I looked up through the lashing rain and spotted the intersection and the road to Ballyneety, near where I had seen Andrew days before. On impulse, I turned. He hadn't said exactly, but I thought I knew where he lived.

Fifteen minutes later, I was sitting in front of a fire, sipping a hot cup of tea, while Andrew's mother fussed over the wet priest who had unexpectedly appeared at her door.

"And where is it you're from again, Father?" Mrs. Toomey asked.

Caught by surprise, I sipped my tea as I thought of my answer. Over the last two months I had used half a dozen names including

that of a long dead friend as well as that of a man whose passport I
had stolen. But for the last few weeks I had been a priest and, for the
life of me, I couldn't remember what I had told Andrew.

"New York," I finally said. "But my family lives in Clare."

She nodded but said no more. She turned back to the fire, having insisted on making me breakfast. I sat in silence while the smells
of ham and bread filled the room. Andrew, she had told me when I
first arrived, would be back shortly, having been sent to a neighbor's
farm to deliver some eggs in exchange for butter and milk. Why he
hadn't waited for me in front of the Royal George, I didn't ask, and
I suspected she wouldn't have known if I had. He had made it home
safely, it seemed.

The ham sputtered and sizzled when Mrs. Toomey placed it in
the pan, and the smell soon filled the room. That a priest was wanting to see her son had left her worried, wondering what transgression he might have committed. I had told her the truth, that I had
met Andrew on the way to Limerick as I was searching for Tim. I
told her I was worried about both of them, about God's children
being caught in the battle that was sure to come.

"Why did Diarmuid join?" I asked, before she thought of another question for me.

I saw her stiffen. She turned slowly, and I saw the same look in
her eyes that I had seen in Andrew's.

"There's no telling with a boy like that," she finally said. "Daft he
is and with no schooling…" She paused and wiped her eyes. "Andrew
is only twelve, but Diarmuid always thought him the older brother."

I frowned. Now I understood why she had been sending Andrew
to Limerick. What we Irish called daft, British doctors called *idiots
and lunatics*. The British send boys like Diarmuid to the asylums,
many expected to labor in exchange for food and shelter. Never one
to rely on the state, the Church provided its own answer. *Idle hands
make for the Devil's work*, the Church believed and the *lunatics*, especially the children were kept busy with lessons and work.

But Mrs. Toomey hadn't done that, preferring instead to keep Diarmuid at home. Caring for the sick, the elderly, and the *daft* had been the burden of Irish women for centuries. She had no intention, I suspected, of doing anything different.

Something nagged at me: Diarmuid was daft, and I struggled to understand why the IRA would want him. My thoughts were interrupted when Mrs. Toomey placed the plate in front of me.

"Thank you, ma'am," I said. I hadn't eaten yet, and the smell of the ham and warm bread had reminded me I was hungry. I reached for my fork but caught myself when I saw Mrs. Toomey frown. I stared at her for a moment before I realized what I had done, or rather what I had failed to do. Scolding myself silently, I folded my hands, bowed my head, and offered a prayer of thanks. When I was done, I looked up. I could see the question in Mrs. Toomey's eyes: *what kind of priest is it that forgets his prayer?*

"And Diarmuid, how is he?" I asked, hoping talk of her son would make her forget about me.

"I don't know," she said. Her sigh filled the room. "He's never been away from home," she continued. "But when Billy Ryan came...." Her words trailed off.

*Billy*, I thought with a frown. It didn't make sense. If there was going to be another war, why had he been recruiting lads like Tim and Diarmuid, boys incapable of fighting? Suddenly I pictured the lad with the red hair spilling out from under his cap, his eyes full of fear, as he marched with the Free State soldiers across Sarsfield Bridge. *Was it a ruse?* I wondered. Were the Free Staters and the IRA filling their ranks with anyone they could, hoping to intimidate each other into surrender with their seemingly larger forces? Maybe. But with Billy, I wondered if it was something more.

No longer hungry. I pushed the plate away.

———

Andrew returned moments later. If he was surprised to see me, he didn't let on. Soaking wet, he warmed himself by the fire while Mrs. Toomey fixed his tea. I gave him a few moments to dry off then smiled and nodded to the chair. He sat down, somewhat reluctantly, it seemed, his eyes downcast as the steam from his cup swirled around his face. The apprehension I had seen when we first met had returned, reminding me of my own experiences with Father Lonagan.

"How's your brother?" I asked.

He glanced up at his mother before answering. She nodded.

"Scared, Father."

"What do they have him doing?"

"Marching," he answered. Then he frowned, and a confused look came on his face.

I nodded again, waiting for more.

"They woke him up in the middle of the night and made him hide in the back of a lorry," he continued. "They left him at the asylum..." His mother gasped at this but he shook his head. "Then they made him march back."

I thought about this for a moment. "Were there others with him?"

He nodded then frowned again. "But they went to a different hotel this time," he added.

"Which one?"

"The Glentworth."

I sat back and took a sip of my own tea as I wrestled with what this meant. I had been right. Billy was marching the same men into the city twice, maybe three or four times, making it appear as if he had a bigger force. But what did this mean for Tim?

———

We set out for Limerick a short while later, Andrew perched on the handles while I pedaled. It had stopped raining—for the moment anyway—but the dark sky told me there was more to come. Still

I had to carefully dodge the puddles that dotted the muddy roads and lanes. The ham and the bread I hadn't been able to eat were now wrapped, tucked below Andrew's coat. Worried that the other men might take advantage of him, Mrs. Ahern wanted to make sure Diarmuid was fed.

"His name is Tim," I reminded Andrew as we passed the cemetery. "He's..." My words trailed off when I spotted the commotion in front St. Joseph's Asylum. Dozens of men stood around, most in small groups, talking and smoking. Most wore trench coats, and many had bandoliers stretched across their chests. These men weren't sitting like the men I had seen two days earlier. They were getting ready to march.

I had heard that Tom Barry and the men from Cork had come to help defend the city against Brennan's forces. *Are these Barry's men?* I wondered. They wouldn't know me, I didn't think, and we were far enough away that no one would recognize my face. Still I unbuttoned my coat, letting my priest's collar show, and kept my head down as we pedaled by. I could feel their eyes on me the whole while.

As the asylum faded behind us, I continued. "He's my size. Tall and thin, with curly black hair."

Andrew nodded.

"And he has a scar on his chin."

Andrew glanced back, and I drew my finger across the right side of my jaw, showing him where.

"I know, Father," he said and I said no more.

———

As they had for the last several days, lorries, Crossley Tenders, and armored cars raced through the city while troops marched to and fro. I avoided them—turning down side streets—when I could. And when I couldn't, as I had done at the asylum, I turned my head and prayed no one would recognized me. We passed O'Mara's Bacon, and I turned on Catherine Street. One block from the Glentworth, I pulled to the curb and let Andrew off.

"I'll meet you in the park," I said. I had wanted to say something to lift his spirits—that everything would be grand—but knew he would see it for a lie.

He nodded, then, without looking back, he made his way up the street.

I waited in People's Park, sitting on a bench. The path circled around the memorial—a Greek limestone column topped with the statue of a man named Rice. Who he was I didn't know, but the memorial was almost one hundred years old. I watched a mother, across the way, bent over her pram, fussing with her baby. After a moment, she stood, smiled, and said something to the child, a mother's soothing words I was sure, then turned the pram and began walking again. I watched until the path and the woman and her pram disappeared into the trees. Even in the middle of a city arming itself for war, life went on.

It all made me think of Sean Murphy. He and I had sat on this very same bench, on IRA business, some eighteen months before. While old men with their race cards, mothers with their prams, and couples holding hands strolled by, we sat in wait for a man from Dublin—the same one who would show me how to make the bomb that would end Sean's life. As it had then, it had rained earlier, and as I stared at the still wet stone of the path, I couldn't help but think how much had changed since that day.

———

Andrew found me an hour later. I watched him as he appeared from the trees then wound his way around the monument. As he had on the day I met him, he walked as if the weight of the world was pressing down on his shoulders. When he looked up, his eyes found mine. As he drew closer, I could see that he had only just wiped the tears away moments earlier.

I stood. "What's happened," I asked.

"They hurt him," he blurted out.

"Who?" I asked, but I already knew.

"The IRA," he said as he stared down at the ground. Then he looked up. *Why did they do that?* his eyes seemed to ask. He turned his back to me, and he wiped away another tear. When he turned around again, he told me that Diarmuid's nose had been broken. After several questions, it was clear what had happened. For the first time in his life, Diarmuid was away from his home, away from his mother, away from his protective younger brother, and away from the comforting routine his life had become. Confused by the change and overwhelmed by the discipline expected of him, he had earned the wrath of one of the officers. I pictured the IRA men I knew, wondering which would strike a frightened child. There was only one man who would do that.

"He wanted to come with me," Andrew said. He let out a sigh, and I knew before he told me what happened next. Seeing his brother again—his only connection to the only life he had ever known—Diarmuid had tried to leave. Billy had ordered him to stay and, when he refused, Billy had used his fists, a lesson both to Diarmuid and to anyone else who might defy one of his orders.

"He was a big man, was he, the one who did this?" I asked, picturing the thin upper lip, the square jaw, the crooked nose from Liam's stone those years ago, the hooded, menacing eyes, and the broad shoulders.

"Aye," Andrew said. "It was Billy Ryan."

———

We left Limerick quickly, Andrew once again perched on the handles, me pedaling silently, lost in my thoughts. British versus Irish, landowner versus tenant, Catholic versus Protestant, Unionists versus Republicans, Free Staters versus Anti-Treaty—we Irish were forever choosing sides, preparing to fight. Trapped in our own history, it seemed, it was the only thing we knew how to do. As we passed by a column of troops marching on Limerick—the men we had seen earlier at the asylum—I didn't bother to turn my head. I stared into each of their eyes and wondered how many of these young men would have to die before we finally laid down our guns.

Yet as these dark clouds chased me, I could still see my father's face, could still see the earnestness in his eyes, could still hear his words: *When a thing is wrong, you have to make it right.* But how could I do that? I wondered. As if he had no answer himself, Andrew silently swayed and bounced on the bar in front of me. The only thing I had done, I realized, was make things worse.

I was lost in these thoughts as I pedaled down the rain-soaked lanes, over the hills and around the bends, past the farms and the sheep, past the whitewashed cottages and the women churning butter while the men struggled to hold the plows straight in the rocky soil. At the road to Ballyneety I stopped, intending to let Andrew walk the rest of the way. I didn't want to speak to Mrs. Toomey, for there was little I could tell her. As if he knew this too, Andrew hopped down.

Consumed as I was with my own thoughts, I didn't hear him the first time.

He stared up at me. "I saw him, Father."

It must have been the confusion in my eyes that made him say it again.

"I saw him," he said as he searched my eyes. "Tim. He was there."

# Chapter Twenty-nine

I lay behind the tree just below the ridge, the church and the stream that ran past it below me. Through the field glasses that Mr. Maloney had given me, I watched as Seamus, Mick, and a handful of other lads carried Liam's coffin out the front door, the line of mourners making the sign of the cross as the coffin passed. I shifted the glasses slightly until I found Father Lonagan at the head of the cortege. Liam's mother, a black veil over her face, followed the coffin, Liam's father holding her arm. Tara and the family were behind them, followed by the Sheehys, Mrs. Murphy and Martin. My mother walked with Mary and Sinéad. Last came Mick and Padraig, behind everyone else, Padraig having trouble with the rough ground.

In the middle of the crowd was Billy—a bandolier stretched across his chest and revolver in a leather holster riding on his hip—upset I'm sure that he hadn't been asked to carry Liam. My own anger rising, I watched two men who had no right to be there, one leading, the other following, as my friend was carried to his grave.

I knew why Father Lonagan was here. But what was Billy doing? Why wasn't he in Limerick? Had he come here looking for me?

I watched Father Lonagan praying by the mound of fresh dirt and the hole—a raw wound in the ground that would soon hold my friend. I couldn't hear the words and didn't need to: words of comfort that held no meaning; the same Latin prayers I had heard countless times, a hypnotic monotone from the mouth of a man who, I was now certain, didn't believe them himself. The rain began to fall, but I didn't budge as I watched my friend being lowered into the soil. One by one, first Liam's mother, then his father and then Seamus tossed handfuls of dirt over Liam's coffin. When the last prayers were done, two men with shovels began to fill in the grave. Liam's parents left first with Seamus and Tara, the other mourners following as they began the long trek to Liam's parents' house.

I watched Billy leave, Kevin by his side, then slid my glasses back to Father Lonagan. *When a thing is wrong*, I heard my father say, *you have to make it right.*

———

I found him in the rectory, standing in front of the window, head bowed, staring outside or praying I didn't know. He startled at the squeak of the door but didn't turn and I wondered for a moment whether he had been waiting for me. Finally, he turned and I could see both the fear and the resignation in his eyes.

"Do you think any of that made a difference?" I asked as I gestured with the gun, to the window behind him and the mound of freshly turned dirt in the distance.

He said nothing.

"You betrayed us." I had to fight to keep my voice even. "At a time when we needed you most, you betrayed us."

Father Lonagan shook his head, but I raised the gun before he could speak. I gestured out the window again to Liam's grave.

"You betrayed him."

He let out a sigh and hung his head.

"You betrayed the collar you wear." I nodded to the cross on the wall. "Do you think there's any forgiveness for what you've done?"

He lifted his head, his eyes pleading, but he said nothing.

"There's not an ounce of mercy in you, so don't be expecting any from me."

His head hung again and his shoulders shook. I waited. When

he finally looked up, his eyes were wet. He sniffed, then wiped his nose and then his cheeks. I shook the gun at him.

"I'm already going to hell, Father, is that it? How many times have I heard that? Surely one more killing won't make any bit of difference."

"Please," he begged, his voice cracking as the tears ran down his cheeks.

I shook my head.

He let out a sigh then made the sign of the cross. With his hands steepled below his chin, he shut his eyes and bowed his head. He was praying—praying while he waited for the bullet.

"Look at me," I hissed.

He flinched and his eyes snapped open.

I stared at him for a long moment, at this man I had come to hate. I heard my father's voice in my head. *When there is a wrong, you need to make it right.* I thrust the gun at Father Lonagan.

"It's time for your penance, Father."

———

I knelt in front of Liam's grave, staring at the small puddles forming in the mound of newly shoveled dirt. One by one, they overflowed their sides, and little streams of muddy water snaked their way down to the wet grass that surrounded the hole that held my friend. The rain dripped off the brim of my cap, and I could feel the water soaking into my trousers.

"You were a better friend to me than I ever was to you," I said softly as my own tears fell with the rain.

I don't know how long I knelt there, the rain soaking through my clothes, weighed down by the guilt that my friend was in the coffin instead of me. Had I died that night in Argyll Manor, along with Dan, Tom, and Sean, Liam never would have been captured by the British. But it was more than that, I told myself again. When Billy had chosen to sacrifice me to save his cousin, Liam's fate had been determined. Father Lonagan wasn't the only one who needed penance.

I finally stood and, as I shook the water off my coat, a chill ran up my spine. Through the heavy, wet air, I caught the faint smell of a cigarette. I reached for the revolver as I spun on my heel. Mick was standing by the gate to the graveyard. He waited a moment until I lowered the gun and nodded. He walked over to join me. I stuck the revolver back in my pocket.

"I figured you would be here," he said softly.

I nodded.

"He was a good man," Mick said.

"Aye. He was."

We both stared silently at the mound of earth, at the *Celtic* cross—a simple iron cross with a ring circling the intersection. It was the only marker.

"How have you been?" he asked.

It took me a moment to realize what he meant. I told him what I had done since I'd last seen him and what I had left to do.

"Billy was asking about you," he said. "At the waking." He nodded toward Liam's grave, "And here today."

I said nothing, my anger starting to build again.

He cleared his throat, a smoker's cough. I glanced over.

Hands in his pockets and collar turned up against the rain, he gestured with his chin toward the trees and the hills and the country beyond.

"There'll be another war soon," he said. "But we still haven't finished the last one." He paused for a moment before continuing. "I spoke to the lads. There's not a one that agrees with what Billy did."

I stared at him for a moment.

"Aye." He nodded as if he read my mind. "When a thing is wrong, you have to make it right."

———

I had intended to go back to the castle but spent the night at Mick's instead.

"Who's with us," I asked.

We were sitting in his cottage, the horses and animals fed and watered. I wore one of Mick's shirts and a pair of his trousers. My own wet clothes hung by the fire. I felt like a child dressed in his father's clothes—Mick's shirt and trousers hung from my small frame. But they were dry, and the heat from the fire finally began to thaw the chill in my bones.

"Padraig and Martin," he said, ticking them off on his fingers.

"And Seamus," I added. "Maybe."

"Aye. And, with you, that makes five."

I smiled for the first time that day. The weight that I had felt pressing on my shoulders suddenly felt lighter with Mick and the men behind me. But it wasn't enough.

"We don't have any guns." I said, frowning. "Just the one," I added patting my pocket.

Weapons had been in such short supply that we rarely kept our rifles and revolvers after an ambush. The quartermaster would store them in the cache, but they were often lent to other units for their own raids. After the ceasefire, the quartermasters of all units quietly gathered any remaining weapons from the men, lest they fall into the wrong hands. Now, with another war looming, it had been a wise move—for Billy and the troops in Limerick. But still it left Mick and me in a quandary.

"We can get guns," Mick said as if he were talking to himself. "Enough to do the job, anyway."

I stared at him, frowning. *How?* I wondered.

"A half dozen revolvers," he continued as if reading my thoughts. He blew a stream of smoke up toward the thatched roof above. "And maybe one or two rifles." He paused and looked at me. "But revolvers would be better in Limerick."

"How?" I finally asked out loud.

Mick leaned forward. "Padraig had a cousin in the Tans."

*The Tans?* I hadn't known that.

Padraig's cousin, he said, had been in the British Army. He had fought in France but had stayed in England after the war, the only place he could find work. When the British began to recruit former soldiers for the new police force they were sending to Ireland, Padraig's cousin—thinking he would be a policeman and not a bully—saw it as a way to return home. When he realized what the Tans were all about, he left, but not before stealing weapons and setting fire to the barracks himself.

I chuckled. I had always thought the IRA were responsible for burning that barracks.

"He gave the guns to Padraig," Mick continued. "And then he fled. The last I heard"—he paused as he sucked on the cigarette—"he was working on a steamer out of Sydney."

Padraig, for one reason or another, never turned the guns over to the IRA; he had kept the secret well.

We discussed our options, looking at each from a military standpoint. A direct attack would be foolhardy. Although Billy had lads like Tim and Diarmuid, we knew he also had a full company of men who had seen battle. Andrew's descriptions of what he had seen inside the Royal George and the Glentworth had told me as much. Billy had set up a defensive position in front of the hotel—the furniture and the men with rifles in the windows I had seen myself. But now, apparently, the temporary barricades had been fortified with concertina wire and sandbags. We would never get past the front door.

"Could we get Billy by himself?" I asked.

Mick shook his head. "I've never seen him travel without Kevin and one or two other men." He gestured with his cigarette, pointing out the door. "And with what's happening in Limerick, he would be foolish to go off by himself."

Billy was anything but foolish. I sighed. I had the men and guns, but I still didn't have a way to free Tim and Diarmuid. I looked at Mick, unsure what we were going to do. Mick, as I had seen him do countless times, sat back, stared at the fire, and let the thoughts tumble around in his head. Every now and then he sucked on his cigarette then blew rings of smoke up toward the roof.

Just when I was ready to give up, he smiled.

"There may be a way," he said, "if the story I heard is true."

And for the second time that night, Mick surprised me.

# Chapter Thirty

"Father Lonagan is gone," Mick said as he examined the revolver. "He's not been seen for days."

"Good riddance," Seamus hissed.

"Where did he go?" Padraig asked.

"And what does it matter?" Seamus responded.

"You never liked that one, did you?" Padraig said with a laugh, poking Seamus in the ribs.

Seamus shot him a look. "He's the devil himself, that one."

I listened but said nothing. Mick's eyes shifted between Seamus and me, as if he couldn't make up his mind between the two of us. I ignored him as I studied Seamus. *What had he done?* I wondered.

With a grunt, Seamus stood, his chair scraping on the stone floor.

"What does it matter?" he asked again, softer this time, as if he were asking himself. A moment later, the door banged and Seamus was gone.

I pushed my chair back, wanting to follow, but Padraig grabbed my arm.

"Leave him," he said. "He's not been himself."

I nodded and sat again, turning my attention back to the guns on the table. Liam's death had left me angry and bitter and hollow inside. I could only imagine what it had done to Seamus. I sighed. Where Father Lonagan was I didn't know. I hadn't given him a choice, telling him he had to leave—Limerick, Ireland, the Church—he had to leave it all. Maybe he had, I thought.

Still, as I glanced back at the door, I wondered.

———

We waited by the crossroads, outside of town, knowing that he had to come this way. Mick and I crouched behind the walls with our revolvers. Padraig was across the lane, a rifle held ready. Seamus and Martin were on the opposite corners, both of them unarmed.

Martin had wanted a gun too but didn't put up too much of a protest when I told him he wouldn't be needing one. Whether he knew how to use one or not wasn't something I wanted to find out in the middle of an ambush.

Seamus saw it differently.

"I'll have no use for one," he had said when Padraig had tried to hand him a gun. He held up the club. "I won't be needing it anyway."

Seamus would be fine. But it was a long wait, and I worried about Padraig. The crouching and hiding wouldn't be good for his leg, even if it was no longer there. I had told him that we could manage without him, but he wouldn't hear of it.

"Sure and what do you know about an ambush?" he asked, the grin spreading across his face. Despite the grin, I knew it was more than the thought of action that made him stay.

The night dragged on and my thoughts wandered. *Why had he come back?* I wondered. It was a foolish thing to do. Sure, the same could be said about me. But my return was to marry Kathleen and to right the wrongs of the past. As for his return, I could only guess. Our paths had crossed only a handful of times, the last on a cold December night a year ago, and my life had changed forever. Now, his was about to change too.

It was a quarter past midnight when I heard the curse then the faint sounds of steps on the wet road. I watched as the shape appeared, weaving side to side, feet heavy with drink—we had seen him go into the pub earlier—or dodging the puddles from the earlier rain, I couldn't be sure. Either way, he was alone which would make our task easier.

He passed by and, in the faint light, I saw him. Tall, thin, his light hair pale in the glow that seeped through the clouds. He wasn't drunk, I could see now, just a cautious man on a wet road. Either way, it didn't matter.

I slipped silently over the wall, the wind masking any noise I might have made. I came up behind him.

"A fine night for a walk, Rory." I said.

He spun around, a look of alarm on his face. Then I saw the soldier in him. His eyes darted around, weighing his options, until he saw the gun. His eyes flashed from the revolver in my hand up to my eyes then back to the gun, trying to decide, I guessed, whether he should take his chances. I gave him a moment, to build up his hope, then whistled softly. There was a rustle and a curse—the curse coming from Padraig as he climbed over the wall. A moment later Rory was surrounded, but his eyes still darted around, looking for an escape.

"Three good men, Dan, Tom, and Sean were," I said, breaking the silence. Rory grimaced at the names. "They're dead now because of you."

"I had no choice," he said defiantly.

"Ah, but you did," I said as I stepped forward. "Many a man before you and many a man after took their torture," I added, thinking of Liam. "And many died without ever betraying the Republic."

He cringed at my words.

"Traitors, spies, and informants," I continued, my words heavy in the wet air, "they're all treated the same."

Rory's eyes flashed to Seamus then Padraig then Mick before returning to me. I saw the change. He dropped his arms by his side, and I saw the slight shake of his head, a dismissive gesture that told me he thought he knew something I didn't. It wasn't much, but I caught it. Then he smirked.

"And what do you think Billy will do?" he asked. "When he learns what you've done."

Before I could stop him, Seamus lunged forward. "Shut your gob hole, you little shite!" he hissed and brought the club down on Rory's head. There was a sickening thud and Rory's eyes flashed wide before he collapsed to the ground.

Seamus stood over him, staring down at the limp body lying in the mud at his feet.

———

The light from the oil lamp cast long shadows in the cottage. The room had grown cold, and Mick was busy stacking more peat on the embers in the fire. He stood, brushed his hands off on his pants and sat again, a cigarette dangling from the corner of his mouth. The room brightened, the shadows from the lanterns fading like the spirits at first light. A few minutes later, I began to feel the warmth.

I listened to them debating: Seamus, Padraig, and Martin. Only Mick was silent, staring off at some unseen spot on the wall, puffing, as he usually was, on a cigarette.

"It's all of us or none of us," Padraig insisted.

"Ah, you're crazy," Seamus said. "You'll just get us all killed."

"Seamus is right," Martin interjected. I was surprised; I had expected him to side with Padraig.

Mick looked up but said nothing. He turned to me. We stared at each other for a moment then he gave me a small nod, knowing, I'm sure, what I was about to say.

"I'll go alone," I said, and they all turned. "I'm the one he's after and, besides, Tim is my nephew."

"Diarmuid's there too," Padraig said.

"I know. But he's my worry, not yours."

"What Billy does is all our worry," Padraig insisted. He had a point. Each had lost something because of Billy, if not directly then through the chain of events he had set in motion.

I shook my head. "Sure and Billy will come after the lot of you, Padraig. If I go myself," I added, "Billy will never know you were involved.

His eyes narrowed. "Aye, he wouldn't," he said as he nodded toward the door. "Not if you put a bullet in him."

I sighed. Padraig was right. Outside in the stable, Rory lay on a bed of hay, his hands and feet bound, a strip of cloth stretched over his wounds. Padraig was right; Rory knew us all. But as much as I wanted to leave him by the side of the road—bound and shot, a traitor with a note pinned to his chest—without him I had no chance of freeing Tim and Diarmuid.

The cottage was quiet for a moment, the only sounds the crackling of the peat in the fire and a soft groan from Padraig as he rubbed his leg.

"Someone needs to stay here," I said, gesturing toward the door.

Padraig looked up, frowned, but said nothing.

"And if something goes wrong…" I continued, the sentence unfinished but the thought clear.

The four of them sat silently for a moment. Finally, Mick nodded again, having made up his own mind, it seemed, and leaned forward. "Frank's right," he said.

Padraig's eyes darted back and forth from Mick to me. Finally, he sighed then nodded. Still, it was clear that he wasn't happy with the decision.

———

We spent the rest of the night discussing our plan. Going to Limerick now was foolhardy but we had no choice. Padraig had reluctantly agreed to stay and guard Rory. He was upset to be missing the action, but I had been watching him for the last few hours.

Lying in wait for Rory had taken its toll. Since we had returned to Mick's barn, he had been rubbing the stump of his leg, where his real one ended and his wooden one began, a grimace on his face the whole while.

Seamus and Mick would go to Limerick with me. Martin would too. But as he wasn't a soldier, he would serve as a lookout. He would bring word to the others if anything went wrong.

In the fowl-house outside, the hens began to stir, and the first gray light of day filtered through the windows of the cottage. Seamus looked at each of us.

"It's done then," he said. Not waiting for an answer, he stood and stretched. As if it took all of his energy, he slowly lowered himself to the floor. Close enough to the fire to be warmed by the embers but not close enough to catch a stray one, he closed his eyes. It was no more than a minute before he began to snore. Padraig was next, limping off to Mick's bed while Martin joined Seamus on the floor, hoping for a few hours' rest.

Too tired to sleep myself, I followed Mick outside into the cool air of the morning and stopped for a moment to watch the sky brighten over the hills to the east.

"I'll look in on him," I said and Mick nodded, lost in his own thoughts as he usually was.

I left him staring at the hills and slipped quietly into the barn.

Rory was where we had left him, asleep now, bits of straw stuck to his bloody hair. The cloth we had used to dress the wound was dark with blood and had begun to work itself loose during the night. His hands were bound behind him, and his feet were tied to the post. He was asleep, his mouth open, his breathing heavy to match that of the horses. I stared down at him for a moment, in the darkness of the barn, and couldn't help but think of Tim. He looked more a boy now than a man, Rory did, asleep before me in the hay. What he had done was surely a sin, worse than the many I had committed. It would be so easy, I thought, to end it all here, to avenge

Dan, Tom, and Sean. To avenge Liam. In my pocket I rubbed my hand along the handle of the revolver. It would be so easy.

"Don't do it, Frank,"

I turned at the voice and there was Martin.

"Without him, we haven't a chance to free Tim and Diarmuid," he said.

I sighed. I turned back to Rory. He must have heard the noise; he opened his eyes. He let out a low moan, the throbbing in his head awaking as he did. After a moment of confusion, a struggle to remember—where he was, why he couldn't move his hands and feet and, surely, about the pain that was coursing through his head—his eyes found mine. They were glazed and unfocused in the dim light. He shook his head as if to clear it. With a sudden hiss of breath and a loud moan he closed his eyes and lay still again.

I stared down at him, unable to feel anything but contempt.

"He'll kill you," he hissed quietly through clenched teeth. His eyes were still closed, but he knew I was there.

I said nothing. Finally, he opened his eyes again. I stared at him a long moment before he looked away. His eyes took on a downcast look, one that said he knew his fate was coming and there was little he could do to stop it.

I turned on my heel, brushing past Martin on the way out.

# Chapter Thirty-one

Dressed as a priest again, I sat next to Seamus as, one-handed, he gave the reins a slight tug, calling ahead softly to the horse. The horse stopped with a snort and dropped its head, content to wait for Seamus's next command.

Behind us, the hay was piled high in the back of the cart, Mick hidden below along with the guns I hoped they wouldn't need. My own was in the burse that hung heavy at my side. The bible, the Holy Water, the oil, and the bread I'd left on Mick's table. I stared at the front of the Glentworth Hotel, hoping Tim and Diarmuid hadn't been moved again. A group of men, ones I didn't recognize this time, stood out front behind the sandbags that had been stacked in front of the door. Two carried rifles but several were smoking, their backs to the street. I glanced up. The two men perched in the windows regarded us for a moment. One of them turned and said something and both laughed as they glanced back at us.

I stared back at them and their smiles vanished. They bowed their heads—from the shame of mocking the giant man in the cart and the short priest with him. One made the sign of the cross.

"What do you make of it?" I asked Seamus.

"I don't know," he said as his eyes narrowed.

We had been wondering ever since we had passed the asylum earlier. There had been no troops marching through the streets to-day. Like the men before us now, those we had seen were sitting on the sandbags, talking and smoking. Most had given us only a casual glance. But it was the smiles that really seemed odd. *Had a truce been reached?* I wondered. Had the Free State withdrawn their forces? Not sure what to make of it, I climbed down.

"Mind yourself now," Seamus said. He called softly to the horse then gently flicked the reins.

I watched him for a moment until the cart turned the corner. If everything went according to our plan, Seamus would see Martin coming the other way. Out of sight, Seamus and Mick would wait while Martin crossed Catherine Street, stopping on the corner for a cigarette. From there he would be able to see the front of the hotel. I could only trust that he would be there, I told myself, as I turned and began to make my way across the street, dodging the motorcars and lorries that raced across the cobblestones.

Wearing caps and dressed in trench coats—the uniform of the IRA—the four men in front of the hotel turned to watch me. Younger than me, they couldn't have been more than nineteen.

"Good day, Father," one said as another held the door. "The lads will be glad to see you."

I stopped short.

"And how are the lads, son?" I asked, trying to cover my surprise.

"Grand," he said with a smile, "everyone's grand." He stepped out of my way.

Still I hesitated.

"Forgive me, son. I've been all night with a sick child. Has something happened?"

"Aye, Father." He smiled. "Brennan, that shite." He spit on the ground. "He's leaving." An agreement had been reached, he told me, and the war that had seemed certain had been averted. Brennan's Free State forces would retreat from the city and the Strand, and Castle Barracks would be turned over to the local IRA, men from the Mid-Limerick Brigade, men I likely knew. All other barracks would be turned over to the city government while remaining IRA divisions—forces from Clare, from Tipperary, and from Galway—would retreat to their respective counties.

"The lads and I," he said as he gestured to the men beside him, "are from Cork."

"Tom Barry's men?" I asked.

"Aye," he answered proudly.

"And the Limerick men?" I asked. "Are they here? In the Glentworth?"

"Aye. Some are, Father. But most left last night."

"I'm looking for a lad named Tim Reidy," I said. "From Kilcully Cross. St. Patrick's Well Parish."

He shook his head. "I'm sorry, Father. I don't know him."

When I had asked about Diarmuid, the answer was the same.

———

I left the Cork men there, confused, I was sure, at my abrupt departure. I breathed a sigh of relief, thankful that Tim and Diarmuid would be spared the fight that neither would have survived. *But where are they?* Would Billy have let Tim or Diarmuid go? If the fight wouldn't come to him, would he set out to find it?

I walked along Catherine Street, glancing across but not seeing Martin. *He must be with Seamus*, I told myself. I turned at the corner, expecting to see them both. The street was filled with motorcars and lorries and horses and people, busy going about their business—but Seamus and Martin weren't anywhere to be seen. *Where have they gone?* I wondered. I turned around and crossed Catherine again. They must have gone to the Royal George, I thought as I tried to shake the feeling that something was wrong.

In the noise of the street—the clip-clop of the horses, the squeaks and rattles of the drays, the roar of the motorcars, and the shouts and sounds of daily life returning to normal now that the war had been averted—I didn't hear the lorry until it was upon me.

With a screech of brakes, the lorry skidded to a stop. I turned to the men jumping from the side, their rifles held ready. I stared at their faces, at men I once knew, dressed in their trench coats and wearing their caps, pulled low now over hard eyes. In the middle of the men stood Billy. He stepped forward, stopping two feet away.

"So the traitor has returned," he said, loud enough so all would hear. I stared back but said nothing. His eyes were darker than I remembered. The muscles in his jaw twitched, betraying the violence within. Two men stepped past him and grabbed my arms. I stared back at Billy, watching his hands, knowing what was coming, knowing there was nothing I could do to stop it. The fist came at me, and I turned my head. A second before a rainbow of colors and a flash of pain exploded inside, I saw him in the lorry.

Sitting with his arms folded across his chest and wearing a scowl was Martin.

# Chapter Thirty-two

A wave of panic hit me and I coughed and spit out a mouthful of blood. Gasping, I gulped a lungful of air. My head was spinning and I struggled to think. I could feel the cold dirt of the barn floor pressing against my cheek, the pain pulsing through my arms, my legs, my chest. I opened my eyes and stared at the black earth before me. Lying inches from my nose were two small chunks that looked strangely familiar. Red or black, I couldn't tell, but a moment later I realized what they were. I coughed again and ran my tongue over my gum, where my teeth used to be.

"Where is he, you traitor?"

I didn't answer, and the boot came at me again, slamming into my ribs this time. There was a burst of pain, and I heard something crack, or maybe I felt it, I couldn't be sure. I struggled to breathe, each mouthful of air like a knife in my side.

"Where is he?" the voice demanded again.

I didn't answer—I couldn't have even if I wanted to, struggling to hold on as waves of pain swept over me. The darkness was coming—I felt it as much as I saw it—and this time I wasn't sure if I had the strength to hold on. But I had to.

*This is Mick's stable*, I told myself, something to focus on other than Billy's boot.

The boot came at me again, and my head exploded in a rainbow of blues and purples.

*This is Mick's barn*, I told myself again. Billy had brought me there, looking for Rory. But Rory was no longer there.

"Get him up," I heard, and rough hands grabbed me below the arms. I screamed as the pain tore through my body. I took several breaths, fighting to hold on.

*Mick's barn*, I told myself again. But Rory wasn't there. The frigid water hit me, and I gasped again, struggling to breathe. I coughed and spat once more and there was Billy before me, the empty bucket dangling by his side. I shivered, the water soaking through my clothes but clearing my head.

He stared at me, his eyes dark with violence, but there was something more. I had known him long enough to see the worry hidden in his eyes.

"You're a daft man, Kelleher." He shook his head. "You should have stayed in America."

I looked up at him through swollen eyes. It was a foolish thing to do, but I did it anyway. I waited until he leaned close, his dark eyes piercing, his mouth a sneer. I spit a mouthful of blood. He flinched, but he wasn't fast enough. He wiped his eyes as the blood, *my blood*, ran down his cheeks and chin and dripped onto his shirt. His eyes flashed and he raised his hand.

"Do they know what you did?" I shouted, then wondered if I had said it at all.

The fist slammed into my head, another flash of colors, and I told myself that surely I had said it. Out loud. I slumped forward, the only thing that kept me from falling were the hands that held me up.

Rory wasn't there, I told myself. He was in Adare. I felt the rough hands again, pulling then pushing, as I was forced back into the chair. My arms were stretched behind my back, and I screamed out again as the pain coursed through my ribs. I closed my eyes and waited for the fist, certain this time it would send me away.

But it never did.

"He's here," I heard from the darkness.

Unsure what that meant, and knowing I could do nothing about it, I focused on what I knew.

*I helped Mick with the morning chores, letting the hens out of the fowl-house while he tended the horses. I thought Martin had gone back to sleep, next to Seamus by the fire. I was returning from the well, the bucket of water for the horses sloshing at my side and there was Martin, pedaling the bicycle up the lane. Mick was watching silently.*

*"And where's he off to?" I asked.*

*"The pub," he said as Martin disappeared around the turn. "He'll be back by midday," he added, although I could hear the doubt in his voice.*

*By the time he returned, Padraig and Rory were gone, on their way to Padraig's shop in Adare, where Rory now was surely still bound and gagged.*

———

I heard the metallic click, the cock of the revolver, and opened my eyes.

Billy pointed the gun at the ground before me. Then he turned and motioned to the shadows.

"You've a job to do," he said.

"I can't." I heard, the voice, soft and high. A shiver ran up my spine.

Rough hands, the same ones that must have held me earlier, pushed the boy from the shadows.

I stared at the boy who would have been my nephew, had I only married Kathleen. Tim's eyes darted back and forth from Billy to me. Billy held the revolver out and, when Tim didn't take it, Billy grabbed his hand and wrapped it around the gun. Then Billy grabbed his shoulders and turned him toward me.

"Are you one of us?" Billy asked before pointing at me. "Or are you a traitor like him."

Tim shook his head, and the tears slid down his cheeks. Time slowed, and I watched as he raised his arm, the gun shaking in his hands. He pointed it at my chest. I stared up at him and something flashed across his eyes.

"No, Tim," I said, my voice barely a whisper.

"Shoot him!"

He flinched at Billy's shout, his eyes pleading with me, telling me he didn't have a choice.

"Shoot him!" Billy yelled again.

Tim raised the gun until it was pointing at my head. He took a breath, wiped his eyes, and let out a long sigh. The gun stopped shaking.

"No, Tim," I said again, for the first time feeling scared.

Tim just shook his head and I could see he had made up his mind. Then, before I could say anything else, he spun, faster than I ever thought he could, dropping into the crouch that Billy had taught him.

The metallic click of the hammer falling on an empty chamber was loud in the barn. Billy stared back at my nephew, at the gun that was now pointing at him. Tim pulled the trigger again only to be rewarded with the same empty sound. His eyes went wide, a look of panic, as Billy calmly reached for the gun. As he grabbed it, his eyes never left Tim's.

"I had my doubts about you," he said as he pulled the bullets from the pocket of his coat. One by one, he loaded these into the gun.

Tim was crying again.

"You're a traitor," Billy said, "just like he is." He turned the gun again and held it out. I wasn't surprised when Martin stepped from the shadows.

Martin grabbed Tim's arm, leading him outside. Before he disappeared, Tim's eyes caught mine. Like those of an animal that finally gives up, deciding it's time to die, Tim's eyes were filled with defeat.

"It's me you want, not him." I pleaded with Billy.

He stared back at me, his face clouded in darkness.

"He's just a boy," I said again.

Billy said nothing as he stared back at me, his eyes narrowed—a look of arrogance I had seen many times before.

I felt the panic flood my stomach. Tim's cries and pleas from outside, loud at first, now seemed to fade. Time seemed to hang still for a moment, and there was nothing I could do to stop what happened next. I flinched at the bang of the gun and let out a wail, knowing I had failed him. I pictured Tim slumped in the dirt outside, the young lad who had wanted what he could never have—to be a soldier. I had failed him. I had failed Mary.

There were two more shots followed by voices, hushed, urgent. I looked up at Billy and saw him flinch. Suddenly he lunged to the side as the barn door slammed open. Mick rushed in, his gun searching before he found Billy. He fired twice. Billy stumbled, grabbed onto the post to keep from falling, then slumped to the floor.

Padraig hobbled over, his own gun held ready as he stared down at Billy.

"He's alive," he said, glancing back at Mick.

"I know," Mick said softly. "I told you no more killing."

Defiant as ever, Billy pushed himself off the floor, first to his knees, then to his feet. He turned slowly, and I saw where Mick's bullets had struck him. The stain on the shoulder of his trench coat began to spread. His eyes fell on Mick, then on Padraig, then me before settling back on Mick. They were filled with hatred.

"So what's it going to be now, lads," he said as he placed his hand over the wound, pressing to stop the bleeding. "Which one of you is man enough to finish it?"

Mick shook his head. "There'll be no more killing."

I heard the door of the barn and, a moment later, I saw Tim step from the shadows. The tears were gone. His eyes were clear now, the look of determination I had seen only moments earlier now back.

I shook my head. "No," I said but no one heard me.

Tim stepped calmly forward, the gun steady in his hand.

"No," I said again, the words nothing more than a wheeze.

Billy, Padraig, and Mick glanced my way before their eyes shifted to the door.

"No, Tim," I said, louder this time.

Whether he heard me or not, I don't know. I could only watch, helpless as the gun roared, flames spitting from the end of the barrel.

# Chapter Thirty-three

*New York City*
*July 1924*

I held my son's hand as we climbed down the long series of stone steps to the banks of the Hudson. There, we found a lighthouse perched on the rocks and, as we stood near it, I marveled at a river that made the Shannon I had grown up with look like a stream. Our new neighborhood was named, we had learned, for the fort that had once stood high up on the bluffs above us. Long after America's own war for independence, the fort had been abandoned. Eventually, rich families had built their summer houses where the soldiers once stood. For reasons I had never learned, those families had left and, now, the brownstones and houses of Washington Heights had become home to immigrants like us.

"Boats!" my son said, eyes wide as he pointed to the river.

I smiled and told him what they were: the steamers, the tugboats, the barges and the skiffs that seemed to fill the river. Black clouds billowed from the smokestacks, trailing for a while before disappearing in the wind. The sun glistened off the surface, a gray-brown that reminded me of the Shannon. Beyond rose the rocky cliffs of New Jersey. The papers said that one day a bridge would span all the way from New Jersey, what Americans called the Palisades, to the banks where Kathleen, my son, and I now stood. I stared out over the water, trying to imagine how such a thing was possible. But men with big dreams were determined to build it, and already there was talk of naming it, like our neighborhood, after America's first president. Maybe one day, I thought, the Irish would build a bridge and name it Michael Collins and wouldn't that be grand.

"Up," my son commanded and I reached down and grabbed him in my arms. We had named him Eamon, after my father.

Kathleen watched with a smile as Eamon, head leaning against mine, pointed to the gulls that swooped and dove along the rocky shore, searching for their next meal. Two years old, my son was, an age of excitement and wonder. I watched him, pointing now to the lads who were climbing down the rocks, scattering the gulls in their way, off for a swim in the river.

He turned to me, and I smiled. His own smile faded and his eyes took on a serious look. He reached up and touched my mouth, as he had done dozens of times, and pointed to where my front teeth had been.

"Gone," he said.

"Aye," I said, offering a toothless smile. "Gone."

Satisfied that we were in agreement, he turned back to the water and the wonder it held.

As I watched him, I thought back to our journey, from the fields of Ireland and the life it would have held for us had we stayed, to the shores of the Hudson River and the dreams that now lay before us.

———

Although the civil war had been averted when Brennan's forces retreated from Limerick, the tenuous peace wasn't meant to last. A month later, Anti-Treaty forces—what the newspapers called the *Irregulars*—had seized the Four Courts in Dublin, an ominous sign that foretold of the bloodshed to come. It didn't take long. In June, after a general election in which Irish citizens approved the Treaty, fighting broke out when Michael Collins's forces unleashed their eighteen-pound guns on the Four Courts. As if a force all its own, the fighting quickly spread, and soon blood was spilling in Sligo and Roscommon, in Tipperary and Wexford. By early July, the buildings in Limerick were ablaze while gun battles raged in the streets below smoke-filled skies.

We were gone by then, Kathleen and I, standing on the decks of a steamer as the fighting spread to Galway and Mayo, to Cork and Donegal. When Limerick fell, a week after the National Army—what we had called the Free State forces—turned their guns on the Artillery Barracks, the damage was done. Then when Michael Collins was killed—ambushed by men he knew—it was the beginning of the end. Waterford, Cork—one by one the counties fell and when the last bullet was fired, more blood had been spilled fighting each other than had been shed in the war with the British.

It was only luck that we got out when we did.

The inquest had been quick; the Sínn Féin courts had found Tim not guilty in Billy's death. Billy had killed Martin, the Court had ruled, when he refused the order to kill me. Then when Tim had been given the task, had been ordered to kill his own uncle, he knew what fate awaited him if he too refused. Faced with no other choice, he had turned the gun on Billy. By the time Mick and Padraig had arrived, Billy lay dying in the dirt. It was close enough to the truth. When I was called to testify—my broken ribs and my swollen face evidence of Billy's boot and my missing teeth evidence of his fist— and I told the story of Argyll Manor and the long chain of events that followed, any doubts had been quelled.

We were still in court when Diarmuid was found wandering the streets of Limerick. After the inquest, I visited Andrew and his mother, this time without a priest's cassock. If they were surprised, they didn't show it. The three of us watched as Diarmuid chased the dog with a stick, a carefree smile on his face, the dog's playful bark echoing off the hills. Whatever wounds he had suffered at the hands of Billy had healed, but the lines on Mrs. Toomey's face and the worry that still clouded Andrew's eyes told me that, for them, it would take far longer than a few weeks.

In the middle of it all, Rory's body was found, floating face down along the banks of the River Maigue, outside Adare. His death was ruled an accident, that of a man blind with drink who had stumbled into the water while poaching fish in the middle of the night.

I could only imagine what had happened to him.

"What's done is done," Padraig had told me, refusing to answer my questions. "It's over now."

*Maybe*, I thought. Despite my misgivings, the new government had set about to restore order; from the ashes of war, they set out to rebuild Ireland. But the buildings and bridges that had been set afire and now lay in rubble and the train tracks that had been torn and twisted by IRA bombs would be far easier to mend than the divisions that had turned us against each other. Historically divided by counties and clans, years of servitude below the British had also left us divided by religion and class. It would take generations for the wounds to heal.

––––

"He's asleep," Kathleen said, dragging me as she often did back from Ireland to the life we now had in New York.

"Aye," I said with a smile. Eamon's head was nestled by my neck, and I could feel the steady rhythm of his breathing as he slept.

After one last look at the river, we turned and began the long climb back up to the streets of Manhattan.

"Mary wants us to come in September," my wife said.

"Aye, that's grand."

Kathleen hadn't seen her sister since we left. Mary and Tim had left a week after us, settling in Philadelphia near her brother, Declan. Kathleen's brother too, I reminded myself, but she barely knew him. He had left Ireland when she was only three.

"I'll have to ask," I added.

"I know," Kathleen said. For her it would be easy. Kathleen had been able to find work as a seamstress, mending and sewing she could do at home while she minded Eamon. The sewing could wait for a week or two.

As for me, I worked in the stables on Amsterdam Avenue, a stone's throw from Central Park. When I had first asked for a job, the head groom smirked, commenting on my size and my missing teeth, assuming I had lost them to a horse I couldn't handle. He didn't know that my father had kept two draft horses, large hulking animals, for pulling the heavy ploughs through Limerick's rocky soil. I had learned how to handle them at a young age and felt quite at home in the stables. The groom shook his head, but I was persistent. After a few minutes with a horse, he realized I was far more capable than he had thought and quickly offered me a job.

I didn't think he would begrudge me a week or two away from work.

There was a noise above us and we moved to the side as three young lads raced down the steps, their voices filled with excitement at the afternoon before them. The clatter of their feet on stone and their high pitched squeals and shouts were soon lost to the wind behind us.

When we reached the top, I turned and stared back down at the Hudson and, once again, my mind drifted along with the currents back to the Shannon. A large steamer was chugging up river, the brown water churning up behind it, thick, black smoke billowing from its stack. Sailing up to Poughkeepsie or Albany or somewhere north, the steamer continued on, undaunted by the other boats that lay before it. Far larger and more powerful, it wouldn't alter its course. The low moan of its horn sent smaller boats scattering. Those that didn't would be crushed below its hull or sucked into its wake.

So like Ireland, I thought. Guided by men I knew, the new country ploughed forward, the dead and wounded that had tried to alter its course left in its wake. It was a powerful force, a people who had been enslaved for centuries suddenly set free.

I heard another low moan and this time felt the vibrations in my chest. I glanced north and saw another steamer, aided by the current, charging down the river. The horns on both ships sounded—like the tips and taps of the telegraph, a language I didn't understand—and then it happened. The ship sailing upriver yielded, the evidence in the slight curve of its wake.

Would the peace last? For a while anyway and only until a more powerful force rose up and changed the country's course. Until we laid down our arms for good, Ireland would always be on the brink of war.

"Will you go tomorrow?" Kathleen asked me.

I turned and nodded.

Kathleen smiled and linked her arm in mine as we turned away from the river. I had begun going to church again. I wasn't sure what drew me back. It may have been Kathleen, it may have been my son—then again, it may have been something more. Tomorrow, as I had done for the last several weeks, I would go to mass with Kathleen and Eamon. I would stand and kneel with everyone else, and the Latin would roll off my tongue as it had done countless times before. But the whole while, my mind would be elsewhere. I would think of the rain falling softly on the green hills. I would think of the rich, rocky soil soaked with the blood and holding the bones of so many before me. As the scripture was read I would see the Shannon flowing and I would think of Tom and Sean and Dan, smiling in another time. I would think of Margaret, the daughter I had never known and I would think of Liam and my father. I would think of the ones who had survived and who were still there, building anew from the ashes of those who had fallen.

I would think of Ireland.

* * * *

# Author's Note

When most people think of *The Irish Republican Army*, they think Northern Ireland and Ulster, terrorists and bombs, Catholics fighting Protestants. Figures like Bobby Sands, Margaret Thatcher and Gerry Adams come to mind along with images of heavily armed British troops and tanks patrolling the streets of Belfast. Many remember the nightly news stories during the *Marching Season,* of bloody clashes between the Green and the Orange. This period, during the latter half of the last century, is what the Irish refer to as *The Troubles.*

But long before *The Troubles*, on the Monday after Easter in 1916, a relatively small force—a rag tag group of freedom fighters—took over the General Post Office in Dublin and declared their independence from Great Britain. The Crown was quick to restore order, arresting hundreds within weeks and swiftly executing the leaders. By most accounts, the *Easter Rising* was a failure but Britain's harsh response spurred widespread discontent and, in the turmoil that followed, the IRA was born. In 1919, vastly outnumbered, undertrained and short on guns, the IRA set out to achieve the independence that those who gave their lives in Dublin three years earlier had envisioned.

Family legend held that my grandfather fled Ireland with a price on his head by both the British and by the IRA. That my grandfather served in the Irish Republican Army during the War for Independence is a fact. Whether he left under an assumed name and with the British and the IRA hot on his heels is unclear. But my research paints a picture of a very tenuous time where the temporary alliance cobbled together to defeat the British crumbled easily under the weight of ancient divisions; where suspicion of disloyalty often resulted in death; and where past sins were rarely forgiven.

As many authors of historical fiction do, I took some liberties with time and place and with the events that occurred to craft my story. The villages of Kilcully Cross, Drommore and Mullins Cross exist only in the pages of this book. Most of the events depicted were based loosely on real accounts of IRA raids and battles with British Forces. But the broader context of the war and the civil unrest that followed is true, to the best of my knowledge.

L.D. Beyer
June, 2016

# Maps of Ireland

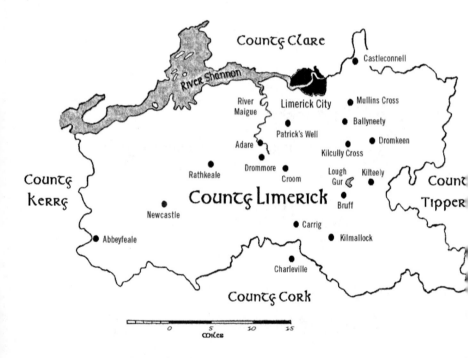

County Clare

River Shannon

River
Maigue

Limerick City

Castleconnell

Mullins Cross

Ballyneety

Patrick's Well

Dromkeen

Adare

Kilcully Cross

Drommore

County Kerry

Rathkeale

Croom

Lough
Gur

Kilteely

County Limerick

Bruff

Newcastle

County Tipper

Carrig

Abbeyfeale

Kilmallock

Charleville

County Cork

0    5    10    15
Miles

merick City

Kings Island

Castle Barracks

Strand Barracks

Union Workhouse

RIC Post

RIVER SHANNON

ABBEY RIVER

Canal

DUBLIN ROAD

Sarsfield Bridge

Cannock's

WILLIAM ST

RIC Post

HENRY ST

Royal George

BISHOP'S QUAY

CECIL ST

Artillery Barracks

Post Office

O'CONNELL ST

CATHERINE ST

Glentworth

MULGRAVE

Peoples Park

Rail Terminal

Gaol

Lunatic Asylum

New Barracks

To Cork

To Waterford

# Historical Cheat Sheet

**Ancient Order of Hibernians** – The Ancient Order of Hibernians (the *Hibernians*) was and still is an Irish Catholic fraternal organization. Staunchly Catholic, they were strongly opposed to the secular ideologies of the Irish Republican Brotherhood and similar organizations.

**Anti-Treaty Forces** – The Anti-Treaty Forces were an offshoot of the IRA that refused to accept the Treaty with Great Britain that ended the War for Independence. They vowed to continue fighting until all of Ireland—both the north and the south—was free from British rule.

**Black and Tans** – The Black and Tans, also known simply as the Tans, were a group of former World War II soldiers sent by Great Britain to supplement the Royal Irish Constabulary (RIC) and counter the guerilla war waged by the IRA. There was a belief in Ireland at the time that many Tans had served time in British prisons before being conscripted into the RIC. While this was never proven to be true, the Tans were brutal and harsh in their methods and targeted citizens and suspected IRA soldiers indiscriminately, often killing with impunity.

**Civil War** – The Civil War was fought between former IRA divisions and allies from June 1922 to May 1923. This followed the Irish War of Independence and the establishment of an Irish Free State under the Treaty with Britain. The IRA was divided on the Treaty, which resulted in the partition of Ireland. Many IRA soldiers, particularly in the south and west, vowed to continue fighting until all of Ireland, including the six counties in the north, were free from British rule. These units were referred to as Anti-Treaty forces. In contrast, units that supported the Treaty effectively became the newly formed nation's—or Free State's—army.

**Cumann na mBan** – The Cumann na mBan (the *Cumann* or *Irish Women's League*) was an Irish republican women's paramilitary organization formed in 1914. They operated as an auxiliary of the Irish Volunteers and, later, the IRA.

**Easter Rising** – An armed rebellion in Dublin led by Irish Volunteers to declare independence from Britain. The Rising began on Monday, the day after Easter, April 24, 1916. Although Britain was caught off guard, after five days of heavy fighting, they succeeded in squashing the insurrection. Over 450 people were killed and 2,500 wounded. Irish opinion and support for the independence movement surged after Britain's swift arrest and execution of the Rising's leaders.

**Fenians** – Fenian was a universal term for the Fenian Brotherhood—a U.S.-based organization sympathetic to the Irish cause that provided financial and moral support—and the Irish Republican Brotherhood (IRB), which operated in Ireland.

**Free State Forces** – Following the signing of the Treaty with Great Britain in December 1921, ending the War for Independence, the IRA split between supporters and opponents of the Treaty. The Treaty resulted in the partition of Ireland with the twenty-six counties in the south and west forming the new Free State, while the six counties in the north—most of Ulster—remained part of Great Britain. The Anti-Treaty faction of the IRA did not support the Treaty and, within months of its signing, went to war against their former comrades, who had sided with the Free State.

**Gaelic League** – A social and cultural organization that promoted Irish culture, heritage, and the revival of the Irish language, in defiance of British attempts to eradicate a separate Irish identity.

**Irish Citizen's Army** – The Irish Citizen's Army (the *ICA* or the *Citizen's Army*) were volunteers from the Irish Transport and General Workers' Union established in Dublin to defend protesting workers from the heavy-handed tactics of the RIC. They assisted in the planning of the Easter Rising in Dublin in 1916.

**Irish Republican Army** – The Irish Republican Army (the *IRA*) evolved from the Irish Volunteers, a group of nationalist-leaning rebels that had fought in the Easter Rising. The Rising's leaders were quickly arrested and executed by Great Britain. Consequently, it took several years for the group to reform. When it did, it changed its name to the IRA.

**Irish Republican Brotherhood (IRB)** – The Irish Republican Brotherhood (the *IRB* or the *Brotherhood*) was a secret oath-bound fraternal organization founded in 1858 and was dedicated to achieving independence from Great Britain. They helped establish the Irish Volunteers as a military organization. The IRB were the key architects of the Easter Rising.

**Irish Women's League** – See Cumann na mBan.

**Irish Volunteers** – The Irish Volunteers (the *Volunteers*) was a military organization established in 1913 by Irish nationalists seeking independence from Great Britain. Membership swelled to 160,000 by 1914. They were the primary fighting force that took part in the Easter Rising in Dublin in 1916.

**Peelers** – A nickname for the Royal Irish Constabulary (the *RIC*).

The term Peeler was in reference to Sir Robert Peel, British statesman and former prime minister, who is considered the "father" of policing in Great Britain. Interestingly enough, the term Bobby, used to refer to constables in Great Britain, is also a reference to Peel.

**Royal Irish Constabulary** – The Royal Irish Constabulary (the *RIC*) was the Irish police force. They were loyal to British rule, and their job was to maintain law and order in Ireland. They were referred to as *Peelers* by the IRA.

**Sínn Féin** – Sínn Féin was a political party that sought to achieve independence through political means. In the 1918 United Kingdom general election, Sinn Fein won the majority of the seats, effectively representing Ireland in British parliament. Although operating independently, Sínn Féin did support the IRA during the War of Independence.

**Tans** – See Black and Tans

**War for Independence** – The Irish War of Independence, fought from January 1919 to July 1921, was a guerrilla conflict between Irish nationalists and British forces in Ireland. The war ended in a Treaty that effectively partitioned Ireland into north and south. The twenty-six counties in the south and west formed what today is known as Ireland or the Republic of Ireland, achieving independence from Britain. The six counties of the north remained below British rule. This partition, above all else, is what led to the civil war that followed.

For a preview of *The Deadliest of Sins*,
the next installment in the Matthew Richter Series,
read on...

# THE DEADLIEST OF SINS

*New Delhi, India*
*May 1992*

Thomas Braxton, III jumped at the noise, the sound sharp in the confined space, the loud crack seeming to bounce off the tiles, sucking the air out of his chest. The heavy wooden rolling pin spun once on the tile floor then rolled below the cabinet. He raised his now empty hand, his eyes wide as he stared at it, his fingers curled around the rolling pin they no longer held.

*What have I done?*

The young woman lay crumpled at his feet. She coughed several times—more of a gurgling, choking sound—then her eyes rolled into the back of her head. She shuddered for a moment then suddenly went still. His breath came in ragged gasps, and Thomas fought the sudden wave of panic. Head swimming, he reached behind him, searching for something to hold onto, to steady himself, before his hand finally found the countertop.

*What have I done?*

He closed his eyes and counted to ten, trying to will away the nightmare. But when he opened them again, the grisly scene was still there, splayed out on the gray tile floor of the butler's pantry. The floor appeared to have been dusted with flour, the ceramic storage canister lying in shards. The pool of blood grew before his eyes, spreading across the tiles, dark red-black tentacles stretching out in a geometric grid along the grout lines, leading the way for the advancing puddle that followed. It seeped around the broken pieces of ceramic until they looked like they were floating. It formed small piles of dark red sludge when it reached the flour.

Thomas turned away, gagging, and barely reached the sink before he was sick. Hands on the countertop, head low as if he were prostrated in prayer, he sucked in mouthfuls of air. He squeezed his eyes shut and counted to ten again, trying to slow his breathing, trying to will away the growing hollowness in his belly—that terrible feeling that threatened to consume him.

After what seemed like an eternity, he lifted his head. He reached for the faucet and splashed water on his face. Unable to find a cloth, he raised the sleeve of his monogramed shirt to wipe his mouth. His arm jerked short at the sight of the dark red splatters that ran up his arm.

*What have I done?*

He took several deep breaths again. *Think!* he told himself. He could make this right. He had to make this right. *He was a Braxton, damn it!* Isn't that what his father had told him time and time again? He could make things happen. He was better than the rest!

He forced himself to turn and face what he had done. The girl's arms and legs were splayed at odd angles, her brightly colored sari—ripped by his own hands—was now, like his own shirt, splattered with blood. He stared at her face, at the bindi, the bright red dot between her dark eyebrows. Once the only adornment on the girl's face, now there was a series of red spots and smears that extended from her nose across one cheek and jaw then down her neck.

*Why did she have to fight?*

Her mouth was open slightly, as if she were moaning, and several strands of bloody hair were stuck to her face.

*Why didn't she understand her place?*

He shook his head, chasing the thoughts away before the panic overtook him again. His mind raced as he debated what to do. After a moment, he awkwardly stepped across the girl's body, careful not to touch her, careful to avoid the blood. He stared down at her face again, just for a moment, before he looked away.

*Christ!* He couldn't even remember her name!

He shook his head and reached for the phone on the wall. Mechanically he punched in the extension.

"Maloney," he heard after a click.

He turned his back to the girl, took another breath, and lifted the receiver to his mouth.

"It's Thomas," he said. "I, uhhh...there's..." he stammered, then paused. "Something's happened." He paused again, not sure how to explain. Finally, he blurted, "I need help."

"Stay where you are," he heard before the phone disconnected. He let out a breath, relieved at the sound of the crisp, efficient voice that would take care of everything. Just as it always had.

He hung up the phone, leaned back against the wall, and shut his eyes. The overpowering stench of the girl's released bowels suddenly filled the air. As if that weren't bad enough, he smelled the acidic stink of his own vomit. He clasped his hand over his nose as the bile rose in his throat again. He took a few more breaths then tried breathing through his mouth, hoping that would help. Strangely, on top of the stink, he noticed a metallic coppery smell. Before he had time to figure out what that was, there was clatter of shoes on tile, and the door burst open. Gun held in two hands, Gene Maloney stopped on the threshold. His eyes darted around the room, taking only a moment to figure out the sequence of events that had led to the grisly scene before him.

"Christ," he muttered under his breath. He looked up at Thomas. "Are you hurt?"

Thomas shook his head. Then it came to him. "It's Anupa," he blurted, suddenly remembering the girl's name.

"I know who she is," Maloney snapped as he holstered his gun. "It was just you two?" Maloney asked as he carefully stepped into the pantry. "No one else?"

Thomas shook his head. "No one else." He opened and closed his mouth several times looking for words to explain what had happened. "I told her..." He paused. "I just wanted..."

"I know what you wanted!" Maloney hissed, his eyes dark.

Thomas shrank below Maloney's glare. He leaned back against the wall and, with his face in his hands, stifled a sob. Maloney barked a series of orders into his radio. Thomas only half listened. There was little he could do. This was now in Maloney's hands.

"I need a cleanup team," he heard Maloney say.

Thomas dropped his hands. *A cleanup team?*

"And you'd better wake *Castle*," he added before he disconnected.

Thomas felt the sudden hollowness in his belly again. "Hey, wait. You don't need to wake him," he said, suddenly standing straighter, trying to be the man his father kept telling him to be. "We can handle this."

"Not another word," Maloney snapped, his finger pointing like a gun. His eyes scanned the room again, looking for anything he might have missed. They settled on the rolling pin sticking out from below the cabinet. "Is that it?" he asked.

Thomas followed Maloney's eyes. He looked up and offered a weak nod, knowing what Maloney was asking.

Maloney pulled open several drawers, searching, before he found a dishtowel and a plastic garbage bag. He carefully stepped over the dead girl and picked up the pin with the dishtowel, dropping both into the bag.

There was noise from the kitchen, and the door behind Maloney opened. Two more security officers stepped into the room. Like Maloney, their eyes quickly took in the scene. They exchanged a glance, then one opened the bag he was carrying and pulled out the things they would need. As they slipped on the white biohazard coveralls, gloves, and booties, Maloney explained what needed to be done. They nodded silently.

Once they were suited up, they unfolded the body bag and laid it on the floor next to Anupa, careful to keep it out of the growing pool of blood. One at each end, the two men lifted the girl and gently—surprisingly so—placed her in the bag. Then they carefully folded her arms across her chest.

Two more men entered the room. They too stopped to survey the scene before they looked at Maloney for instructions.

"Get him cleaned up," Maloney barked, pointing his thumb over his shoulder at Thomas. "I want him on the next plane back to the States." Maloney's eyes darted back and forth between the two men. "One of you will need to go with him."

One of the men—Romano? Thomas could never remember his name—slipped on a pair of latex gloves then stepped around the two men in white suits. They were now on their knees, trying in vain to clean the floor, picking up shards of ceramic and spreading towels. *God, there's so much blood!* The cleanup crew stuffed the blood-soaked towels into the body bag with Anupa. Anupa's sightless eyes stared up at nothing.

*God forgive me!*

Thomas flinched when Romano grabbed his arm, harder it seemed to Thomas than he needed to.

"Take off your clothes," Romano snapped. "Now," he added before Thomas could object. His eyes, like Maloney's, were dark. Meekly, Thomas complied, handing his shoes, pants, and shirt to one of the white-suited men on the floor. These were stuffed into the body bag alongside Anupa.

He was handed a pair of white booties and, after he slipped them on, Romano grabbed his arm again and led him around the body bag. The pool of blood was now gone, and the men were spraying something on the floor then wiping again to remove the last traces.

What had repulsed him only moments before now mesmerized him. Anupa's head had tilted to the side, the hair above her ear matted and sunken, where her skull had caved in. Unsure why, he reached down but was suddenly yanked back. He continued to stare as Romano, a vise-like grip on his arm, dragged him toward the door. As they stepped around Mahoney, Thomas saw the security chief hand the white-suited cleanup crew the plastic bag he had been holding. *That's the rolling pin*, Thomas said to himself, unsure why that was important. The men stuffed this too in the body bag with Anupa. One of the men grabbed the zipper.

Thomas shivered at the sound but watched nonetheless, fascinated as the bag was closed. *Just like that*, he thought. Anupa and the mess he had made were gone.

As the door swung shut behind him one of the men said something—he couldn't quite make out the words—but there was no mistaking Maloney's response.

"Burn it. Burn it all"

*Copyright © 2016 by L.D. Beyer*

# Acknowledgments

I am indebted to many people for their assistance, support and encouragement in bringing *The Devil's Due* to life. Jennifer Stolarz, Pat Galizio, David Leahy, and Jeff Beyer all read early drafts and provided their thoughts, corrections and perspectives. Without them, this book would still be an unfinished manuscript.

During a visit to Ireland, Doctors John O'Callaghan and Gavin Wilk of the University of Limerick were gracious enough to spend time with me and answer my numerous questions, as was local historian Thomas Toomey. I am also indebted to Cpl. Andrew Lawlor, who works for the Irish Military Archives, for providing my grandfather's military records and steering me towards other research sources such as the witness statements by IRA soldiers, now published online.

To get a better sense of the IRA and the war, I read numerous accounts by the men who fought it, including *My Fight for Irish Freedom* by Dan Breen, *Guerilla Days in Ireland* by Tom Barry, *When Youth Was Mine* by Jeremiah Murphy and *Victory and Woe* by Mossie Harnet.

I also read historical perspectives including *The Battle for Limerick City* by Pádraig Óg Ó Ruairc, *Limerick's Fighting Story, 1916-1921, Told By The Men Who Made It*, published by The Kerryman in 1948 and John O'Callaghan's *Revolutionary Limerick*.

Movies such as *The Wind That Shakes the Barley*, written by

Paul Laverty and directed by Ken Loach, and Neil Jordan's historical biopic, *Michael Collins*, as well as the many documentaries on the *Rebels of Ireland Channel* on YouTube helped fill in the blanks.

*The Dead Republic* by Roddy Doyle and *Children of the North* by M.S. Power provided a glimpse into The Troubles that continued to plague Ireland well after the time frame of my book. David O'Donoghue's *The Devil's Deal* shed light on the links between German Military Intelligence and the IRA in the 1930s and 1940s, a little known chapter in Irish history that could have greatly altered Ireland's course.

To get a sense of the Irish experience, I also read *Angela's Ashes* by Frank McCourt and *Don't Wake me at Doyles* by Maura Murphy.

I owe many thanks to my editor, Faith Black Ross, to my graphic designer, Lindsey Andrews, and to Amani Jensen and Maggie Elms, for providing another set of eyes.

Again, the advice and counsel I received was outstanding and any mistakes in the finished work are mine and mine alone.

While the above people and sources were invaluable, my ability to pick up a pen and write in the first place would never have been possible without the support of Mona, Kaitlyn, Kyle and Matthew.

Thank you all.

**L.D. BEYER** is the author of two novels, both part of the Matthew Richter Thriller Series. His first book, *In Sheep's Clothing*, was published in 2015 and was the #1 bestseller for Espionage Thrillers, Assassination Thrillers and Terrorism Thrillers on Amazon Kindle.

Beyer spent over twenty-five years in the corporate world, climbing the proverbial corporate ladder. In 2011, after years of extensive travel, too many missed family events, a half dozen relocations—including a three-year stint in Mexico—he realized it was time for a change. He chose to chase his dream of being a writer and to spend more time with his family.

He is an avid reader and, although he primarily reads thrillers, his reading list is somewhat eclectic. You're more likely to find him with his nose in a good book instead of sitting in front of the TV.

Beyer lives in Michigan with his wife and three children. In addition to writing and reading, he enjoys cooking, hiking, biking, working out, and the occasional glass of wine.

If you enjoyed this book, please consider writing a review on Amazon, Goodreads, or the platform of your choice.

You may also sign up for L.D.'s mailing list on www.ldbeyer.com. Thank you.

# Connect with Me

**Twitter:** https://twitter.com/ldbeyer

**Facebook:** https://www.facebook.com/ldbeyer

**Subscribe to my blog:** http://ldbeyer.com/blogs/

**Instagram:** www.instagram.com/ldbeyerauthor/

**Tumblr:** www.tumblr.com/blog/ldbeyer

**LinkedIn:** www.linkedin.com/in/ldbeyer

**Pinterest:** www.pinterest.com/ldbeyer/

**Goodreads (Author Page):** www.goodreads.com/LDBeyer

Printed in Great Britain
by Amazon

22536782R00179